UNDONE
THE HENRY BROTHERS

AMY KNUPP

CHAPTER 1

AVA

My eyes were gritty with fatigue and dread as I climbed out of the taxi in front of the Honeysuckle Inn.

I'd dozed on the hour-plus drive from the Nashville airport, knowing I'd need every bit of strength to face this place and the memories steeped within it. My red-eye from the West Coast had landed at just the right time to be slowed by rush-hour traffic, and I had to admit I'd welcomed the delay.

Time to face the music though.

All I wanted was to get in, figure out exactly how I was going to handle the inn, and get out emotionally unscathed, but I suspected that was a long shot.

As the driver retrieved my suitcase from the back, I stood on the damp pavement, the rain down to a barely noticeable sprinkle, and took in the century-old building, attempting to see it through objective eyes instead of as someone who'd once lived in the innkeeper's cottage.

The hand-carved welcome sign above the double wooden

doors of the main building had its summer cloak of sunflowers and wildflowers draped over the top. The porch welcomed guests with rockers and Adirondack chairs, giving the place a quaint, homey feel. The landscaping in front of the porch, however, was barren in spots and in need of new plantings. As I walked closer, I noticed the exterior paint was past due for a refresh. Both issues would be easy enough to spruce up.

For the nine-hundredth time since I'd received the call from Loretta Lawson telling me of my dear aunt Phyllis's unexpected death, I shoved away the threatening steamroller of emotions and focused my brain on all the pressing practical matters.

I pulled my determination around me like a protective cloak, went up the two steps to the porch, and pushed open the door of the inn.

The first thing that hit me was the smell.

Banana muffins and cinnamon, plus a hint of humid lake air.

Oh, God.

How was it that, out of all the things—thoughts, memories, sights—a smell could be what nearly leveled me?

I held on to the door for an extra couple seconds and greedily sucked in a breath, loving and hating the aroma at once.

"Good morning. You must be Ava." It wasn't the full, sixty-something voice I'd expected but a younger woman's.

I turned my attention to the familiar check-in counter straight ahead. A woman with long strawberry-blond hair had her gaze fixed on me and a questioning look on her pretty face. She looked to be close to my thirty-seven years old, maybe a little younger. Her expression was neither warm nor chilly, more guarded, and I realized I hadn't replied.

"Yes," I said as I strode across the area toward the desk. "Ava Dean, Phyllis's niece. I'm sorry, I expected Loretta or one of the other ladies in the Diamonds to be here. But thank you. Thanks for covering." I glanced around the area, which was deserted at the moment.

"I'm Magnolia James."

She came around the desk and extended her hand. I took it, racking my brain for why the name was familiar. She must be a townie. I'd known a lot of them at one time, but since moving away, I'd let as much of Dragonfly Lake go from my memory as possible—with the exception of Aunt Phyllis.

"Are you an employee here?" I asked, knowing Aunt Phyllis didn't have many. She'd always been one of those people who kept her costs down by doing as much as she could herself. It was only recently I'd convinced her to hire someone to man the front desk overnight, but I thought she'd hired a man for that position.

Though this wasn't a bed-and-breakfast but more of a boutique hotel—with a central common area and two wings of twelve rooms each that jutted out from either side, providing each room with a lake view—Aunt Phyl had worked the front desk, baked and served the breakfast goodies, ensured the guests had whatever they needed, and had been known to help with housekeeping even though she had Gretchen Morris as the head of Housekeeping and, last I knew, a handful of part-time cleaners. Her other longtime employee, Halstead, was the head of Maintenance. I'd known the man who was probably close to seventy now since I was a kid, but I still wasn't sure whether that was his first or last name.

"I'm a friend," Magnolia said. "Just trying to help out."

I was trying to wrap my head around the *friend* bit. My aunt had a tight-knit group of the dearest ladies, the Dragonfly Diamonds, as they called themselves, a nod to their weekly poker nights. They were all in their sixties or thereabouts. Loretta Lawson, Dotty Jaworski, Kona Powers, Rosy McNamara, Darlene Lionetti, and Nancy Solon had been her tight friendship circle for years, since before I'd moved out, but as far as I knew, those ladies didn't hang with the under-forty crowd.

My confusion must've shown on my face, because Magnolia continued, "I'm sort of in the Diamonds. A recent addition. It's a long story." She flashed a smile that was full of nervousness. "I...don't have a lot of friends. Not super-close ones, for, well, reasons. When I went through a rough patch a few months ago, Dotty gave me a job at the Lily Pad and leased me the apartment over the store. She was so sweet, knew I was mostly alone, so she invited me to poker night, and"—she laughed—"I had so much fun. They were all so kind to me and welcomed me in and, well, it stuck." Sobering, she said, "Phyllis was such a sweetheart. I'm so sorry for your loss."

Magnolia's eyes teared up instantly, telling me the loss was also hers.

"She was," I said. "A sweetheart." Exactly the type who would welcome Magnolia into the group if she knew she was lonely or alone. I didn't allow my mind to go too far down the road of how wonderful my aunt was, because I couldn't afford to break down. "I'm sorry for your loss too. Everybody's loss."

Magnolia let out a sob that took me aback for a second, and then I couldn't help but hug her. She accepted it, wrapped her arms around me, and held on, her body heaving silently for a few seconds. I tried hard not to let it get to me, but my eyes filled with tears and my chest welled up with grief.

After a few moments, Magnolia pulled away with an embarrassed half smile as she swiped at her eyes. "I'm sorry. It's been a quiet night here and it's just...sad, and I've tried to be strong, but then—"

"No apologies," I said. "Have you been here all night?"

"We divvied it up into shifts. Deshon, the night shift guy,

his wife is eight months pregnant and their two-year-old daughter's been sick, so we told him to stay with his family. I took the midnight shift because those ladies don't need to be here in the middle of the night, and I don't sleep much anyway…" She shook her head as if trying to stop rambling. "It's been slow. Peaceful. There's only a handful of guests at the moment, so it was no work at all."

"But I bet you're exhausted." I knew I sure was.

"Grief does that to a girl, doesn't it?" She looked self-conscious, and I wondered what her story was. She had a sort of flawless beauty about her, even with fatigue lining her eyes, her skin milky and perfect, her wavy hair enviable, particularly to someone with thin, board-straight, plain brown hair like me.

"Grief sucks," I said half to myself, and I fought down another surge as I walked behind the counter and spotted the ancient padded stool Aunt Phyl had used in more recent years.

Magnolia followed me behind the counter and picked up her bag. "There's a guy coming to look at the air conditioner for the west wing sometime this afternoon. We have all the guests on the east side. I guess it's a good thing there are only six parties at the moment, two of which already went out for the day. Oh, and Olivia is bringing donuts from Sugar for breakfast all week so we don't need to bake."

"That's so nice of her." Sugar was the bakery on Main and had never disappointed, but I didn't know who Olivia was. I needed to start a list of people to thank.

"Also, just so you know, the left-side door to the deck is sticking. I locked it and put a sign on it to use the other one, like Halstead said to, and he's going to check on it this morning." She flashed a nervous smile. "Sorry. It's a lot to walk into on top of…everything else."

"Halstead's the best. I know he'll take care of it."

A checklist was starting in my mind, and that was fine.

That was good. Checklists were actionable. I'd get this place all fixed up and beautiful so I could find an on-site manager to run it for me. Someone who would appreciate it and love it and care for it as much as my aunt had. I could never sell it—I was well aware of the numerous offers Phyl had received over the years. She'd never once given any consideration to them, staunchly believing a chain would ruin the small-town lakeside inn she'd poured the last third of her life into. Selling this place would be dishonoring Phyllis Sharp, and I wouldn't do it. However, there was no way I could move to Dragonfly Lake and run it.

There was a pang in my chest that I couldn't be that person, but I reminded myself Aunt Phyl would understand. She knew I was *this close* to realizing a lifelong dream.

"I need to get to the Lily Pad to cover for Dotty's weekly hair appointment," Magnolia said, "but let me know if there's anything else I can do. I know Loretta will be checking in soon. She's kind of the group leader, bless her."

"Thanks, Magnolia. I know Aunt Phyl will"—I closed my eyes briefly—"would've appreciated your help."

With a tired wave, Magnolia was out the door with a black umbrella that had a big hot-pink flower on the underside, and I could hear the rain coming down hard again, which seemed perfectly appropriate for this day. Not giving myself time to sit and acclimate, I smiled sadly when I found the "master file box" on the counter.

"Dear Auntie," I said quietly.

There was a hitch in my breath as I remembered our discussion the last time I'd visited. I'd tried for the hundredth time to convince her that some inn management software would be worth the expense and would make her life easier. She'd assured me something like that would derail her and ruin her whole system. Investing in software would be a priority going forward.

I picked up that old "system" now—the long, skinny file

box—and opened it. It was so old that the clasp no longer functioned. Inside were dividers for every guest room. In each section were color-coded index cards, a different color for each month. I located the six with paper clips, which marked current checked-in parties, marveling yet again that this was how the woman had functioned since buying the inn for her and my mom to run together twenty-five years ago.

Noting which rooms were occupied, I grabbed the keys to a couple that weren't—yes, honest-to-god old-fashioned metal keys—and set off to look into them to see if there was anything else to add to my checklist.

I came out from behind the counter and took a longer look around now that I was alone. When guests came in the main door, the ornately carved staircase on the right was the first thing they usually noticed. To the left was a cozy area with a couple of chairs, a sofa, and a luggage cart at the ready. The carpet in this area was tired and would need to be replaced, maybe with some homey wood planking.

To the left of the check-in counter was the arched doorway to the common area, which opened up into a high-ceilinged room lined by windows on the lake side and a giant stone fireplace backing up to the front desk. I walked through to the gathering room, as Aunt Phyl had called it, my eyes drawn to the windows even though it was anything but a lovely day.

The rain poured into the lake in sheets, the wind whipping the tree branches around dramatically. By most vacationers' account, not a pretty day, but I'd always loved the rainy days, from the drama of a storm to the peace of a quiet rainfall, as much as the sunny ones.

One of the tables-for-two in the breakfast area caught my eye because there was a wadded-up napkin on it. I went over and threw it away, and my gaze veered back to the weather out the window.

I'd been twelve when my mom and I had moved from St. Louis to Dragonfly Lake, into the cottage with my aunt Phyl.

As a teenager, I'd helped around the inn each day, then gradually spent more time caring for my mom over the years, but whenever it rained, if I could slip away for a few minutes, I would find an unrented room, let myself in, and sit out on the covered private balcony to watch the storm.

I knew there'd be no time for such a luxury today. I was beginning to wonder if I'd be able to arrange all the necessary improvements before I flew back to LA next week. I had a funeral to plan, and I needed to dive into the search for a full-time manager. The projects were adding up and needed to be taken care of before I hired someone, and I hadn't even made it past the common areas yet.

To say I was conflicted was an understatement. I needed to do this place—my aunt's pride and joy—justice by finding the perfect person to run it and care for it. My conscience and my heart wouldn't allow anything else. But the timing couldn't be worse.

Three days ago, I'd been on top of the world after my agent had pitched my TV series to an exec at Stream, a not-so-creatively-named up-and-coming streaming company. That meeting had gone well, so well that we had another one next week to discuss me being the head writer, and I'd been floating...until Loretta's call about my aunt's unexpected heart attack at the Country Market, of all places.

I squeezed my eyes shut, trying not to think too hard about what her final moments must have been like.

My poor aunt, though... She'd been such a good human, such a caring woman. She'd put everything she had into this inn, and it was up to me to make sure it wasn't sold off and it didn't go broke.

This was her legacy. That she'd left it—and everything she owned—to me wasn't a surprise as I was her only family, but I'd never expected this to happen *now*. She'd only been sixty-six years old. I knew better than most not to count on anything, but I always thought that dear woman would live to be a hundred.

I could still hear her voice Friday night when I'd called her to tell her about my agent's promising meeting. *Oh, Ava, I'm so proud of you. It's your time, hon. I can feel it. You've spent too many years putting your dreams on the back burner, first with your mama, then with that no-good ex-husband of yours. It's time for Ava to Ava the heck out of the world.*

I sniffled and choked out a laugh as I turned from the view of the lake and attempted to get back on task.

With a glance toward the underused kitchen, I headed out toward the hall that connected to the east wing. I entered the old elevator and pushed the button for the second floor.

When the elevator doors opened, I heard a racket out in the hall. As soon as I craned my neck out, I spotted Halstead, the head of Maintenance, at the other end of the hall, pushing a large heavy-duty garbage can under a stream of water pouring out of the ceiling.

"Halstead!" I called, my joy at seeing him battling with concern over what looked like a waterfall where there wasn't supposed to be a waterfall.

"Little Avie, I wondered when you would get here." In spite of what appeared to be a roof disaster, his weathered face morphed into an affectionate grin, his eyes brimming with warmth and concern. "Get over here."

I would've run to him even without the directive, and within seconds, I was wrapped in the big, burly man's grand-fatherly arms.

"How you holding up, little one?" he asked when I buried my face in his chest.

To everyone else, Halstead was gruff, quiet, and focused on his responsibilities of making sure everything at the inn worked as well as it could. To me, he was the giant teddy bear who'd always made time for me. I'd suspected for ages that he had deep, unrequited feelings for my aunt, though I'd never asked him.

"I'm doing okay," I said, willing it to be so. "How are *you* holding up?"

"Keeping busy, as you can see." He ended the hug and gestured to the ceiling, and I didn't fail to notice he hadn't really answered my question. "I hate to be the bearer of bad news, but I've been telling your aunt we need to do something about the roof for quite some time."

"What needs to be done?" I stepped back because that was no small trickle, and I didn't care to get splattered.

"Right now? I'll have to patch what I can. We had some wind last night and I suspect some more shingles came loose, but I won't know till I go up and look."

"It's raining too hard," I said.

"Reckon it'll subside soon enough. I need some supplies from the hardware store ASAP while I try to Band-Aid this. You up for that?"

"Sure," I said automatically, thinking I needed to be about three places at once. "What about the front desk?"

"There's a sign behind the desk you can put out. Phyllis had her number on it for emergencies. Change it to mine. It's on the list there."

A piece of plaster fell from the ceiling, as if to emphasize we needed to do more than stand here and chat, so I nodded.

I was no innkeeper, but even I knew this was no way to run this place.

I started toward the stairway, then stopped. "I don't have a car."

Halstead straightened from a crouch. "Phyllis's spare truck key's in the pen cup behind the front desk, where she always kept it."

"Right." Phyllis's truck that was now my truck. "What do you need specifically?"

I pulled out my phone and jotted down items as Halstead

rattled them off, then hurried down the stairs and out the side door of the inn.

I made my way toward the cottage in the trees, where the truck was parked, trying to summon a facade of steel.

Dragonfly Lake and the Honeysuckle Inn had never been easy, carefree places for me, and now, on this dreary, depressing rainy Monday, between the practical challenges of the inn and the emotional trip wire I knew was lying in wait, I had no idea how on earth I would make it through this godforsaken day.

CHAPTER 2

Meetings had never been something I had patience for. Sitting still wasn't one of my strengths, even when the subject of discussion was my lifeblood, my passion.

Trying to bite down on the antsy feeling that seemed to be my constant companion lately, I forced myself to listen to my brother Seth as he explained the ins and outs of our restaurant, Henry's, as well as the Rusty Anchor, the brewery our brother Holden opened last month. We were in the back booth at the Dragonfly Diner, meeting with Kennedy Clayborne about the possibility of her handling our marketing.

"So they're two separate businesses but you market together," Kennedy said, summarizing Seth's long-winded explanation.

"That's right. We revamped our menu in conjunction with the brewery's grand opening. You can sit on Rusty Anchor's beer patio and order from a special Henry's menu. When you eat at Henry's, you can order Rusty Anchor beer."

"And we have several dishes that incorporate Rusty

Anchor beer," I added. "Next time we meet, we'll do it at Henry's and you can sample them."

"Absolutely," Kennedy said, her brown eyes sparkling with enthusiasm. "I appreciate you guys accommodating my schedule this morning so last-minute, but some sampling is definitely in order next time. Tough job I have."

We'd met Kennedy years ago. Her younger sister, Sierra, was best friends with our sister, Hayden. We hadn't known her well, just in passing. We'd recently become reacquainted when Kennedy's husband, Hunter, a former brand manager for a Chicago brewery, took an interest in Rusty Anchor.

Maribella, the server, arrived with our food—skillet scramblers for Seth and me and waffles for Kennedy—the diner's famed Dragonfly Dust waffles.

"This is like a dream come true that I didn't even know I had," Kennedy said as she took in her colorful, over-the-top breakfast.

Dragonfly Dust waffles were the creation of Monty Baynes, the owner. Though he didn't have formal chef training, I respected the hell out of what he'd created here and had no trouble admitting the guy knew food. These were thick Belgian waffles with a dusting of blue, green, and purple sprinkles in the batter, hence the "dust." On top was a layer of homemade whipped cream and another dusting of sprinkles, these in the diner's signature custom-made dragonfly shape.

"My marketing brain and my pregnant brain are fighting it out, trying to determine who's more in love," Kennedy said, dipping her spoon into the whipped cream and sprinkles. "My God, this is genius."

"Monty Baynes has never been accused of being stupid," Seth said.

"The dude can create good food. If you like sugar, you can't go wrong." I much preferred the savory dish I'd ordered, but I couldn't deny the Dragonfly Dust waffles were legendary.

"I'm part owner of a bakery," Kennedy reminded us. "There's more sugar than red blood cells in my veins."

"A bakery and a marketing consulting business and a toddler and a baby on the way," Seth said in his engaging way. "You, Sierra, and Hayden are three peas in a pod as far as badass driven business owners."

"Not gonna lie," she said as exchanged her spoon for a fork, "it took me a long time to figure it all out. I couldn't do it without a supportive husband. I think Sierra and Hayden would agree. And Everly, from what I hear. I don't know her well yet, but I can tell she qualifies as badass too."

At the mention of his fiancée, my brother's fool-ass infatuated grin spread across his face. "Everly's got some badass in her."

"And a good man behind her," Kennedy said, finishing her first bite. "This"—she pointed her fork at her waffle—"is out of this world, as promised."

"No need to inflate Seth's ego," I pretended to grouch. Fact was, if Seth hadn't gotten over himself and gone all out to win over Everly, I would've kicked his ass six ways to Sunday then thrown him in the lake.

Kennedy laughed and said, "It sounds like there's an epidemic in the Henry family. Hayden, Holden, and Seth have fallen hard, all in the past few months, right? Your dad too. What about you, Cash? Are you next?"

"Nah. I've got zero prospects and I'm just fine with that. I'm married to my job."

"He's not lying," Seth added, his tone making it clear he considered that a fault of mine.

"I'm focused on the restaurant," I said, steering the conversation back to a comfortable topic as we all dug into our food. "There's something I'd like us all to discuss that I haven't had a chance to talk to you about yet." I indicated Seth with a nod. "When we're done with everything else."

Seth's brows shot up in curiosity, but he took my cue and

launched into what he considered Henry's strengths and weaknesses and opportunities for growth. We were staring down the off-season and our annual downturn in business. The restaurant wasn't hurting, but now that Rusty Anchor was open, we believed we could become even more of a year-round destination for special occasions, weekend events, and craft beer aficionados.

"Tell me about your social media," Kennedy said, pushing a stray strand of copper-colored hair behind her ear and then leaning back over her food with enthusiasm.

I let Seth fill her in on our accounts and our less-than-stellar attempts to fill them with compelling content. "We fall short pretty regularly," he said. "That's one of the things we'd love help with. Cash doesn't have time to post from the kitchen, and it's too easy for me to get absorbed by supplier issues or staff issues or any of a dozen other things. Before I know it, it's six p.m., I'm home for the evening, and I forgot to post."

"I get it completely," Kennedy said. "You both already have your hands full with the day-to-day. You need someone to head up your social media efforts."

"That's the dream," Seth said.

"That's something I can help you with." She jotted some notes on her tablet. "What about regional advertising?"

I listened but didn't participate much for the next few minutes as they discussed tourism magazines, brochures, and online ads. I was familiar with most of it, but Seth was the one who handled the details. My focus was on the kitchen.

When Kennedy had gotten through her list of questions, Seth pushed his empty plate away and turned his attention to me. "What else did you want to discuss?"

I'd just shoved the last bite of my scrambler in my mouth, so I gave him a *just a minute* gesture while I chewed. Maribella stopped by our table and refilled coffees and waters and asked if we needed anything else.

"Did I see you sell the dragonfly sprinkles to go?" Kennedy asked.

"You did. We have two sizes of bottles," Maribella said.

"One of each," Kennedy said. "Ivy will do something genius with those on cupcakes at the bakery, and my little Stella definitely needs some at home."

When Maribella left to add sprinkles to the bill, Kennedy said, "I'm all ears, Cash."

"Are you two familiar with *Small Town Smorgasbord*?" I asked them.

"That's the show you think Henry's should be on," Seth said.

"I've seen it a couple of times," Kennedy said. "I completely agree. That would be incredible." She added the name to her notes. "I can research how to be featured."

"I've researched it," I told her, "and until now, there wasn't an official way for a restaurant owner to get their attention. They seemed to go by word of mouth, but there was no way to tell who their sources were."

"That's changed?" Seth asked.

"It has. The show's grown in popularity, and it's a hotter ticket than ever before. They have ads running for some new campaign for restaurants to get featured."

I explained to them what I knew after seeing the ads and scouring their website for details. The first step was posting on social media using the right hashtags and telling the producers what made our restaurant worth the trip. Photos of signature dishes were recommended.

"The Southern shrimp and grits," Seth suggested, looking at me. "Made with Golden Sunshine Wheat beer," he explained to Kennedy. "The lager pork chili would be good… The beer-battered walleye and roasted asparagus makes a pretty picture too."

I nodded. "Or there's the brisket."

Kennedy had her phone out and looked to be searching

social media for the hashtag. "It's a good thing I'm not hungry—" She let out a gasp and tapped on her phone. "The Cove at the Marks is here."

"Here?" I asked, leaning forward, my pulse speeding up as my competition mode was ignited. The Marks was the brand-new hotel down the shore from Henry's. The Cove was the restaurant inside. It was the only other place in town with a trained chef, Nola Simms.

"Posting with the hashtag already, saying why they should be on *Small Town Smorgasbord*," Kennedy reported.

"Hell no. If anyone from this town gets on the show, it's going to be Henry's," I vowed. "We've been here for decades. They've barely set up shop."

Nola Simms was admittedly good, but that didn't mean I wanted her hogging the national spotlight on the show I'd dreamed of being featured on since its debut.

"I figured they'd be some friendly competition, but I didn't foresee them being a problem this fast," Seth said, leaning his elbows on the table. He shook his head like it didn't compute, which was my opinion exactly.

"I'm not about to let them waltz in here with their corporate budget and new restaurant and steal our opportunity," I said.

"You need to get your pitches out there right away," Kennedy said. She had her phone out and was tapping and swiping in a frenzy. "If you decide to hire me, I can help."

While her eyes were on her phone, Seth met my gaze with a questioning look. I gave a subtle but adamant nod.

"We're hiring you," Seth said.

Kennedy's head popped up and she looked from him to me. She must have seen we were serious as a heart attack, because a grin spread across her face. "Awesome. Let's do this," she said. "And let's start by doing everything we can to get the show producers' attention. We need to get high-quality food photos ASAP and the best, most enticing copy on the planet, which I can help with. Do you have a food photographer you use?"

I'd never *not* liked this girl, but right now, I wanted to stand up and hug her and swing her around for jumping in with zero hesitation.

"We've mostly done it ourselves but if you know a professional—"

"I've got a guy. I'll see if he can get out here... When could you have at least three dishes camera-ready?"

I glanced at my smart watch, ran through our options for which dishes to use, and did some calculations. "I could have them ready this afternoon, before the dinner service. Or any day this week," I added as I realized getting someone to Henry's that fast was a long shot.

"Like three p.m.?" Kennedy asked. "Would that give you enough time to prepare, say, six options?" Her thumbs were flying over her phone screen as she appeared to be sending a message to someone—her photography guy?

"I can do three o'clock, but are you sure you can?"

"I'll postpone the meeting I had at one. We could go to Henry's right now and you can tell me more about the dishes so I can start tailoring some copy for the social media posts. If you guys are up for it."

"I need to run home and change," I said. "You want to take her in?" I asked my brother. We normally had a Monday morning meeting, so I was pretty sure he had the time if we canceled that.

"I'm ready as soon as we cash out," Seth said. "Kennedy and I can head over and start on the hard part."

Laughing quietly at the long-running battle between us regarding which job was harder, cooking or running the business, I craned my head to signal to Mirabella that we were ready for the bill. She was at our table in less than thirty seconds with it and a Dragonfly Diner bag with Kennedy's sprinkles.

I reached for my wallet, but Kennedy smacked down a card before I could pull it out.

"This is my treat. You're hiring me. I'm stoked to work with you," she said. "I can't wait to rock *Small Town Smorgasbord's* world and get them to Henry's."

"I like the way you think," I said. I stood and extended my hand. Kennedy gave it a sturdy shake. "I'm going to be the rude one and run home to put my whites on. I'll see you both at Henry's in a few."

I made my way out of the diner, nodding at the people I knew as I went by. I could tell by the growing line to be seated that it was just after nine. That was when tourists started the daily infiltration.

Though it was mid-August and school had already started throughout the state, the rest of the month was still busy in Dragonfly Lake with couples and childless groups squeezing in an end-of-summer trip to our town. Most of the shops opened at nine or before, so people filled the rainy sidewalks as I made my way toward my loft apartment above the hardware store. I barely saw them as I wove in and out, though, my mind going a thousand miles an hour on how to win the war the Cove had just started.

Six dishes wouldn't be a problem, but I needed to be strategic and pick the most photogenic ones, the ones I had all the ingredients for on hand, the ones that were most unique. The ones that would blow Nola Simms out of the water, and ultimately, the ones that would allure the *Small Town Smorgasbord* producers in.

As I walked past the hardware store's front windows toward the stairs up to my place, I was lost in a debate in my head between the apple fritter cake and the stout cake as I wondered if I could get Kinsey in early to pull this off. I took out my phone to send her a message, but before I could unlock the screen, I collided smack into someone coming out of the store. Multiple bags crashed to the ground, the contents scattering across the sidewalk, as I automatically reached out to steady the petite woman I'd plowed into, grasping her elbows.

Cussing at myself for being so wrapped up I'd nearly run someone over, I said, "I'm sorry—"

Oh, holy Jesus. My heart stopped as her dark-chocolate-brown eyes met mine. Familiar eyes.

"Ava?"

"You've got to be kidding me," she said, and it wasn't in a friendly way.

Then again, Ava Dean had no reason to be friendly toward me and every reason to hate me.

"I'm sorry," I said inadequately, unsure whether I was apologizing for bulldozing her over on the sidewalk or for ending our relationship so poorly all those years ago.

She was shaking her head, as if laying eyes on her worst nightmare, backing away from me, and fuck if that didn't make me feel like an ogre.

"I'll help you pick this stuff up," I said, but as I glanced around us, I realized someone else had beaten me to it.

Rosy McNamara straightened, holding out three Bergman Hardware bags stuffed with merchandise to Ava, looking between Ava and me, assessing.

"Ava Dean?" the intuitive woman in her late fifties asked. "Stars above. Are you okay, honey?"

Ava pressed her lips together as she averted her gaze from mine, and I could swear her eyes filled with tears.

"Did I hurt you?" I asked, looking her over. She wore calf-length leggings, a long white shirt with a thin gray unzipped hoodie over it, white sneakers, and a ball cap. I couldn't see any outward sign of injury.

She continued to shake her head, quick, frantic shakes, as she backed farther away. "I'm fine. I just"—her eyes met mine for another second—"I can't do this. Not today."

Without taking the bags from Mrs. McNamara, she turned and scurried toward the old truck parked a few spots down.

Mrs. McNamara sent a concerned look my way, then her brows shot up. "I've got her. It seems obvious she doesn't want your help."

Swallowing, I nodded once. Even though the woman's tone was compassionate instead of judgmental, I didn't like how it felt to have Ava run away from me.

Before I could say more, Mrs. McNamara caught up to Ava and put an arm around her shoulders reassuringly. Since Ava let her and I needed to get my ass to work, I headed up to my apartment to get on with my day.

There was no reason a chance collision with Ava Dean after seventeen years should affect me for more than a minute, so I sure as hell didn't know why I was still seeing those hurt brown eyes in my mind when I walked into the kitchen at Henry's thirty minutes later.

CHAPTER 3

'd like to think that, on any other day of my life, I'd be able to handle seeing Cash Henry just fine.

Today, though, I was so not even in the same zip code as fine.

Running into his broad chest, feeling his big hands on my shaky arms, looking into those dreamy hazel eyes that had once been my entire world had taken the last little bit of my heart that was still intact and crushed it.

Not for any logical reason, mind you. It'd been seventeen years since I'd seen him. Seventeen years since he'd snapped me out of my naive twenty-year-old self and helped me learn that even the person you felt closest to on this earth could let you down.

I'd gone to college in California, grown up, and married and divorced someone else during that time. From what I'd heard through the grapevine—my aunt and her beloved friends, the Diamonds—Cash had stayed in the Navy for a few years, returned to Dragonfly Lake eventually, and had married and divorced himself.

One look at him, though, and all those years had disappeared in an instant. Logical thought had been sucked out of my head, and my heart had taken over for about three beats. Just long enough for the composure I'd been fighting tooth and nail to hold in place for the past eighteen hours to collapse.

Those three heartbeats had been enough for me to register that Cash Henry was one of those guys who looked even better at almost forty than he had at twenty-three.

Then my eyes had filled with goddamn tears. There was no hiding my annoyingly fragile state from anyone on that sidewalk, so I'd done the only thing I could do. I'd retreated, like a turtle pulling into its shell.

Before I could reach the refuge that ancient Chevy offered, I felt a gentle feminine hand on my back.

"Darling girl, you're not alone."

Even if I hadn't recognized Rosy McNamara's voice, the jangling of her multiple bracelets would've given her away. Relieved that it wasn't Cash who'd followed me, I let her pull me into her side as we kept walking, not daring to attempt words.

Even though I hadn't seen this woman for several years, she was one of my aunt's people, a member of her tight circle of friends. I felt closer to Aunt Phyl just being near Rosy, and I allowed her to guide me to the truck. When I started toward the driver-side door, though, she took my hand and stopped me. I had no choice but to meet her gaze, and I swiped at my eyes as I did so.

"Let me drive you to the inn, Ava." The compassion in her voice and the kind concern in her crystal-blue eyes nearly did me in.

I cleared my throat in an attempt to break through the grief that was finally leveling me. "I'm fi—"

"You're not fine, darling girl. No one would expect you to be fine. I've got your bags from Bergman's here." She looked into the plastic bags I'd totally forgotten about in my rush to retreat. "These look like something Halstead would ask for. Am I right?"

I nodded, my determination to resist her help weakening by the second. I didn't even know what half the stuff in that bag was and had only made it through Halstead's list with the help of Jake Bergman, who'd also recognized me, offered condolences, and unknowingly helped set the emotional stage for the shit show that had just happened on the sidewalk.

"Let me take you home. I'll deliver these things to the maintenance god himself, and you can steal a few minutes alone," Rosy said.

"I need to cover the front desk—"

"I'll take care of that too. I know my way around dear Phyllis's antiquated setup."

That elicited a bittersweet smile from me. I'd never questioned how close those women were. It gave me a measure of peace to know that Phyllis had had good, caring people in her day-to-day life. My aunt and I had FaceTimed weekly, but I always felt bad about not seeing her in person more than once or twice a year. Those women, the Diamonds, had been here every day for her and she for them.

"I'll take you up on covering the front desk," I said, "and I'll take these to Halstead. I need to keep busy—and there's plenty to get done."

Rosy took a gentle hold on my arm and steered me toward the front end of the truck. "You're facing a lot, darling girl. You're smart to let us Diamonds help you. Phyllis was one of ours, and we'll do anything for her and, by extension, you."

Because her kind words had my throat swelling with a ball of emotion, making it impossible to speak, I nodded and went around to the passenger side. I kept my eyes to the ground, my hair draping over the sides of my face, and I didn't look back once to see if Cash was still nearby. I didn't want to know. Didn't want to care about him any more than I cared about a stranger on the street.

My aunt's fifteen-year-old truck was huge, but Rosy handled it easily, as I was pretty sure she handled most things. The woman had raised a handful of boys and taken over running the marina when her husband passed away. She was the free spirit of the Diamonds, a senior citizen flower child, with her arms full of bangles and beads and her fingers accented with large-stoned rings—in citrine yellow today to coordinate with her moss-green, tunic-length, short-sleeved shirt, her botanical-print baggy pants, and a flowy cape thing in the same print that hung over one shoulder. She looked eccentric and put together at once.

When she caught me studying her from the side, she sent me a sympathetic smile.

"Pretty rings," I said to head off more condolences.

"I love the splashes of color," Rosy said with a glance at her knuckles on the steering wheel, "and they pack a heck of a wallop when I punch someone."

A halfhearted, disbelieving laugh gurgled out of me. "You punch people often?"

"Only when I have no other choice." There was no hint of humor and no sign of exaggeration in her tone. Just matter-of-factness. She turned off Honeysuckle Road onto the inn's property, following the short but windy road through the trees, past the overflow lot and the main parking area. With an easy familiarity, she took the gravel drive to the cottage and pulled the truck up where I'd found it. She reached over and squeezed the back of my hand before I could open the door and escape. "How are you holding up, Ava? Phyllie's passing is quite the shock."

I swallowed, my glance going out the windshield and landing on my aunt's home. *My* home until I was twenty. It looked...empty. Lonely.

After a slow, shaky inhale, I said, "I was doing okay until

back there…" I shook my head. What the hell had that been on the sidewalk with a guy I no longer knew? Ridiculous, that's what. "I've been holding everything at bay, trying to get as much done as I could…"

I sensed Rosy nodding next to me. "Sometimes when something awful happens and there's no way to make it better, it helps to keep yourself busy."

"There's so much to do," I said, making no move to get out of the truck. "I think Loretta said something about planning the funeral on the phone yesterday. I haven't even had a chance to think about it…"

"You've traveled across the country on top of hearing tragic news. Of course you haven't thought about a funeral. I'm sure Moses over at the funeral home will meet with you whenever you're ready."

My aunt and I had arranged my mother's funeral together when she'd died seventeen years ago, but I barely remembered any of it. Now I had to get through the process alone.

I glanced at the side mirror, where I could see the inn reflected.

"The inn looks…sad," I said, noticing the exterior paint on this end was peeling and the stonework was noticeably dirty. "Was Aunt Phyl happy?" Again, my throat thickened with sorrow as I voiced the question that had been dogging me since the taxi had dropped me off.

A thoughtful sigh sounded from Rosy as she leaned back against the seat. "I think she absolutely was. She loved this place with all her heart. In a lot of ways, she *was* this place, and when she passed, it's like the inn lost a little bit of its soul."

I wasn't sure about any of that, but it made me feel marginally better that Aunt Phyl had derived happiness from this place. "It needs a lot of work before I can find someone to run it."

"You're going to turn it over then. We wondered."

"I'm not going to sell it." My gut hardened into a knot. "But my life is in LA. My career. Aunt Phyl understood that —" My voice broke. Damn, it was exhausting to fight off these nonstop emotions. "I'm this close to getting the job of my dreams," I said, my voice lower, thicker. "My agent is on the verge of selling my screenplay to Stream, and there's a chance they're going to hire me as the head writer."

"Stars above, Ava. That's remarkable!"

I blew out a breath, worried I would jinx it if I told too many people. "It's a long shot. They don't usually hire a newbie, but the company's young and my agent has pull with one of their executives and they apparently love my idea."

"Sounds like a good agent to have. Phyllie didn't tell us any of this!"

"It's new. I just told her Friday night…"

I'd just FaceTimed with her three days ago without knowing it was the last time, our final goodbye. It was impossible to wrap my head around it. It made my chest literally hurt.

Rosy let out a pained sigh. "She had to be so pleased for you. She just never had the chance to tell us."

Because less than twenty-four hours later, she'd had a heart attack. The only solace in anything was that the medical people said she'd gone instantly, with no suffering.

"This could be the break I've been hoping for since my first year of screenwriting school," I explained. "Some people work for forty years and don't get an opportunity like this—"

"You deserve it, Ava."

Her words stopped me, because I'd been expecting her to try to persuade me to stay in Dragonfly Lake. "I don't know if *deserve* plays into it, but if I don't pursue this, I might never get another chance. It might sound selfish, but I finally have the opportunity to focus on what *I* want—"

"Ava." She squeezed my hand again. "You don't have to defend your decisions to me. Stars above, you spent years caring for your mother, and from what I gather, you sacrificed a lot for that ex-husband of yours as well. I'd say it's past time for you to tend to your dreams and goals."

My affection and appreciation for this woman grew tenfold. "Thank you. I'm sure most people won't see it that way. They'll say it's a travesty for me to put someone else in charge of my aunt's legacy."

"Anyone who says that doesn't know you and doesn't have a clue what you've been through."

"Nobody here ever really knew me," I said matter-of-factly. I suspected this town might judge me and judge me hard. I was still working on not caring. "But I know Aunt Phyl would understand. She'd never want me to feel forced to stay here because of her inn. She'd want someone to take it over because it was their heart's desire."

"You're absolutely right. She loved you so much and would want you first and foremost to be happy."

"Writing makes me happy," I said, nodding, fighting down another surge of feelings that talking about my aunt in the past tense brought on. "Anyway, if you know of anyone who might be interested in managing the inn full-time, have them contact me. I don't suppose you or the other Diamonds would be?"

"Most of us have our own businesses to run. I've all but handed off everything to do with the marina to my boys. Loretta has the yarn shop, Dotty the Lily Pad. Darlene'll never leave the Country Market—I just thank God she wasn't working when Phyllie..."

I gasped and was also glad my aunt's good friend wasn't on the scene when she'd collapsed.

"Nancy likes her solitude and Kona has her husband and dogs to keep her busy."

Nodding, I said, "It was worth a try. Speaking of busy, I need to get this stuff to Halstead." I went for the door handle but paused when she spoke again.

"One more thing, Ava. What happened back there? With Cash?"

There were apparently no easy topics on this Monday morning. "I...don't know. Nothing, really, other than I've been blocking out all the feelings for two days, just trying to get through without losing it. Crashing into *him*... It's like it hit the release valve or something."

"If I remember right, he broke your heart," Rosy said, her voice brimming with compassion.

"We were young. I was naive. On the scale of life, it wasn't a big deal."

Which was a lie, but it was ancient history.

Rosy didn't hesitate a second before saying, "I remember we all thought he was on the verge of proposing to you."

I pressed my lips together and figured this intuitive woman could see through me, so I might as well just level with her and get back to my inn checklist. "I thought he was too." I flashed a smile. "See? Naive. And seventeen years ago."

"It looked like whatever was there seventeen years ago might still be there today."

I forced a little laugh. "He's still good-looking. I'll give you that, but that's all it was. My life is in California now, not Tennessee."

She raised a questioning brow. "I don't know if you've heard my history, but I grew up in California, went to college there. My girlfriends and I took a VW Bus cross-country just before finishing grad school. I had every intention of going back, but then I met Tom McNamara at a music festival, fell in love, and here I still am, nearly forty years later."

"That's sweet," I said, because it was, but it was her story, not mine. "My story's the opposite. I left Dragonfly Lake to get away from the guy. I have no interest in getting him back."

With a shrug I hoped was conspiratorial rather than a

blow-off, I opened the door, picked up the bags, and set off through the light rain to find Halstead to deliver his requests.

I could feel Rosy watching me, probably putting way too much thought into the Cash thing. There wasn't a Cash thing, truly. I'd just been stunned to run smack into him of all people. I'd forget all about it within five minutes of returning to my to-do list if only we stopped talking about him.

I was overwhelmed by everything I needed to get done in the next week. I barely had bandwidth to pee, let alone plan a funeral and update the inn and find the perfect person to run it. The sooner I could get everything here in Dragonfly Lake handled, the sooner I could get back to my career.

The last thing I had room for was mooning over Cash Henry. And yet, as I went in the east-wing door of the inn, I couldn't get the image of his rugged face and compassionate eyes out of my damn mind.

CHAPTER 4

CASH

Family meal was new at Henry's.

I'd finally convinced Seth to close down at three thirty each day for dinner prep, and that included one of the kitchen staff cooking a meal for the rest of us to share before reopening at five.

Seth had cringed at losing a little income for that hour and a half. I'd argued it would foster camaraderie. The reasoning that had finally convinced my business-freak brother, though, was that it would help retain employees in an industry where turnover was high. We were two weeks into it, and though we were still adjusting to the new rhythm, family meal was turning out to be a positive thirty to forty-five minutes that built up morale and allowed the staff to get to know each other even better. And my staff had been cooking up some damn good food. It had quickly become one of the best parts of the day for me.

Today, however, it'd been a struggle to get through. My mind was stuck in other places.

The session with Kennedy and her food photographer had

been a success, according to Kennedy, who was without question an expert at marketing. The posts we ended up with looked tantalizing, and her copy was scores above our usual attempts, but in my mind, the only way to gauge success would be to wait and see whether we were selected to be on the show. It could be weeks before we knew anything.

My sous chef, Zinnia York, sidled up next to me as I triple-checked Mead's mise en place work. He'd been with Henry's for less than a year and had happened upon this job, with no chef training, but I'd liked his attitude and his work ethic, so I'd given him a chance. So far, I didn't regret it. I still checked his work and in fact checked everything that went out of the kitchen when I was here, which was almost always.

"Jelena rocked the chevapcici, don't you think?" Zinnia asked as she kept a watchful eye on tonight's staff. She was my right hand and fully capable of running a service without me. I'd allowed it from time to time, but generally I was here for most lunches and dinners. Not because I didn't trust her but because I burned to be here.

"If we ever decide to serve Serbian food, she's got us covered," I said. "That spread was unforgettable."

"Ajvar, she called it. I could eat that on her flatbread every day."

Mead, who'd been chopping more onions, went into the walk-in for something, and Zinnia took that opportunity to butt into my business.

"What's wrong today, Cash? You seem uptight, like beyond all levels of Cash Henry uptight. Our social media posts for the show look amazing. You've never made prettier plates in your life, so what's up?"

I might've grunted—definitely shrugged—as I spun around to the meat station to see how Perry was doing. She was, of course, on top of things, as I'd come to expect. That didn't mean I wouldn't keep checking. It was *my* last name on the sign. My full name on the door as head chef.

There were people who believed I didn't measure up simply because my grandmother had handed this place over to my brothers and me. People who believed I didn't deserve it. Seth said it was all in my head and had accused me many times of wasting mental energy on something that was pointless, but I wasn't about to let my guard down. Being featured on *Small Town Smorgasbord* would be a big step forward in my credibility.

And yet Zinnia was spot fucking on. I was uptight even now, when we'd done everything we could for the time being, and my tension had little to do with the pursuit of national TV coverage.

The reason, undoubtedly, was my literal run-in with Ava.

It was irrational. I'd put her out of my head for years now. When word had spread Saturday that her aunt died, my siblings had been all over me about it, but I'd managed to stuff those memories, those regrets, down even with their harassment. Seeing her this morning, though, in the flesh… touching her… Those ninety seconds on the sidewalk had opened the vault in my mind where I'd shoved all things Ava Dean.

Remembering I needed to check the schedule for the rest of the week to account for Joey going out of town for a memorial service, I headed into my office, not upset by the prospect of getting away from Zinnia in case she had more questions. On a piece of scratch paper, I jotted down Joey's remaining shifts so I could find someone to fill them. I stood and shoved the note in my pocket as my pixie-sized sous chef appeared in the doorway.

"We open in twenty-two minutes," I grumbled to her.

"Which means you should just be straight with me so I can get back to work." She sat on one of the visitor chairs on the opposite side of my desk and gave me a challenging look even as I remained on my feet. "Those photos from earlier look fantastic, Cash. And the copy Seth and Kennedy cooked up…it's so good. The best advertising I've ever seen come out of Henry's. It represents the dishes perfectly and conveys what we are—a foodie's dream marriage of Southern cooking, craft beer, and vacation on a plate."

I grinned in spite of myself. "You've been listening to Kennedy all day, huh?"

"The woman nailed it, as she herself would say. We could not present Henry's in a more accurate, tempting light. Whatever you're paying her, you're getting your money's worth."

"We'll see if we get on the show."

"If we don't, it's because we're not the right fit, not due to anything lacking on our part."

I nodded, knowing what she said was true even if I didn't like it and would have a hard time accepting it.

When Zin didn't make a move to get back to work, I glanced at my watch. "Nineteen minutes."

"The sooner you tell me what's really wrong, the sooner I can return to my duties."

I inhaled slowly, gathering my patience, sizing her up, determining how deeply she was digging in. She'd worked here for three years. I knew her well. She was at least as stubborn as Seth when he was in money-manager mode.

"Does it have something to do with running into your ex in front of the hardware store?" she asked, bold as can be.

"Since you weren't in Dragonfly Lake back then and wouldn't know my ex from the Virgin Mary, I can only assume you've been listening to gossip," I muttered. I'd been in the kitchen all day and hadn't been tuned in to the outside world—or the bullshit the locals brought in with them.

"Interesting stories going around," she said with a spark in her knowing eyes. "You can tell me the truth."

Because this was Zin and I trusted her more than I trusted most people, I took the time to explain. "There's nothing to tell. I bumped into my ex, who's in town for her aunt's funeral—"

"Phyllis Sharp, right?"

With a nod, I continued. "I was sidetracked, thinking about which dishes to do for the *Smorgasbord* posts, and I nearly ran her over on the sidewalk. End of story."

"Except...not. Otherwise you'd be more on your game today."

"You said yourself I've never plated prettier," I threw back at her.

"There was too much salt in the grits."

Fuck. She'd noticed that. Kennedy had sung its praises, as had Mead, who'd taken a few minutes to watch the process. But Zin was correct. I suspected I'd salted the grits twice.

"Uncharacteristic mistake for you," she said, crossing her arms.

I sank into my chair, letting out an exhale, not really knowing what to say, because though Ava had flitted around in my thoughts all day, I hadn't had a chance to think clearly about her, about why that collision was affecting me this much.

"I heard she ran away from you today." Zin's tone was compassionate now, not teasing.

"She was pretty much horrified to see me." Just saying that out loud made my chest tighten, and that pissed me off.

"Did you hurt her in the past?" When we were in the kitchen, I appreciated Zin's directness, but right now, I hated it. "You did," she said quietly when I didn't answer.

"I mean, I don't know."

Hell. I did. I'd always known. I'd just buried it all for so long I liked to tell myself none of it mattered anymore. In my day-to-day life, it didn't. It hadn't, anyway, until she'd come back.

"What did you do, Cash?"

The concern in her tone had me scowling at her. "What the hell are you thinking I did? I was young, stupid, and scared.

We'd talked about getting married, but the night before I left for basic training, I broke up with her instead."

Zin let out a gasp. "That poor girl."

"I know. I handled everything poorly."

I shook my head as I allowed myself to recall that time in my life. Self-doubt had plagued me at every turn. I'd been searching, trying to figure out what to do with my life. I'd had a short stint in minor league baseball, but after a season and a half, it'd been clear the majors were not in my future. It'd felt like a big, hairy failure.

At loose ends, with no college degree and no desire to go to school, I'd taken a job as a beverage distributor, driving a truck all over the region. The Honeysuckle Inn had been one of my stops. The attraction between Ava and me had been immediate, and we'd spent whatever time we could steal together.

"I still had a lot of growing up to do back then," I told Zinnia.

"Did you purposely lead her on?" She narrowed her eyes at me.

"Of course not. I wasn't conniving, just clueless. Part of me wanted to marry her and live happily ever after."

"But the other part?"

"You know we open in twelve minutes, right?"

"Better finish the story fast then, Chef."

I blew out a breath, wondering why I hadn't hired a sous chef who minded her own business. Meeting her eyes, I cut straight to the chase. "I was worried I couldn't be what she needed. Not long-term, not while I was halfway around the world on a ship. I didn't know how long I'd be in. I'd like to say it was a selfless act, but I was just scared."

"That's fair," Zinnia said. "It sounds like it wasn't the right time."

She made it seem simple enough, but I knew I could've

handled it better. Like a man instead of a freaked-out boy. I'd been twenty-three. There was no excuse for it.

I was about to remind Zin of the time once again when she said, "It seems like you have regrets."

Regrets weren't something I spent a lot of time on, but…I shook my head. "I don't know. Seeing her just took me back. The way she looked at me…" As if I was the dead-last person she ever wanted to see again… I hated that the most.

There wasn't anything romantic left between us, but I couldn't stomach the thought of being someone she dreaded running into. I stood abruptly. "I need to clear the air. Apologize for being a douchebag all those years ago." I glanced out the office door to the kitchen staff, who were all on task and looked to have everything under control. "Are you okay handling dinner service?"

Zinnia's brows shot up her forehead, and I knew what she was thinking—that I rarely skipped a dinner shift unless I had a scheduled event that couldn't be avoided. I was thankful she only said, "Of course. Do what you need to do, Cash. You know I could handle this in my sleep."

I nodded, thanked her, and brushed past her to rustle up some dinner for the woman who, years ago, often forgot to feed herself. Tonight, I was going to feed her and clear the air so I would be one less problem for her to wrangle.

CHAPTER 5

AVA

wasn't sure if it was late afternoon or early evening. Definitely still Monday. Grief had a way of wringing all sense of time and place out of a person, and it'd had its wicked way with me for the past few hours.

I'd spent the afternoon at the funeral home, working out the details for Aunt Phyl's service with Loretta Lawson's kindhearted help. I'd insisted on writing the obituary myself because how could I not? I was Phyllis's last living family, and as a writer, I wanted it to convey the spirit of her life perfectly.

No pressure.

My aunt's spirit was a beautiful, generous one and was intricately wrapped up in this inn and this town. Every word I wrote about her made me cry harder, and by the time I'd composed the last lines, my eyes burned and my chest hurt. I had zero tears left as I sat out on the balcony of unit number seven, watching the lake through the persisting drizzle. Number seven had always been my refuge of choice growing up. It was smaller than the other rooms, so it was usually the last one we rented out.

Apparently the weather thought it should take over where I'd left off with the tears, because the rain started pounding down and the wind gusted, changing it from a peaceful, soothing rainfall to the precursor to a storm. As if on cue, a knock sounded on the main door to the room, loud enough to hear through the open slider even with the rain.

I jumped up, worried it might be Halstead. While he'd Band-Aided this morning's roof leak, he'd made it clear a new roof was a must.

I carried the notebook with the handwritten obituary inside and tossed it on the bed. Running my hands over my swollen, sore eyes to make sure they were no longer wet, I walked to the door and opened it…and blinked stupidly when I saw Cash standing there, soaking wet, staring down at me.

"Don't slam the door on me," he said, holding his hand out as if to block it if I tried. When I didn't move, he held up a Henry's bag, and I caught a whiff of fresh food.

"What are you doing here?" I attempted to keep my tone level. He didn't need to know about the emotional shitstorm seeing him evoked in me.

"You and I need to talk."

"How did you know where to find me?"

"I went to the registration desk. Kona thought you were in the cottage. When nobody answered there, I suspected I'd find you here. How many storms did we watch blow in from that balcony?"

He nodded behind me as memories flashed like lightning through my mind's eye—us on the balcony, us in the bed that was mere feet away. I'd lost my virginity in that bed, to the man still standing in the doorway with an unsure expression on his face.

I didn't know if it was because I'd cried every last tear and had none left for him or because I was curious about what he thought we could possibly need to talk about or because that bag of food smelled good enough to make my stomach growl, but I stepped back to let him in.

At that moment, it was as if the clouds opened up to prove they could rain even harder. A shift of the wind had drops pounding against the glass slider and, since I'd left the door open, into the room. It snapped me out of my stupor.

I rushed to the door and slid it shut, closing out the rain and muffling the noise of the storm. There were no lights on in the room, as the sun hadn't set yet, but it was suddenly almost as dark as night.

Cash closed the door to the hallway, sealing us away from the world, and my heart pounded. I wasn't afraid of him, not physically, but I'd never, ever expected to be this close to him again, let alone shut in a small inn room crammed full of memories.

I watched in silence as he took the few short steps to the dresser and set down the bag—two bags, I realized. Then he reached to the lamp and flipped it on low as if it hadn't been a decade and a half since he'd been in the room.

"You're drenched," I said stupidly, taking in his wet navy-blue T-shirt that molded to his thick chest and flat abdomen.

"Yeah." He shook his head as if it couldn't matter less. "I want to apologize for this morning. I was distracted and nearly plowed you over."

"It's okay. Barely a blip on my radar," I lied, crossing my arms over my chest and leaning against the glass door.

"I'm sorry about your aunt."

I nodded curtly and said, "Thanks. I appreciate that, but you didn't have to come all the way out here to say it."

He studied me for a moment with those greenish-brown eyes that I'd long ago thought of as dreamy. I didn't want to like them now, but I couldn't deny there seemed to be genuine concern in them that threatened to get to me.

"That's not the only thing." Cash cleared his throat, leading me to believe he was uncomfortable. He turned his back to the dresser, resting his butt against it, his hands braced behind him on the edge of it, looking...so painfully handsome.

He couldn't have caught me at a weaker moment. I was raw and barely breathing, waiting for him to say more or leave. Preferably leave, because no matter how irrational it was that he could affect me in any positive way after all this time, oh, fucking hell, did he affect me. My mouth was bone-dry and my heart raced like a thoroughbred horse in Kentucky.

I'd been back to town a few times over the years, but I'd tried to stay close to the inn whenever possible. This—*he*—was one of the biggest reasons.

"This is awkward," he said, his voice a low rumble.

"You brought food?" I prompted, hoping to hurry him along.

"I'll get to that. Ava, I'm sorry I was such an asshole before I left for basic training."

I pressed my lips together, trying to figure out how to respond. I hadn't expected an apology, hadn't expected him to bring up the past at all, and I wasn't sure how much good it could do now. "That's water under the bridge, don't you think?"

"The look on your face when you saw me this morning said otherwise."

My burning eyes popped wide open. Did he think I still had feelings for him? After all this time? I let out a hollow laugh. "It's been seventeen years. I was married to another man, Cash. I haven't been pining away—"

"That's not what I mean. There was anger or maybe dislike in your eyes, and I get it. I deserve that. But I'd like to try to make peace."

"Just...wipe out the past? Just like that? I don't know if I can do that. You…" I sucked in a breath. Were we really doing this? Right now? After all this time and when I was so wrung out I was verging on numb?

"I what? What were you going to say?" he asked.

He wanted to go there? Okay. Maybe I did have some things to air out. "You not only broke my heart, Cash, but you cured me of my naiveté. You made me feel like a foolish little girl who'd woven my dreams around a big, fat load of BS. We'd talked about getting married, even after you decided to enlist. I actually thought you were going to propose that night before you left, not dump me."

His lids lowered and his expression seemed regretful, but what did I know? I'd read him wrong all those years ago. I liked to think I was wiser now, but maybe Cash Henry was an expert at making me believe whatever he wanted me to believe.

Before he could say anything, I continued, "Five weeks after you left, my mom died. As you know, we were aware that was coming for a long time, but I still wasn't prepared for it. I always thought you'd be there to help me through it, so when it happened and I was on my own…" I'd thought I was out of tears, but my eyes gushed full again. I couldn't have hidden it if I wanted to. "I was doubly devastated."

"Fuck, Ava," he let out, meeting my eyes again, his expression laden with regret and sympathy. "I don't blame you if you hate me."

"You hurt me, then life hurt me by taking my mom." I sucked in a shaky breath. "I was brokenhearted, but I never hated you." Sometimes I thought hating him would be easier.

"You should have. I handled everything wrong."

I let out something close to a laugh. "Breaking up is breaking up. Is there a right way to do that?"

He brought his hands to his face, ran them over it, then crossed his arms. I couldn't help noticing the way the sleeves of his tee were tight over his bulging biceps. The Navy—or life—had done a heck of a job of filling him out.

"Saying I'm sorry doesn't do you a bit of good," he said, "but I am. I hate that you had to go through your mom's death by yourself. When my mom died, I was surrounded by family and friends and I still didn't know how I'd ever get through it. I can't imagine how hard it was for you."

"I'm sorry about your mom too." I'd heard the news from Aunt Phyl when it happened a few years back and couldn't remain indifferent, but I'd kept my sadness to myself and had merely allowed Phyl to add my name to the flowers she sent to Cash's family.

He nodded. "I still don't know what to say to that. Thanks?"

With my lips twitching upward in the beginnings of a sympathetic smile, I said, "Always awkward."

"There's something I want to clarify. The times we discussed getting married? I meant everything I said. I wasn't bullshitting you."

I tilted my head, studying him, wondering yet again if I could believe him. When we were together, I'd never questioned his character, never doubted the things he said, but his blindside of a breakup had left me questioning everything. I didn't want to be made a fool of again.

"I bought a ring, Ava. I had it in my pocket that night."

Everything crashed to a standstill—my heart, my breathing, my brain. I blinked, sucked in air. "Then *what happened?*"

He shoved away from the dresser and paced toward the sliding glass door, pausing a couple of feet from me and peering outside. I watched his face in the dim light, noting the furrow of his brow, the slight pressing together of his lips, barely enough for me to see.

"I got scared," he said quietly, still gazing out the window. His Adam's apple bobbed as he swallowed. "Of everything. Of enlisting. Of finding yet another career I wasn't cut out for.

Of letting you down. I was worried I couldn't be what you needed. Not long-term, not while I was halfway around the world on a ship. I wasn't sure I'd be a good husband even if I didn't enlist."

"So...like pre-game jitters?" That was so much to unpack, and I couldn't begin to sort through it now.

Cash shook his head. "It went deeper than that. As much as I never wanted to hurt you, I don't think I was ready, probably not for any of it. The military doesn't give you much choice but to get ready fast, but..." He shrugged, still not looking at me. "I've since proven I don't know how to make a marriage work."

"Something we have in common," I muttered.

"Live and learn, right?"

"Something like that."

Cash turned ninety degrees and faced me, leaning a shoulder against the glass, shoving his hands in his jeans pockets. "I hate that I hurt you, but for some reason, I'm glad we're not divorced. From each other, I mean." He offered a halfhearted half smile. "Which makes no sense at all."

I nodded, because it didn't make sense and yet I knew what he meant.

"I don't want to be one more bad thing you have to deal with now that you're back," he said.

I straightened and swiped a finger under each eye, trying to level myself out. "To be honest, I don't know *what* you are."

I had a lot of years of hurting to overcome. I didn't want to hold on to that pain, but my heart needed time to catch up with my brain, which did understand we'd both been young and stupid. Maybe he'd outgrown it. I certainly hadn't, if you considered I'd made another bad relationship decision when I'd married Wes. I liked to think I'd finally learned the lesson that I needed to rely only on myself and make myself happy.

He studied me for several seconds, then said, "I guess that's fair. Maybe I can curry favor with dinner?" His whole manner changed as he pushed off the window and went toward the food. "I was guessing you haven't eaten for a while. Unless you've changed."

He'd guessed right, I realized, as I tried to think back to my last meal. I'd had pretzels on the plane this morning, which seemed like a week ago. I kept that to myself, a little shaken that he remembered my tendency to forget to eat.

"I threw together a turkey BLT croissant sandwich. Pretty simple but Kinsey's croissants make everything next-level."

My stomach rumbled again, and I didn't think it would matter what he pulled out of that bag. When he popped open the to-go container and handed it to me, my brows rose. The croissant was picture-perfect—puffy with golden-brown layers.

"Soup too?" I asked, noticing a steaming Styrofoam cup with a lid.

"We don't do a lot of soup in the summer, but the weather today called for a summer minestrone."

I picked up the sandwich and took a bite. The flavors came together to nearly make my eyes tear up again. It was that good.

"You're not eating?" I asked when I'd swallowed the first bite, then quickly took another.

"We have a staff meal before the dinner shift."

"So you're the chef, huh?" Another bit of gossip I'd inadvertently gathered on a trip home, after Guinevere Henry had turned her restaurant over to her grandsons. I'd told myself none of Cash's news was relevant to me anymore, but with a town like this, you could never avoid hearing bits here and there.

"I am."

"I knew you liked helping your grandmother when you were really young, but I didn't see this coming."

"It wasn't my lifelong plan, but the first one didn't pan out."

"Baseball," I said unnecessarily. I hadn't met him until after that dream had crashed and burned. "So how did you get from the Navy to cooking? Someone had to cook when your grandma was ready to retire and you stepped up?"

An expression flashed across his face, something I couldn't read, but it wasn't a happy one. Closer to a cringe.

"Did I say something wrong?" I asked.

"You made the assumption a lot of locals make. That my grandma decided to call it quits, so I picked up the apron and started cooking." His jaw ticked, and I waited for him to say more, because surely there was more. He didn't, though.

"No?" I prompted.

Cash straightened. "I went into the Navy not knowing what I wanted to do, in the service or with my life."

"I remember."

We'd talked for long hours about the decision. I'd planned to stand by him regardless. I could be a military wife. I could do the long periods without him, as long as I knew he was coming home to me.

Or so I'd thought.

"I was a culinary specialist, maybe because I mentioned working with my grandma as a kid. I don't know. It wasn't a dream job, and most guys in Culinary hated it, but it sparked something in me. After my four years were up, I came home and enrolled in culinary school."

"You figured out your new plan."

His answer was a single nod, and I was starting to get the message loud and clear that this was a sensitive issue.

"So culinary school and then what?" I asked, trying to figure out what I was missing.

"I worked in kitchens in Nashville for a few years under some damn good chefs. When my grandma was ready to retire, she offered up Henry's to my siblings and me. Holden, Seth, and I took her up on it."

"Not Hayden?"

"She'd earned a degree in design and was following that path."

"So the three of you took over the family restaurant." I loved that they'd kept it in the family.

Though I hadn't eaten there often, Cash had brought me carryout frequently—back when he'd first figured out regular mealtimes weren't my strong point. I myself wasn't good in the kitchen and had relied on things like microwave popcorn, frozen pizza, and toaster waffles to keep my mom and myself fed. She'd preferred to drink her calories, and I'd tried to keep food in her stomach, thinking it would help soak up the alcohol. Her palate had been like a three-year-old's, though, and I'd taken the path of least resistance to get her to eat.

"Seth runs the business end. Holden was our front-of-house manager until he left to open Rusty Anchor Brewing, and I took over the kitchen. We did a major overhaul of the building, doubling the size of the kitchen, and updated the rest of the place."

"So people think you just inherited and assume you didn't earn your chef chops?" I asked.

He blew out a breath. "In a nutshell. It's stupid to let it bother me. I know what I've been through. I know I'm a damn good chef who held my own in two of the best restaurants in Nashville." He shook his head as though frustrated with himself.

"Your work speaks for itself, Cash." I held up the cup of soup, which I was currently devouring. "Your food is excellent."

"Says the girl who has a top-twenty list of PopTart flavors."

I laughed. "Had. I got tired of them during college. Haven't had one for years." Sobering, I muttered, "My ex wouldn't have wanted them in the pantry anyway."

I could feel Cash staring at me, like he wanted to know

more, but Wes Winchester was the last topic I wanted to get into today.

"I take it it wasn't an amicable divorce?" he asked.

I shrugged. "It was amicable enough." Thanks, in part, to my dad being my ex's mentor in their law firm. "Just glad to get away from him."

"He's in California?"

I nodded as I stuck the last of the turkey croissant in my mouth and savored the salty taste.

"Dragonfly Lake is definitely 'away,'" Cash said, one side of his mouth twitching upward.

"I'm not staying," I clarified.

"You're not moving back?"

"I'm trying to get into screenwriting," I said. "There's a new-ish streaming company that's looking for series and movies. Stream. They're interested in a series I wrote."

"I've heard of it. That's impressive as hell. Congratulations."

"Nothing's signed yet." I knew better than to count on anything before the signatures were dry and the money was in the bank. "My agent is optimistic though. In part because they're also considering hiring me as the head writer for the show. I have a meeting with an executive next week that could springboard my career."

He sent me a smile that took me back nearly twenty years, when it felt like it was him and me against the world. "I'm happy for you, Ava. They'd be idiots to let you slip away." His eyes burned with intensity, as if there was a deeper meaning to his words. I couldn't even begin to think about that. "You always talked about wanting to write someday."

"Talking was all I had time to do until after my mom died," I said frankly. "I ended up going to film school in LA. Anyway..." I'd finished the soup and sandwich—all while standing because I didn't want to get too comfortable with him—and closed the cup inside the bigger container. I stepped toward the dresser, where he'd left the empty bag, and stuffed the containers inside to throw away when I left the room. "I need to get back to work."

Cash closed the distance from the window to the dresser. "You didn't think I'd forget dessert, did you?" He picked up the second bag, took out a square container, and held it out to me.

The familiar gesture struck me, even though so many years, so much of life had passed since he'd done that. Before I even opened the box, I knew.

"Hummingbird cake?"

"See for yourself."

I opened the box to a triple-layered slice of fluffy, cream-cheese-frosted cake. Without trying, I could smell the pineapple and bananas and sugar. Hummingbird cake was packed chock-full of comfort, like a grandmotherly hug— unless you were eating it in bed with the baker's grandson after sex, which had been the case many times in the past.

With memories dogging my mind, I made the mistake of glancing up at Cash. He was closer than I'd thought, maybe a foot away, and peering down at me with—I could swear it— heat in his eyes, as if he was remembering those nights too.

"It smells amazing," I said. "I'm going to save it for a midnight snack." Mainly because I needed him out of here, away from me. It was too tempting to fall into the easiness and affection we'd had in the past, and whatever had been was irrelevant now. I needed to remember that.

Breaking eye contact, I closed the cake box, spun around, and walked toward the door. "Thank you, Cash. You're in the right career, for sure." I reached the door and opened it, then smiled to soften that I was, in essence, kicking him out after he'd done something so kind for me.

"I like to think so," he said as he joined me at the door. "I'm glad we cleared the air about the past."

Before I could react, he leaned down and kissed my forehead, just a quick touch, but it had the impact of a punch to the chest.

"Good night, Ava."

I don't even know if I said goodnight back to him, but within seconds, I had the door closed between us, and I leaned my back against it, lying to myself that Cash Henry no longer had any hold over me.

CHAPTER 6

t was just after ten o'clock Thursday evening, and I was perched on Aunt Phyl's stool behind the front desk, reflecting on a very difficult, draining day that had also filled my heart with love and made me feel supported.

Aunt Phyl's funeral had been this morning. It was a fitting tribute to her, with a funeral-home full house, so to speak, and many tears, laughs, and memories shared during the service and afterward at the lunch in the church.

The Diamonds had closed ranks around me like the mother hens they were—well, mother hens plus Magnolia. They'd stood by my side throughout, making me feel like I wasn't the only surviving family member, and that was fitting since Aunt Phyl had considered these women to be her sisters.

Loretta was the eternal ringleader, ensuring everything worked smoothly, that the receiving line kept moving, and the service started on time. Dotty was quietly efficient and had taken charge of the meal, making sure everyone's donated dish was on the right section of the table—mains, sides, or desserts—and had a serving utensil. Rosy had hovered by me like a cross between a mom and a best friend, prompting me with names and coming up with the right thing to say when I couldn't. Kona, Nancy, and Magnolia had always been nearby and quick to offer a reassuring hug.

Afterward, Magnolia and Dotty, who'd closed the Lily Pad for the day, had brought me back to the inn and insisted I take a nap. I'd been so depleted in every way that I'd done exactly that while they covered the inn. I had to admit I wouldn't be able to stand up now without that hard-core pass-out nap.

This evening was poker night for the Diamonds, as every Thursday was. The ladies had all gathered here at the inn, where they normally met, and spent the past few hours remembering my aunt, laughing, sharing, and yes, there were more tears shed, including mine. They hadn't gotten the cards out, just needed to be together.

It'd taken quite a bit of convincing, but I finally got them all out the door, leaving me here on the stool, breathing. Though I was exhausted, I resisted heading back to the cottage for the night. I'd slept there the past three nights, but I knew tonight, in my current mental state, it would echo with loss and emptiness, and I dreaded going inside. I intended to sit here and continue planning and researching for all the tasks on my inn to-do list.

I was still dedicated to not selling the Honeysuckle Inn, but there were some inherent challenges in that.

Obviously, my life was on the West Coast. I couldn't move back here. Even if, God forbid, the Stream opportunity went south and they didn't offer me the head writer job, I needed to be in LA.

I'd made countless in-person contacts over the years, through school, through former classmates who now worked in various positions in the industry, and through my dad, an attorney who represented several key players in the entertainment industry. Compelling screenplays were obviously a necessity, but being seen, networking, those counted too. You never knew what or who would bring about a big break. I'd landed my agent after Kelsey, one of my best friends from film school, introduced us at a party, and look where that agent had gotten me so far. Hopeful and on the cusp of something big.

When I'd made the decision to find a full-time manager, it had been approximately four thirty in the morning after no sleep and the shock of learning about my aunt's death. I stood by that decision now, but in reality, finding the right person was going to take time.

Before I could begin the search, though, I needed to overhaul the inn. No one in their right mind would want to take charge of an out-of-date, tired, in-need-of-shit-tons-of-maintenance inn. It was just like real estate. If you wanted to sell, you had to make sure the property shone and looked pretty. If I wanted to find a new manager to nurture and love this place, it had to look hopeful and attractive.

Until I could hire a couple people to help at the front desk, I wouldn't be able to fully dedicate myself to Operation Inn Overhaul. I didn't know how my aunt had done it with only Deshon, other than posting her phone number and making herself continually on call. A few of the Diamonds had pitched in for the past three days, bless their golden hearts, yet I was still overwhelmed by the growing to-do list.

Deshon's daughter hadn't fully recovered, so he hadn't been able to work.

Halstead had gone home for the day a couple of hours ago after coming back post-funeral, insisting he needed to stay occupied. Gretchen and her housekeeping staff had been gone for hours, so when I heard a noise in the gathering room on the other side of the stone fireplace, I got up to make sure it was an inn guest and not an intruder. I was ever wary of the lack of security on the lake side of the inn, as my aunt had been too trusting and, again, resistant to any kind of tech update that would require guests to access the deck door with a key card.

When I peeked around the wall, I spotted the guest I'd seen chatting with Loretta earlier. He was the only one of the six parties I hadn't met yet, but I knew from checking out the index cards his name was Knox Breckenridge.

He sat in a worn, comfy easy chair that faced away from me, at a diagonal toward the floor-to-ceiling windows that looked out onto the lake during the day. A low end table sat in front of his chair and a second matching one. The dark-haired guy had a laptop on his lap, an open notebook on the table, and his gaze focused off in the distance.

I walked toward him and he looked up as I approached.

"Hello," I said, flashing my friendly inn-owner smile I'd been working on. I held out my hand, noticing he was maybe forty, good-looking, and smiled back easily. "I'm Ava Dean, the new owner. I don't want to bother you but wanted to introduce myself and make sure you're having a good stay."

"Knox Breckenridge." He stood, holding his laptop with his left hand and shaking with his right. With a laugh, he said, "I've been staying here for so long it feels like home. I'd call that a good stay."

"Oh," I said, surprised. The index cards went by the week, and I hadn't looked into anyone's history, assuming most were here for the typical Saturday-to-Saturday stay. "That sounds positive. I'm glad."

His expression went serious. "I'm sorry for your loss. Your aunt was an amazing, hospitable lady. The service today was thoughtful and fitting from what I knew of her."

"Yeah, thanks." I searched for a way to change the topic. "Are you a writer?" I nodded toward his notebook.

"Aspiring. Well, I've been writing my fool ass off, so I guess that makes me more than aspiring, doesn't it? I have a little imposter syndrome hanging out on my shoulder, I guess." He sat back down.

I was all too familiar with imposter syndrome. "Writers write," I said lightly. "What do you write?"

"By day I'm a tech writer in the financial industry. I've recently started writing fiction in my off hours."

Fatigue, grief, and being overwhelmed ceased to matter. This guy was speaking my language, and I lowered myself into the chair opposite him. "Yeah? What kind of fiction are you writing?"

He seemed to turn self-conscious. "Science fiction. It's what I love to read. The financial industry has treated me well, but it's dry as the desert."

"I write fiction too," I said. "I can only imagine how different financial stuff is from making things up."

"It took me a bit to get used to that. So what do you write?"

"Screenplays," I told him. "I'm trying to get into television." I gave him the briefest rundown of my project with Stream.

"That's impressive," he said warmly. "Congratulations."

"Congrats are premature, but thank you. It's taken a lot to even get this far. I went to screenwriting school and live in LA."

"You know what you're doing, obviously. What genre is your screenplay?"

"If I equate it to books, it'd be sports romance. The series features a professional baseball team, so there's a lot of that, but there's also a bunch of hot, single guys who need to find the right women."

"Of course. Sounds like it'll appeal to both women and men with the sports angle."

"I'm hoping so, even though romance is female heavy. I've read romance for years, and everything I write seems to have at least a little in it." Which was weird when you considered my own failure-ridden romantic history. Eternal optimism maybe? "You said you started recently. Are you working on your first book?" I nodded toward his laptop, which he'd set on top of his notebook.

Knox crossed an ankle over his other knee and relaxed into the chair. "Second. I came to Dragonfly Lake in June and wrote fiction for two solid weeks on a vacation from my full-time financial work. The story just sort of poured out of me. I took another few weeks to finish the book after my day job was done, then I sent it off to a content editor and am working on a different story until I get it back."

"Smart."

"I keep getting ideas," he said. "Like, at all hours of the night. So many ideas. I just need to figure out how and when to write them."

Smiling, I said, "Sounds familiar. So you're on an extended stay here while you write?"

"I'm moving to Dragonfly Lake, actually. I'm on the house hunt, just waiting for the right place to come available."

"Wow. I don't know if I can be considered a resident, but welcome to town and good luck with the hunt."

"Thanks. It started out as a vacation and an experiment. Something about the lake air and the slow pace sparks my creativity. I'm still doing the financial stuff—I can work from anywhere—but my dream would be to write fiction full-time."

"We have something in common then," I said. "What's your book that's with the editor about?"

He stumbled around for a couple of minutes, trying to summarize, and I totally got that. I'd done that plenty when people asked me the same. Being able to summarize a full book in a few sentences was a skill set that took time to develop.

Knox explained a little about his world—which was a fictional planet—and his storyline. I hadn't read a ton of sci-fi, but I was intrigued anyway and asked him if I could read what he had.

"Seriously?" he asked. "You don't have to."

I laughed. "Obviously I don't have to. It might take me a while to get to it, because this place is keeping me hopping, but I'd love something to get my head out of reality for a while. If you're up for it."

"It's raw."

"I've been a beginner before too." I told him my email address and he jotted it down in his notebook.

"Okay. You're on," he said as I registered a sound behind us, coming from the front lobby. "Just be gentle."

"Absolutely."

I turned toward the lobby doorway in time to see Cash walk into the room with a frown on his face as he sized up Knox.

CHAPTER 7

CASH

Ava had been on my mind for the past seventy-two hours.

Her aunt's funeral was today, and I hadn't been able to get away from the restaurant even for an hour because Zinnia had something in Nashville that she couldn't skip.

I remembered how draining and awful my mom's and grandma's funerals were. In Dragonfly Lake, people showed up in droves, with everyone wanting to help somehow, and I heard it had been no different today. I was sure there'd been a thousand well-meaning hugs, hundreds of condolences, countless looks of sympathy to endure.

I was absolutely worn out after the funerals in my family. And though the Diamond ladies had rallied around Ava this week, at the end of the day, she was all alone.

Tonight at Henry's, I'd heard from Abe Powers, Kona's husband, that the poker group had gathered at the inn to remember Phyllis, and I was sure Ava had been a part of that.

I realized what she must be going through, and I couldn't stand the thought of her being alone.

Except when I walked into the main room at the inn at a little after ten after closing down Henry's, she wasn't alone. She was with the new chump in town, who I barely knew from Adam. I'd been introduced to Knox Breckenridge by Holden at the restaurant. I might've exchanged a grand total of six sentences with him. I didn't have anything against the guy, just didn't have any reason to be his friend.

It was irrational and unreasonable, but seeing Ava sitting with him, all cozy and locked in intimate conversation, made me grumpy.

"Breckenridge," I said with a somber nod as I walked up between their chairs.

"Hey, Cash." He stood and offered a hand. I had to summon every bit of my upbringing to shake it and play nice. It was late, I'd had a long couple of days, and I wasn't the friendliest guy on a good day.

I turned my attention to Ava and found smiling easier. "Hey, Ava."

"Hi, Cash." She managed to smile back. "What's going on?"

"I was worried about you," I said pointedly, then held up the Henry's bag. "Brought you something."

Her eyes lit up as she took in the sack, and I'm not proud to admit that made me stand up a little taller, as if I'd scored one on the lanky dude sitting with her.

"Pull up a chair and join us," Ava said.

"Actually, I need to head back to my room," Knox said, apparently understanding I had zero desire to be a third wheel. Credit to him.

"I hope we didn't scare you away. You barely got started writing," Ava said.

Knox closed his laptop, then picked up his notebook. "I was on the deck for a couple hours, until the bugs got too thick. Got a few hundred words in."

I realized they must have bonded about writing. That

should've made me relax, should've made me glad Ava had made a connection with someone, but there was something about that guy I didn't trust.

"That's great—all but the bugs," Ava said, frowning. "I need to screen in a section of that deck. Anyway, it was great talking to you."

He stood. "You too. Good to meet a fellow writer."

"Don't forget to send me your manuscript," she said as he went toward the door with a wave over his shoulder.

Once he left, I released my breath and really looked at Ava. She was harried and exhausted, with shadows under her eyes, her hair pulled up in a messy knot, and a faint smile. She wore shorts, a turquoise T-shirt, and a lightweight, over-sized, short-sleeved jacket thing that I'd heard my sister refer to as a kimono wrap. On her feet were sandals with wedge heels and straps that went around her ankles. In spite of enduring her aunt's funeral today, she looked casual yet professional and so damn pretty. Time had been kind to her, if not the day, and in my opinion, she looked even prettier now than she had at twenty.

"It's late." Her tone said, *You shouldn't have come.*

"I was betting you haven't eaten."

The bluster seemed to drain out of her, and she gave me a sheepish smile. "I haven't eaten. Not since the meal at the church."

Holding up the carryout bag again, I asked, "Will you?"

Ava looked between the bag and my face. "I wouldn't want to be rude by not eating what the chef brought."

"Good answer. I brought a little for me tonight too. Long shift. I forgot utensils though."

She held up a finger and walked over to the dining area. When she returned, she had utensils and napkins. "You just got done with work?" she asked, as she came up to the couch where I sat.

I nodded, then patted the cushion next to me. "Take a load off."

Ava looked toward the doorway to the lobby. "I can't see if someone comes in from here."

"But you can hear. Besides, it's a Thursday night, going on eleven. It looked like the whole inn was tucked in for the night when I drove up." Except for Breckenridge.

She bit her lip for a second, eyeing the doorway again, then she strode over to it, reassured herself the small lobby was deserted, came back, and sat down on the other half of the couch.

Finally. My goal wasn't just to feed her but to get her to relax. One glance at her told me she needed it.

I handed over a container with brisket and homemade beer-battered onion rings and opened my own of the same, leaving the large slice of hummingbird cake in the bag.

We ate in silence for a couple minutes, then she said, "You don't have to keep doing this, you know."

With an onion ring halfway to my mouth, I paused to say, "I'm not doing it because I have to," then bit into the crispy ring.

"Why are you? Are you trying to make up for the past?"

I stopped chewing as her words sank in. After swallowing the bite, I said, "I thought we'd laid the past to rest."

"We did."

"Did we though? If that's what you're thinking…"

"I'm sorry. I just… I don't understand why you're doing this."

"What is 'this'? Bringing you food two times now when you haven't eaten for hours and hours?"

"Acting like it's your responsibility to take care of me. I can take care of myself, Cash. I've been doing it for practically my whole life." She shrugged like it was no big deal, simply a fact.

It was a fact, I realized. Her parents had divorced when

she was young, eleven years old if I remembered right, and that had forced her to grow up too early. She'd been devastated when her dad moved to the West Coast, leaving Ava and her mom alone. Ava's mom had been heartbroken and had self-medicated with alcohol.

Phyllis Sharp had swooped in and given Ava and her mom, Pamela, an opportunity to recover and start fresh at this inn she bought with her late husband's life insurance money, inviting her younger sister and niece to move to Dragonfly Lake and run it with her. But Pamela had never gotten over her husband leaving. She'd helped at first, mostly at the front desk, but as the months and years passed, she'd relied more and more on liquor and worked in the inn less and less.

Ava had stepped in to compensate for her mom's lacking, helping Phyllis after school, in the evenings, and on weekends, the two of them becoming jacks-of-all-trades and juggling nearly all the responsibilities between them. The way I understood it, Ava had worked almost full-time while in high school and had never had time to make lasting friendships. As the years went by, her time had become split between inn duties and caring for her mom, who'd eventually died of liver disease.

Her mom had relied on Ava to cover for her and care for her. Her dad had all but deserted her, managing phone calls a couple times a year. I didn't know anything about the guy Ava had been married to, but obviously, if they'd split up, he hadn't given her the love or care she deserved. Not that I had any room to talk. I'd screwed up with Ava before he had.

Bottom line, no one had taken care of Ava the way she deserved. There was something in me that still wanted to be the one who did.

My family liked to say food was the way I cared for people and showed affection, and it was probably true. I just hadn't realized I still cared about Ava. I hadn't let myself think about her. She'd been a checkmark on my lengthy failure list.

"I know it's not my responsibility," I finally said in between bites. "Damn straight you can take care of yourself. But I wanted to tonight. I can't imagine how hard your day was, and here you are, what? Pulling the overnight shift at the desk?"

Ava pulled her legs up and crossed them on the couch in front of her as she shoved more food in her mouth, and I let her eat in silence. The answer to my question about the night shift was evident.

"There's so much to get done here," she said after several minutes. She'd finished her onion rings and was picking at the leaner parts of her brisket.

"Here? At the inn?"

"Updating it. Getting a new roof. Painting. Fixing. Plus finding someone to manage it."

"No leads on that yet?"

"I just posted it yesterday, thanks to help from Loretta and Dotty. I haven't checked for responses."

"You've had other things to tend to today," I said. "Pretty hard things."

"Yeah." Her chest rose and fell with a deep breath.

"I wasn't able to get away for the service but I heard the turnout was big."

The corners of her mouth tilted up into a sad, wistful smile and she nodded. "So many people loved my aunt. This town still turns out en masse for funerals, huh?"

"They're can't-miss social events around here. Bigger than weddings because you don't need an invite."

She let out a quiet laugh, then her expression fell, and she sucked in another big breath and blew it out. "I don't want to think about it right now. I'm tired of crying."

"Understandable. But if you need to cry more, my shoulders can take it." I finished my dinner and closed the foam container. After pulling out the cake container, I tossed the empty one into the sack. I set the closed cake container on the oversized ottoman between my legs and hers. "How much of your to-do list needs to be finished before you can hire someone?"

"In an ideal world, all of it, but that's not realistic. I need to buy a property management system and get it installed first and foremost. My aunt's systems were archaic."

"Still with the index cards?"

"Color-coded and sorted by week."

"A computer system sounds expensive." I knew the one we'd put in the restaurant when my brothers and I had taken over had cost an arm and a leg. "So is a roof. Did your aunt leave the funds to take care of these things?"

Ava shook her head as she closed her empty container and added it to the bag. "I'm learning she had a huge heart but not so much of a business mind. I don't suppose there's cake in there." She pointed at the box on the ottoman.

"Maybe cake." I picked it up. "There was only one big piece left. I'll get clean forks if you'll share it with me."

"Deal," she said with no hesitation.

I hopped up and brought two forks from the dining area. When I sat back down, I moved closer to the center of the couch as I picked up the cake box and opened it. Ava scooted to my side, and I breathed in her scent like a starving man who hadn't realized how hungry he was. She smelled of vanilla and light florals. I was certain it was the same fragrance she'd worn seventeen years ago, and damn if it didn't take me back to the time when we'd been in love. I wanted to lean closer and bury my face in her neck and breathe it in fully.

"Are you actually going to share or just sit there and stare at me?" she asked, holding out her hand for a fork.

I handed her one, then extended the box for her to take to the first bite.

The sweet, fruity scent of hummingbird cake had nothing on Ava Dean. Just saying.

Since I couldn't take a bite out of the woman next to me, I settled for a little cake and took pleasure in her enjoyment of what I'd made. With her first forkful, she let out a sound of appreciation. With every bite after, she closed her eyes to savor it.

Hummingbird cake was the only thing I baked, if I could help it. I left the rest to Kinsey on a daily basis, and though I'd shared my grandmother's recipe with my pastry chef under strict confidentiality and she could do it just right, it was something I insisted on doing myself.

"So what are you going to do if your aunt didn't leave money for improvements?" I asked. "If that's not too nosy."

Ava eyed the bite she'd just forked as if it was the meaning of life. She stuck it in her mouth, did the eye-closing thing as she chewed, then said, "I hope to get a loan, and I also have money I can put toward it."

My surprise must have shown on my face, because Ava explained, "My dad is my ex's mentor in their law firm. He made sure I got a generous settlement."

"You don't think it would've worked out the same otherwise?" I asked.

"I'm sure it wouldn't have."

"Do you have a job besides writing?"

"I work at a doggy daycare. Enough to pay the rent on my apartment and some expenses each month. I don't have income from writing yet."

"Doggy daycare, huh?" I couldn't help smiling. "You always wanted a dog." She'd never been able to have one because she didn't have time to take care of it on top of the inn and her mom.

"I did, but Wes was allergic, or so he said, and now I live in a small apartment. Anyway, I've stockpiled as much of the spousal support as possible while I get my writing career off the ground. I never planned on the money going to the inn, but it needs it and I have it, and I want to make sure everything is handled perfectly for my aunt."

"I don't mean this in a bad way, but it sounds like anything will be more than what she was managing."

"She loved it as hard as she could, but she didn't have cash or business sense. I plan to make it everything she knew it could be."

Her love for her aunt was evident in the passion behind her words and the sudden glassiness of her eyes. Without thinking about it, I grasped her thigh just above her knee and squeezed it supportively since her hands were full of the cake box and her fork. It was only when I was mid-squeeze that I saw her head whip in my direction out of the corner of my eye and realized I was crossing a line between present us and past us without meaning to. Touching her had just seemed natural.

Instead of apologizing, I acted like it was no big deal and took my hand back, waiting to see if she'd say anything. She didn't.

"This place has so much potential," I said. "It sounds like you're on the right track. Phyllis would be beside herself with love and happiness."

"I just need to figure out how to make it work. It won't be done by next week."

"There's no way. Can you postpone your meeting?"

With a gusty exhale, she said, "No. It's the opportunity of a lifetime. But I'll have to come back afterward, at least for a couple of weeks."

I liked that she'd be around longer. Liked it a lot, whether that was wise or not. Her future was in California, without question, and I wanted her to make her screenwriting dreams come true. She couldn't do that here, obviously. But while she was here, I wanted to spend more time with her, get to know the grown-up version of Ava, spoil her with home-cooked food, and be a better friend than I'd been in the past.

After she finished the last bite, she added the box to the bag of trash and leaned back into the comfortable couch again. Her side was touching mine, and I let myself relax and savor the feel of her, the scent of her, the way she'd appreciated dessert. We sat there in a comfortable silence that I never would've thought would be possible again. The room was dimly lit by three warm-toned table lamps on low settings. No one appeared to be stirring anywhere in the inn. The only sound was the faint whir of the air conditioner. I couldn't remember feeling this content for ages.

"I should get busy," Ava said quietly, unconvincingly.

"What needs to be done tonight?"

"I was planning to research management systems and companies that sell them so I can contact them tomorrow."

Her head sank into the cushion, and when I glanced down at her, her eyes were closed.

"You've been through a hellish few days," I said, my voice a gravelly rumble, barely more than a whisper.

She nodded.

"Why don't you let yourself rest for a few minutes?" I suggested. "You'll work more efficiently if you do."

She didn't respond right away and I wondered if she'd drifted to sleep. It took half a minute, but she finally said, "I need to cover the desk. Anyone could walk in."

"I'll keep an ear out. You can relax and start recovering from your day."

I was betting, if she'd let herself doze off, she'd sleep for a couple hours at least. She needed it, and I wanted to give her that break, so when she didn't say more, I settled into the cushions too, with Ava by my side, listening to her quiet, even, soothing breaths.

When I opened my eyes again, light was beginning to streak across the sky and reflect in the lake, hinting at an incredible sunrise. Even more breathtaking than that, Ava had shifted so her legs were stretched out to the end of the couch instead of on the ottoman, and her head and one hand rested on my thigh.

I knew if all went well for her, she wouldn't be in Tennessee for long, but I vowed to myself right then and there I'd be whatever she would allow me to be while she was here. A friend, a support system, a lover if I was really lucky. She wasn't looking to get involved with me, and if I pushed too hard or went too fast, she'd likely shut me down, so I had to find a way to proceed with caution, but proceed I would. I couldn't not.

We might not have time on our side, but I was going to make the most of the days we had.

CHAPTER 8

AVA

It was shortly after five p.m. Friday, and I'd like to say the inn was hopping with activity, but that would be a lie. The inn, from what I'd observed over the five days I'd been there, was never hopping, and that was yet another problem I needed to solve.

A couple days ago, that realization would've melted me down, but today was different…thanks to Cash.

Last night, on that old, tired sofa in the middle of the very public gathering room, I'd slept hard. I'd had every intention of spending the wee hours doing exactly what I'd told him— researching management systems and software companies. But after filling my stomach with delicious, home-cooked food—and of course, cake—I'd succumbed to exhaustion. The reason that had been okay was Cash's assurance that he'd listen for anyone who needed me at the desk. Of course, the odds were low when we only had six rooms rented, but that didn't mean I could ignore the inn for the night. At a mini-mum, I was somewhat tethered by possible text messages, but Cash's reassurances had allowed me to relax for a few hours.

Apparently I trusted Cash with one of my most important responsibilities, and that was saying a lot. I hadn't just dozed; I'd slept better than I had since I'd been in town. Better than I had in probably the past year, since my divorce was finalized. Come to think of it, I didn't know when I'd last slept for nearly six hours straight.

What a difference six uninterrupted hours of sleep made.

I'd woken up alone, lying fully stretched out on the sofa. I had no memory of shifting my legs from the ottoman or whether Cash had still been there when I did.

The first thing I'd become aware of was the aroma of baked goods wafting to my nose. Sweet, heavenly, tempting breakfast smells had shot me straight up, trying to get my bearings, because my place never, ever smelled like fresh-baked anything.

When my eyes had popped open, I'd been met with the early-morning sunshine over the lake, making the water sparkle and glimmer as pinks and oranges streaked the sky in a breathtaking sunrise. It seemed the universe was trying to tempt me to stay in Tennessee with the most spectacular start to the day, between the view out the window and the scent permeating the air. I was too determined to make my screen-writing dreams come true to succumb to it long-term, but as I'd stood and stretched the kinks out, I'd felt more upbeat and hopeful than I had in a while. Upbeat and hopeful and unable to ignore my rumbling stomach. For once, there had been no way I could forget about my hunger.

Puzzled, I'd gone toward the commercial kitchen, where my aunt used to bake muffins and pastries for guests daily. While a part of my brain had worked out it might be Cash, you know, the *chef*, creating those beautiful smells, I was completely unprepared for what I saw when I reached the pass-through window from the dining area to the kitchen.

There he was, bending over the open oven, sliding a pan in, wearing his jeans and tee from last night, his hair tousled from sleep, looking rumpled, in charge, and, frankly, damn hot.

That was a glorious thing to wake up to, even better than the to-die-for aroma coming off the rack of cooling muffins.

I'd vowed to worry later about the way he was wearing down my standoffishness and warming me up to him.

It was nearly twelve hours later now, and yes, I was concerned about letting my walls down, but I hadn't yet figured out what to do about it. I hadn't had time.

Thanks to feeling renewed by a night of decent sleep, my day had been crazy productive. I'd done the research on management systems, found three companies that sold and installed them, and made appointments for two of them to come pitch to me and, hopefully, save my sanity. I'd interviewed someone for a front desk position, of which I needed three or four, and liked her so much I'd offered her a job on the spot. She promised to give me an answer by Monday. Having a second desk clerk would make a world of difference.

After the interview, I'd met with Halstead about the ongoing maintenance projects, many of which he'd wanted to tackle for months, but my aunt had held him off because she didn't want to spend the extra money. We'd prioritized the list, figured out a means of paying for parts and supplies and extra labor where necessary, and he'd gone off to work, happy to finally be able to dig in. His brother-in-law was a roofer and had come out to give us an estimate on that project.

Finally, I'd booked an airline ticket from LA back to Nashville after my Stream meeting next week. Giving in to the need to spend more time in Dragonfly Lake so that I could handle the Honeysuckle Inn thoroughly and more effectively had helped alleviate some of the pressure that'd been crushing me since I arrived.

So far, I'd had two inquiries about the management position, but neither person was remotely qualified, so the biggest piece of the puzzle still loomed. I had to believe I'd find the right person soon.

I was sitting behind the front desk, where I'd done the majority of my work today, pulling double duty, when the main door opened and Magnolia walked in. Her hair was up in a messy bun, face made up lightly, and she wore a cute summer dress.

"Hello," I said as she entered and let the door close behind her.

"Hi, Ava." She smiled, but I read nervousness behind it, which made me curious. We'd spent a lot of time together yesterday with the Diamonds, so there was no reason for her to be uneasy. "Do you have a few minutes?"

I glanced at the time on my phone. "I actually do. I'm stuck here until Loretta spells me for dinner again."

"You must be so tired after yesterday and covering the desk all the time and, well, everything."

"It's been a hard week, but sleep makes all the difference in the world."

She sighed wistfully as she walked up to the opposite side of the counter. "Isn't that the truth? Funerals are so hard, and they wipe you out." She paused to take in a breath. "Um, I brought something for you." She held out a small rectangular package wrapped in apple-green burlap with an intricate ribbon in yellow and a sprig of live watermelon-colored flowers tucked into it.

"That's gorgeous," I said.

"It's for you, a practical thing I thought you might need after yesterday." She seemed embarrassed for some reason, so I took the package and smiled gratefully.

"Are you sure you want me to mess this up?" I indicated the wrapping, which was unlike anything I'd ever seen.

"Of course. Rip away That's what it's there for."

"It's just so pretty. I'm a terrible wrapper. My presents usually gape at the corners and need extra tape. I'd never think to add flowers but I love this." I carefully pulled out the stems, mindful not to let any of the small petals get caught up in the ribbon. "I'll put these in water. I love the color."

"Aren't they pretty? I got them at Oopsie Daisies. I thought the colors were cheery and summery."

Setting the stems aside for now, I slid the ribbon off the package, then removed the burlap wrap to find a box of hand-painted thank-you cards.

"Oh…" I swallowed down on the unexpected emotions the kind, super-appropriate gift elicited. "Yes. God yes. I have a list on my phone… So many people I need to thank, but I hadn't gotten this far yet. Thank you." I opened the box and my breath caught at the gorgeous floral designs on the cards. "Wow. You have such good taste. These are beautiful."

With a nervous laugh, Magnolia said, "We carry them at the Lily Pad. A local artist keeps us supplied." She shrugged. "It's just a little thing I hoped would help."

"Actually kind of a big thing. I have no idea when I would finally get around to remembering to order cards. This is so thoughtful."

They were almost too pretty to write on, but I would. I absolutely would. So many people in this little town had gone out of their way to help me, from the Diamonds to Olivia from the bakery, who'd thought to bring donuts for my guests, to the mayor, who'd given the most touching eulogy for my aunt yesterday.

"I hope it takes one little thing off your plate," Magnolia said. She shifted from one foot to the other. "And this is more self-serving, and I swear the cards weren't to bribe you…"

I replaced the top on the box and glanced up at her, confused.

She blew out a nervous breath. "I heard you're hiring front desk people. Like for an actual job. I'm interested."

"Oh. You heard right, but I thought you already had a job?

Are you looking to switch?" My interest was sparked. It wasn't every day the right person walked in at the right time.

"I work at the Lily Pad, but we close at five. I was thinking I could do a shift from, say, six or seven until Deshon comes in."

Deshon was working ten to six tonight. I was grateful he was able to make it in, his family healthy again. It was getting to the point where I had to admit I couldn't do it all, even short-term.

"Want to sit down and talk?" I asked.

"I'd love to. And I have an idea. Or Dotty did, really, but I listen to Dotty a lot because she's wise. Anyway, I'm dying for some pizza from Humble's. Dotty predicted you'd try to skip dinner and work while Loretta is here. She thought it would be good for you to get away for a couple of hours and suggested I invite you to dinner. We could talk there?"

Were there no secrets in this town? I laughed quietly at my own stupid question. Of course there were no secrets. I could either be offended by Dotty Jaworski's nosiness or be thankful for the opportunity for a change of scenery and what had always been excellent pizza.

"Sure," I said. "That actually sounds good. I need to get a vase for these flowers and put my laptop away, and then as soon as Loretta gets here, I can go."

"I can watch the desk—as a volunteer, of course—while you do those things if you want."

"Thank you." It felt weird to leave her there, but she'd already proven she could handle it. "I'll be back in five, and there's Loretta now." I spotted her walking from the parking lot.

I rushed off to the cottage, calling out a hello to Loretta on the way, found a small vase, put the flowers in water, and dropped off my computer. After a quick glance in the mirror, I decided I looked fine for Humble Pizza Pie. I had to look better than I had at the funeral yesterday, with my eyes red and my dress rumpled from all the hugs. It wasn't like I had anyone to impress anyway.

That image of Cash, looking every bit like he'd just woken up this morning as he worked his magic in the inn's kitchen, came to mind.

I did *not* want to impress Cash, tonight or ever. Even if the man had previously bought me an engagement ring. *An engagement ring.*

I hadn't allowed myself to think too hard about that since he'd told me. It was too much, and really, what did it matter now? I needed to not let it matter now because this was just a short stay in Dragonfly. A short couple weeks around him. A pit stop that had no bearing on the rest of my life, regardless of what our past was.

Drawing in a deep breath, I ignored the shakiness in it, then fake-smiled at my reflection.

Plain black tank, denim mini, and slides would do just fine.

Ten minutes later, I thanked Loretta and told her our plans, then rode the short distance downtown in Magnolia's cute but older BMW.

Humble's was packed with families, couples, and groups of friends, not surprising since it was prime time on Friday night. I wasn't an extrovert by any means, but it felt good to disappear into a crowd of happy people for a change.

"There are two spots at the end of the bar if you don't mind sitting there," Magnolia said, pointing.

"I'm all for it if it means I can get that pizza in my belly sooner. It smells delicious."

I followed her to the counter, and we each climbed up on a stool.

"Please tell me you're not that girl who orders a salad instead of pizza," I said, setting my clutch on the bar.

"Not tonight," Magnolia said. "We'll be sisters in calorie consumption."

"Perfect."

"Hey, ladies. Would you like a drink?" A short woman, probably in her late twenties, with purple-tipped dark hair, appeared in front of us with an energetic smile. ·

"Hi, Jewel. This is Ava Dean."

"Hey, Ava of the Honeysuckle Inn, right?"

Of course she knew. Everyone knew everything.

"That's me."

"I'm so sorry about your aunt."

"Thanks. I'd like an iced tea if you have it, please."

"You got it. Magnolia?"

"Tea for me too, and we're going to order dinner."

Jewel whipped out some single-sided menus with all the toppings you could get on your slice.

"Was that for the benefit of doing business or are you not a drinker?" Magnolia asked me as we looked them over.

I shook my head. "Let's just say alcoholism runs in my family. I don't care to flirt with it. Am I remembering right that the slices here are bigger than your head?" I asked.

"You're remembering exactly right," Magnolia said.

We each ordered one slice. Jewel set our drinks down, then made her way toward the other end of the bar while we turned to business talk.

I asked Magnolia typical questions, like why she'd be good at the job, why she wanted to work at the inn, and then inquired about her employment history.

Magnolia pressed her lips together and sat up straighter, leaning her forearms on the bar. "The Lily Pad is my first job." She blew out a breath. "I'm going to level with you, because you'll hear everything about me anyway. Might as well get it straight from me."

"Okay..." Intrigued, I straightened too, then glanced to the other side of me, noting the older woman there was completely absorbed in a story her friend was telling her. I couldn't hear a word of their conversation, so I was sure they wouldn't hear ours. "Might as well get it straight from you." I smiled, sensing what she was going to say wasn't all roses and unicorns.

"I grew up in a wealthy family. I didn't have to work." She shook her head. "There's no way to sugarcoat it. I was a spoiled rich girl, and unfortunately I acted like it. I had my problems, but money wasn't one of them. My dad didn't like how it would look for his daughter to 'stoop' to a part-time job, so he made sure I had whatever I wanted and then some. I let him. I'm not proud of it, not proud of a lot of things, but that's why I never worked before."

"But now you do," I said, curious as hell. The rich girl thing made sense in a way. She had a way about her that spoke of a privileged upbringing.

Magnolia took another deep breath. "I should've ordered a bourbon sour for this. I'm only half kidding," she said as an aside. "So I was engaged until a couple of months ago. To the guy my dad wanted me to marry. For business reasons."

My brows shot up my forehead.

"I know. How could I agree to that?" she continued. "My dad threatened to cut me off if I didn't. And I liked Rick well enough at first. We weren't a love match, but I told myself I could live with him, literally and figuratively."

I narrowed my eyes. "Sounds like a but coming…"

"Big but. Rick turned out to be a cheating asshole. He knew all about my dad's threat and thought I'd ignore his indiscretions. That's where he went wrong."

"You dumped him?"

"Like the garbage he is."

"Good for you." I raised my tea and we clinked our glasses. Now the BMW and the retail job made more sense.

"Good for me in the end, but I'm not going to lie. It hasn't been easy to go from spoiled rich girl to destitute. My dad took everything but my car." She let out a self-deprecating laugh.

"At least you can still laugh."

"It's taken me a while to get there, but really, if I didn't laugh, I'd do nothing but cry."

While she and I had very little in common so far, I could so relate to that emotion.

"I know, cry me a river, right? Anyway, my revenge is to make it on my own. I'm sure my dad thinks I can't do it, that I'll come back begging."

"Sounds like he's wrong," I said.

"So one-hundred-percent wrong." She frowned then took a sip of her tea. "I functioned on pure anger for the first couple of weeks. I'm so blessed that Dotty has a good heart—and that she'd been thinking of hiring someone to help for a while. She never thought much of my parents—most of the people in town don't, and my reputation is no better than theirs. But Dotty saw I was in need, saw my determination to change my life, and gave me a place to live and an opportunity to change."

"Dotty's good people," I said.

Magnolia's honesty was refreshing. Yes, I could've easily heard her story from anyone else if I asked, but I respected her for putting it out there, because I could tell it wasn't easy. But she seemed to genuinely want to change.

"So you want a second job?" I asked.

"I don't want to take advantage of Dotty's generous apartment offer forever. She takes my rent out of my paycheck, but it's ridiculously low. I know she could make more from anyone else."

"I get that," I said, thinking about my own goal of living independently, without using my ex's support each month. That was something we sort of had in common. Because yes, my ex was wealthy.

As we ate our slices, we wandered into more usual interview questions, like *what would you do if X* and *how would you handle Y?*

When Jewel came by to see if we needed another slice or a refill, we both shook our heads and held a hand to our stomachs in an *I'm full* motion, then laughed. Jewel cleared our plates, left us the bill, and went on to help another customer.

"I appreciate your honesty about your past and your lack of experience," I said to Magnolia.

"I'm a fast learner," she said, as if she needed to keep selling me on hiring her. I was sure she was, and honesty was one of my top desired traits in hiring someone. That's something I'd picked up from Loretta and Dotty, who both ran their own businesses. Besides, I knew Dotty trusted Magnolia, and that was good enough for me.

"As far as I'm concerned, you're hired," I said.

"Oh!" Magnolia beamed and wiggled on the stool. "Thank you, Ava. Yes! When can I start?"

"Anytime you're able. Want to come in tomorrow evening for a little training? Sunday? If you could be up to speed by the time I leave Wednesday—"

"Tomorrow evening's good," she said. "Oh, yay! Can I hug you?"

Laughing, feeling like she and I could become friends, I said, "Of course," and we leaned toward each other from our stools and hugged.

"I don't want to break up a lady hug," a male voice said behind us.

We pulled out of our awkward hug.

"Hello," he said, looking from Magnolia to me. "Sorry to interrupt, but Magnolia, there's a pool tournament tonight at the Fly by Night. Teams of two. You interested in partnering up?"

"What's the prize?" she asked, raising a perfect brow.

"Five hundred bucks."

"Apiece?" she asked, and he laughed.

"This is the Fly. You know better. Two fifty doesn't suck though."

"Two fifty does not suck. Ava, this is Kemp Essex. He's a pool shark."

"As is Magnolia," Kemp said. "She beat me last month in a singles tournament. Next time I'll get her."

"Good thing you want to be on the same side tonight," I said, grinning.

"That five hundred is almost guaranteed to be ours. What do you think, Mags?"

"I think you're right. Let's do it."

"Sweet. Starts at eight. I'll let you ladies get back to it. See you at the Fly."

"Good friend of yours?" I asked when the guy was gone.

Magnolia laughed slyly. "Let's just say a new friend since I started paying attention to the pool tournaments. He's a good guy, and more importantly, good at pool. I don't suppose you'd come too? For moral support?"

I hesitated.

"I know you want to work, but Loretta and Deshon have the desk, right?"

"They do."

"When was the last time you went out for fun?"

"About 2018," I said, only half kidding. I should've said no, but I'd gotten so much accomplished today, and I deserved to relax for a couple of hours. More importantly, going to the Fly by Night would prevent me from having to spend the quiet evening in the cottage.

"Why not?" I said. I checked my watch and saw it was quarter till eight. "Let's get our butts to the Fly."

CHAPTER 9

The Fly by Night was hopping early.

Jake Bergman, whose family owned Bergman Hardware, and I had been friends since grade school. We lived in separate loft apartments above his store, so technically he was my landlord too. A lot of evenings, after I got home from work, we'd hang out on the back landing, drink a beer or two, and shoot the shit. Tonight, though, I'd taken the dinner shift off, and we were getting our social on in honor of his fortieth birthday.

We'd come to the Fly for dinner, in part because the pork tenderloin sandwiches were big and filling and damn good and in part because Jake had it in his mind his birthday present to himself should be getting laid. I wasn't sure about his odds for the latter, but they were sure as hell better at the Fly than on our back landing.

The food had been cleared an hour ago, but we were still at our table, in no hurry to go anywhere. This was a bar first and foremost that served salty food to keep its customers in drinks, the kind of place that wasn't concerned about table turnover. Our buddy Dylan Copeland had joined us a few minutes ago after getting off work.

The Fly had two sections—tables and the main bar in the front half and pool tables and dartboards in the back. Our table was in the middle of the two. We could see the whole place from here, and half the town had stopped by so far to say hello and wish Jake happy birthday.

Jake didn't need the birthday excuse to get extra attention from women. He'd always been a girl magnet, even in the sixth grade. He, Dylan, and I had played various sports and never had trouble getting dates, but it was tough when you lived in a small town and had known everyone for roughly four decades.

As a trio of ladies a few years younger than we were walked away from us toward the pool tables, Isabel Ballantine, our server, delivered us another round. Jake continued to scan the place, still determined not to end the night alone. I'd never really started searching, and Dylan was seeing someone from the city, so he wasn't interested.

"It's a long shot, dude," Dylan said to Jake. "You're an old man."

"Then so are you," Jake shot back good-naturedly.

"But I'm not the one searching."

"Why aren't you with your better half tonight anyway? She get a better offer?" Jake teased.

"Apparently she did." Dylan laughed. "Front-row seats at a Luke Coombs show."

"Total upgrade," Jake said.

"You've got your work cut out for you," I said to Jake. "Forty years old. It's not like it used to be. You could be the father of half the girls in here."

"Shut the fuck up, man. You're supposed to help me celebrate, not be a grumpy-ass downer." Jake was grinning as he shook his head.

"I was born a grumpy-ass downer," I said.

The main door had been busy all night and had ceased to grab my attention after the first thirty minutes or so. There wasn't anyone I was looking for in particular—or so I thought. I happened to glance that way as a strawberry-blonde came in. Magnolia James, I realized, but then I recognized the brunette behind her, and my awareness snapped right to Ava and stuck.

She looked hesitant, scanning the place as they came inside. She brushed her hair behind one ear, which had always been a nervous habit. There were enough people standing in the way that I couldn't see her as well as I wanted, but I kept my eyes trained on her. Couldn't seem to look away.

Finally, she and Magnolia came closer and I could see her fully. Neither one of them spotted us, so I could check her out at my leisure, and I took my sweet time looking her up and down. Her hair was down tonight, a little tousled. She wore a black tank and a plain denim skirt that stopped at the tops of her thighs. The urge to run my fingers up under her hemline to feel her heated silky skin hit hard out of nowhere, and I clenched my fist under the table.

Magnolia led her past us, toward the back half of the bar. I didn't know Magnolia well, so there was no reason to expect her to stop and talk, and Ava still didn't see me as she walked by.

"Interesting," Jake said, and I realized he was watching me.

I scowled. "What's interesting?"

"The way you zeroed in on your ex the second she walked in the door and didn't take your eyes off her."

"Maybe I was watching Magnolia James," I flipped back, knowing full well he wouldn't buy that. Magnolia had a rep as a spoiled rich girl, so much so that I was fully aware of it even though she was several years younger, close to Holden's age. She was good-looking, but her reputation generally kept guys at bay, although apparently she'd been engaged and recently dumped the dude after some drama. I didn't pretend to keep up.

"I call bullshit," Dylan said, also eying me. "You seeing Ava again?"

"If I was, would I have let her walk by?"

"Never know. You're not the smoothest guy."

"I'm as smooth as I need to be. This one's the one having trouble getting a girl." I pointed to Jake.

"I'm not having trouble getting a girl," he said, as if that was the dumbest thing he'd ever heard. "I'm having a hard time finding one worth getting."

"Maybe try the grocery store," Dylan said. "Older demographic there."

"Assholes," Jake said lightly as I laughed. "Though you do have a point about things being different now. I've lived here my whole life. If there was someone I wanted to take out—"

"A.k.a. screw," Dylan translated.

"—chances are good I already did."

"Valid point," I said. "That's why you should meet women from out of town."

"Worked for me." Dylan had only been with this new girl for a couple of months, so saying it had worked might've been an overstatement. He didn't have a good record for long-term relationships. Then again, none of us did, which was why we were sitting together at the Fly on a Friday night, I guess.

I took a drink of my beer and glanced to the back of the bar, needing to lay eyes on Ava again. Magnolia was standing next to my brother's business partner, Kemp Essex, both of them with a pool cue in hand. Ava sat on a stool at a cocktail table lining the billiards area, engaged in conversation with them.

I checked the marquee on our table, guessing there was a

tournament tonight based on all the energy from the back half, and I was right. It appeared Magnolia and Kemp were partnering up. If I had to guess, Ava was here to watch. She'd never been a big fan of pool. Once the tournament got going, I'd make my way over to her and see if she needed company.

"Hellooo," Jake said, dragging my attention back to the table. "Potential just walked in the door."

I followed his gaze and spotted two women who looked to be early thirties. Still too young for him, but at least they'd been drinking legally for a few years. I could tell right away they were tourists, because I'd never seen them before, and they were dressed up way more than your average Dragonfly Lake resident. Tees and shorts, maybe a casual sundress were what local women wore to the Fly, but these two had heels and tight party dresses on.

"Get your tongue back in your mouth," Dylan said, also watching them.

"I'd like to get my tongue in the blonde's mouth," Jake said. "For starters."

"Now you sound twenty-one, Jacob," Dylan said, even though Jake's full name was actually Jake. We'd called him Jacob for years because it used to piss him off. "I see somebody I need to talk to. Be back in a few." Dylan slid out of the three-sided booth and headed toward the dartboards.

I was about to flip Jake more shit about the blond woman when a guy caught my attention as he stood up at the end of the bar. Knox Breckenridge strode back to the pool tables, and sure as shit, he walked right up to Ava and spoke to her.

She smiled at him, obviously happy to see him, and I clenched my fist again hard enough to crack a couple of knuckles. The place was too loud for Jake to hear them crack, but after a quick glance at my face, he craned around to see what I was glaring at.

"That's that new guy. The writer," Jake said.

My reply was a growl.

Magnolia and Kemp were in front of the table where you paid the entry fee, and that left Ava alone with Breckenridge. He took full advantage and moved in closer to her.

Jake and I watched them for a few seconds, then he turned back to me. "You going to do something about that?"

"I don't have any right to do something about that." That's what my brain was saying, but my gut had a different story to tell.

"Nothing stopping you from butting in on their cozy conversation."

Breckenridge's elbow rested on Ava's table now, and I wondered if he knew a damn thing about personal space. Didn't help that he had to lean in close to her ear every time he spoke to her and close to her mouth whenever she replied.

I was on the verge of scooting out of the booth when Ava tilted her head, nodded, then slid down off her stool. Breckenridge led her to the entry table and said something to the guy sitting behind it.

"They're entering the tournament," Jake said, still gawking like I was. "Guess you'll have to wait to make your move. Are they a thing?"

I grunted and took a long drink of beer, then set down the glass harder than I meant to. "As far as I know, she just met him last night. They talked about writing." It didn't look like they were talking about writing now.

Dylan returned to the table, still laughing at something, then pointing in acknowledgment at someone across the way, happy as could be and oblivious to the storm brewing inside of me. I tried to level myself out and forget about Ava and what's-his-name as I listened to the story Dylan had just heard from Anton White about a group of Dragonfly Lake girls in their late twenties going skinny-dipping and getting caught on video by one of the McNamaras. Instead of covering themselves or diving back into the lake, a couple of them had apparently given him the show of a lifetime. I made myself laugh and finished off my beer.

Even as he listened to Dylan's story, Jake's gaze had flitted back to the blonde repeatedly.

"Just make your move, birthday boy," I grumbled.

He studied me for a few seconds. "Wasn't sure if you needed me to hold you back or what."

"I'm fine." I wasn't a fucking caveman. I could control my reactions just fine. Besides, Breckenridge had been smart enough so far to keep his hands off Ava. I'd made sure of it.

"The stool by the blonde just opened up," I said with a nod in her direction.

"It's like the universe is saying happy birthday to me." Jake stood and added, "Don't wait up."

"Good luck, old man," Dylan said with a smirk.

"Don't need luck." Jake strutted off with his chest out.

"I'm gonna go say hey to Kevin and Jody Rivas," Dylan said as he got up and walked off again, leaving me in the booth by myself with nothing to do but watch the nearest pool table, which was, of course, Ava's.

The two guys she and the writer were matched up against did a simultaneous fist pump as the eight ball sank into a pocket, obviously winning them the game.

Ava shrugged and grinned at Breckenridge, as if to say, *Win some, lose some.* He shook hands with the winners, while Ava told them good game and then walked off toward the hall to the restrooms.

I thought about sitting tight, but if this was my chance to get her to *not* go back to the writer, I wasn't about to let it pass.

I slid out of the booth, not caring that a group of women swooped in and took it over before I was two feet away, and made my way toward the back hall where Ava had disappeared.

CHAPTER 10

AVA

I was so off my social game it wasn't funny.

Going out with Magnolia had turned out to be a welcome change, but it was going on ten o'clock and my week—and my uber-productive day—were catching up to me.

As an introvert, I'd never been a social queen. When I thought back to the parties I'd planned and hosted for Wes's clients and colleagues and the events we'd gone to once or twice a week, I didn't miss any of it now. A small-town bar was closer to my speed, but most nights I'd rather just put on some pajamas and curl up on the sofa with my laptop and write.

I exited the bathroom stall, washed my hands, and touched up my lip gloss. My hair looked stringy and unkempt, so I ran a comb through it one last time. I was ready to bow out for the evening. I didn't think Magnolia would mind—she and Kemp had won their first round and would likely play into the wee hours if they were as good as everyone said. Knox, however, might be a little trickier to convince I was done and ready to go.

I was still considering how best to call it a night when I walked out of the ladies' room. My attention was immediately drawn to the hallway wall opposite the door. Cash stood there, his gaze zeroed in on me, looking intense but not surprised to see me. Before I could process more, he took a light grasp of my wrist and gently tugged me closer. His lips tilted up ever so slightly as he peered down at me.

"Cash," I said, catching my balance with a hand on his chest as my brain played catch-up. "What are you doing here?"

"I was helping a buddy turn forty," he said in a low, growly voice that I felt clear through me. His eyes were locked on mine, then they darted down to my lips, and my heart rate kicked up.

"And now?" My mouth was suddenly dry. When Cash cradled my cheek with one large palm, I was drawn in by some kind of spell that seemed to shut down my brain cells and make it impossible to think.

His eyes implored mine as if he was giving me a chance to put distance between us, but I was locked in place, waiting to see what he did next.

My breath stalled as he leaned his face closer to mine a centimeter at a time. He closed the last bit of space, and his lips crashed down on mine as his hand swept through my hair, to the back of my head, holding me there against his onslaught. I grasped his T-shirt and fell into the sensations that were Cash Henry, tumbling somewhere between the past and the present as it all mixed together—his masculine scent, his decisive kiss, the growl that rumbled up from deep in his chest.

It took a couple seconds for my brain to send the message that this wasn't what I was supposed to be doing with him. It took less than a heartbeat for my lips to part for his insistent tongue and send back the message that it was very much what my mouth wanted to be doing.

For a few magical moments, it was like no time had passed at all and I was twenty again and Cash was my everything. As I tried to get my bearings, I opened my eyes to see an older Cash. It should've stopped me short, but instead, I closed them again and fell back into that kiss. He'd always kissed me like no other man I'd been kissed by, not that there were bunches.

When he rotated us so my back was to the wall and his body was pressing me into it, I let myself be engulfed by his heat. My brain had gone offline, but my body was in full respond mode. An ache throbbed deep within me, and my chest felt lighter than air as I trailed my hands up to the back of his neck.

Cash's intensity lightened, the kiss becoming more tender and thorough, less urgent and have-a-point-to-make, as if he'd reeled himself in or reminded himself we were in the back hall at the Fly.

The thought penetrated the fog in my head and I broke contact enough to say, "Cash…"

"What?" He sounded dazed, and I loved that kissing me had made him that way.

I couldn't help smiling as I put a couple inches between us, becoming more aware of the people who were walking by us en route to the restrooms. "Not here."

"We could get out of here." He pressed a couple of quick kisses to my lips again, as if he hated to stop.

"We can get out of here but not to do more of that." I pushed lightly against his chest, which of course didn't move him an inch, but he did get the message and stepped back.

He caught my hand and wove our fingers together, his broad chest rising as he inhaled deeply. I liked to think he was trying as hard as I was to get his equilibrium back, but who could say? Maybe he kissed random girls in back hallways all the time.

"Are you ready to go home for the night?" He seemed more in control, more like his usual self, the gravel in his voice mostly gone.

I nodded.

"What's what's-his-name going to say about that?"

I tilted my head, trying to puzzle through that. "You mean Knox?"

"Writer boy. Or is it pool shark?"

I laughed. "Considering we got beat in five turns, I think we better stick with writer boy. You sound jealous."

"Hell yes, I'm jealous. You don't even like pool."

Why did I like so much that he remembered that? That he remembered *me*, things about me that not a lot of people on this planet knew?

"You're right. He asked me to play, and I thought, why not? I told him I was terrible, so he went into it with eyes wide open."

My tone was light, but Cash's "Mm-hmm" was not.

"Stop it," I said. "I need to get my clutch and then I'm going home." I took my hand from his, because the last thing either of us needed was to be seen walking through the bar hand in hand, and headed out into the billiards area, toward the table where I'd been sitting.

"How are you getting there?" Cash asked right behind me.

I'd ridden with Magnolia, and I had no intention of interrupting her high-stakes game. "Walking."

"I'll walk with you."

"You don't have to. This is Dragonfly Lake."

"Let me walk you home, Ava," he said just before we got to the table where Knox sat.

"Hey, Cash," Knox said with an easy smile.

"Breckenridge." There was no smile in return, and I

inwardly rolled my eyes, even though jealous Cash gave me a little ill-advised thrill.

As I picked up my clutch, which I'd tucked away behind the table marquee, I checked the tables and saw that Magnolia and her partner were playing a second game. "Are they still looking good?" I asked Knox.

He blew out a sound that said, *No question.* "Only thing slowing them down is the other games. Are you leaving?"

Nodding, I said, "I'm exhausted."

"Need a ride?"

Cash moved into my side at that and said, "I got it."

"Thanks for the offer," I said much more pleasantly. "And for the game, even if I was pathetic."

"Thanks for being my partner. I'm sure I'll see you soon." Knox's parting words were pleasant, friendly, but that was all.

I wasn't getting vibes from him that Cash had anything to be jealous about. There certainly wasn't anything on my end. Though Knox was good-looking and I was excited to have someone to talk writing with, I wasn't drawn to him sexually. Particularly not with Cash at my side, but I wasn't about to tell Cash that.

Cash put his hand on the small of my back as we made our way to the door, and I was torn. Did I like his hand there? Yes. Too much. Did his possessive brusqueness irritate me? More than a little.

I waited till we were outside on the sidewalk and the noise of the bar was all but gone. "What was that all about?"

"I don't like him."

He led me to the right instead of left and took a sidewalk that went toward the back of the bar, across an alley, and through the trees, shortcutting toward Honeysuckle Road. The inn was just under a mile away, but I was glad my slides had flat soles.

"He's a nice guy," I said.

"He might be. Still don't like him."

"What'd he ever do to you?" I asked.

"Nothing until he set his eyes on you."

"His eyes aren't set on me. Not at all. We have writing in common and that's it."

"How do you know?"

"I don't get vibes of anything else. Besides, so what if he was interested?"

"I don't like it."

"You don't get a say." I stopped walking. "What just happened back there didn't mean anything, Cash. We aren't a thing."

He halted a few steps ahead of me, turned toward me, then took slow steps back to me. "We may not be a thing, but we still have chemistry."

In spades, but the last thing I needed to do was admit that. I started walking again and he came with me. "What buddy were you helping celebrate, and isn't he going to wonder where you went?"

"Jake Bergman. He deserted me first for a blond out-of-towner. Dylan Copeland was with us too but he's been fluttering around like a damn social butterfly. I texted him I was leaving. He's fine."

"Jake's turning forty, huh?" I knew him through Cash, and he'd helped me at the hardware store the other day. I'd not spent a lot of time with him in the past—my time with Cash had been limited enough that we stole what we could get whenever we could get it—but he was a friendly guy and I liked him.

"Forty today," Cash said.

"Which means the big four-oh is coming up for you too." It wasn't news to me, but I'd always given him a hard time for being older than I was, jokingly, of course. I nudged him with my elbow.

"Hey, that age joke's not as funny as it was in our twenties," he said with a low laugh.

We reached Honeysuckle Road and turned left, Cash taking the side closest to the road as we walked along the shoulder. It was dark and there wasn't much traffic. I inhaled deeply, appreciating the familiar lake smells and taking comfort in the night sounds—frogs, insects, and the periodic dog bark in the distance. I had to admit Dragonfly Lake was a peaceful place, so opposite of LA.

"You seem...settled these days," I said after a couple minutes. "Like you've made peace with living in a small town, doing what you do." Back when he'd enlisted, he'd been restless, unsure what he wanted out of life.

"I am for the most part. This is my home now, no question. I saw parts of the world with the Navy, figured out what I'm meant to do. Now I'm just trying to build credibility for Henry's and Rusty Anchor."

I envied him that. I'd never felt settled, at least not since my dad left us when I was a kid. Looking back, with Wes, I'd felt more like I was living his life instead of mine. And here in Dragonfly Lake, it'd been much the same. I'd been absorbed with making up for my mom's lacking in the inn at first, and then when she'd gone downhill physically, I'd added her care to my to-do list. My time to myself had been filled with Cash whenever possible. Back then, I hadn't even started writing seriously. Now I hoped to make writing my priority and settle into my own place, my own life, in California.

"Everything I've seen and heard says Henry's has plenty of credibility, along with its top-notch chef," I said. I'd looked online, checked their reviews, seen how popular the place was, and it had nothing to do with how long it'd been open, very little to do with the woman who'd founded it. No question, Guinevere Henry had been savvy and ballsy and a hard worker. She'd laid the foundation, but what Cash was doing now was his own thing, his and Seth's and Holden's too, and it was, in my opinion, impressive.

"We do okay," he said modestly. "I'm on a mission to be featured on *Small Town Smorgasbord*."

"On that cooking channel?"

"That's the one." He told me he and Seth had hired Hayden's friend to do their marketing, and their number one goal was the show. "Our customers are doing their part, sharing posts, posting their own reasons we should be featured, using the show's hashtag. Only problem is the Cove is trying for the same thing. That's the restaurant in the new Marks Resort. Friendly competition most days, but when it comes to representing this town on national TV, that should be us. We've been here decades longer and we're better."

"I agree," I said. "You deserve it." We reached the driveway to the inn and turned down it, the conversation between us easy, comfortable, about his restaurant and my potential TV series.

When we got to the inn, I shook my head and turned toward the cottage instead. "If I go in there, I'll get caught up in work," I explained as we veered toward the path. "Loretta texted me that Deshon is here and has everything handled. I'm going with that."

I felt Cash peering at me. "Taking some breathing time from work. I like it."

"You don't have any room to talk, from what I've seen."

"I took tonight off just to go out with Jake and Dylan."

With a laugh, I said, "What does it say that you deserted them?"

"That a pretty girl wins every time."

Why I was blushing, I had no idea. But my face heated up and my heart turned over a little, proving I was not as immune to him as I wanted to be. I put a couple extra inches between us as we walked.

The cottage was surrounded by trees, as was most of the land the inn was on, so the farther we got from the lamppost in front of the inn's entrance, the darker it got. Naturally, I'd forgotten to turn on the porch light, but the moon was out, filtering through the leaves here and there, giving us enough light to see.

"What's on the infamous to-do list for tomorrow?" he asked.

"I'm getting up bright and early to make muffins for the guests. Any tips?"

"The bakery downtown opens at seven o'clock."

"Smart-ass." Just like cooking, baking skills weren't in my wheelhouse, but Aunt Phyl had left a few recipes, and I wanted to try my hand at them. "I can follow directions."

"That'll get you somewhere with baking. Preheat your oven all the way before you start. Pray a lot."

I whacked his arm as I looked up to find a mischievous grin that was lighter than any smiles he'd sent my way since I'd been back. More like old times when there was no tension or ancient history between us. God, that smile could curl my toes.

When we got to the door, Cash leaned a shoulder against the wall, watching me while I dug out the single key from a pocket in my clutch. Once I'd grabbed it, he held out a hand for me to give it to him. Without thought, I did, and he caught my hand in his, pulled me closer as he straightened, then wrapped his big hands around my waist, settling them on my hips like he owned them.

The movement made me sway into him, a little off-balance, and my hands found his chest like they had earlier. His chest... The years had only made it better. Broader, thicker, harder. Tougher to resist, but I was supposed to be resisting.

"Cash..."

"Mm?"

"Did you hear anything I said back there at the bar?"

"I heard you. We're not a thing. But your body is giving off a different message."

I couldn't deny that, nor could I convince myself to snap out of it. I should be putting distance between us, but it was too easy to stay here. Too comforting. Too familiar. My heart raced with the exhilaration of being so close to him again, and I lifted my gaze and met his heated one.

He lowered his lips to mine, and I let him. I couldn't help it, couldn't resist another few seconds of his talented mouth on mine, this time slow, gentle, persuading.

I let him for more than a little while, losing myself in his kisses, loving being the focus of his attention again. Our bodies were meshed together, his hardness pressing into me, showing me he was as into this as I was. That we could go inside the cottage and have it and my double bed and the whole night to ourselves was at the forefront of my brain, but I refused to give in to that. That was a road I knew wasn't smart and would be so much harder to come back from.

The thought was enough to make me pull back from the kiss and duck my head slightly, still glowing from his affection, fighting myself hard to give it up.

"I'm leaving in a few days," I managed to get out.

"And coming back a couple days after that." He moved his hand up to cradle my face, rubbed his thumb over my bottom lip.

"Only temporarily. You know that."

"I do." He brushed a brief kiss to my lips. "We're just kissing. That's all."

When he put it like that…

"Our lives are on opposite sides of the country most of the time," he continued. "We have a few weeks that we're in the same place. We seem to like each other."

I laughed quietly at the understatement.

"We sure as hell still have chemistry," he pointed out.

"We do," I admitted.

"We're adults. As long as no one's getting hurt, why not spend time together?"

There was nothing I could argue with in anything he said. I looked up into those dreamy eyes that were peering down at me so intently. I nodded. "We can spend time together."

"Okay then."

"Okay. But I need to call it a night. I have to face those muffins at the crack of dawn."

With a sexy, growly laugh, he said, "Why I'm not a pastry chef."

"Smart." I kissed him without hesitation, then managed to stand up straight, putting a little space between us, reluctantly ending the full-body contact. "Thank you for walking me home."

"Anytime, Ava," he said, his voice huskier than usual. "Good luck with the muffins."

He squeezed my hand once, kissed my forehead, and walked off toward the road.

I leaned against the door, watching him go. My body was still aching for him, and there was a big part of me that rejoiced in the thought of kissing him and more. But there was another big part of me that was worrying, thinking I was stupid to agree, because soon I would have to go back to my own life, and that life couldn't include Cash.

CHAPTER 11

CASH

"Didn't figure I'd see you today," I said to Jake Saturday morning as he came down the exterior stairs from our apartments at five thirty a.m., as was our usual.

"Why wouldn't you?" He reached the pavement, tightened a shoelace, then started stretching for our run.

"I wasn't sure if you made it home last night or if you still had company or what." I pulled one foot up in a quad stretch, grinning at him, waiting to hear how his night with the blonde had gone.

"Steamy morning already. Gonna be a scorcher," was all he said.

He wasn't lying. The dog days of summer could be killer in southern Tennessee. It felt like ninety percent humidity right now. But that wasn't nearly as interesting as Jake's dodge.

I finished my stretches as Jake did the same, honoring his desire to not talk about last night, at least for now.

With a glance at each other, we took off down the street on our usual route around the square first.

Saturday morning meant senior sunrise yoga on the square, put on by the senior center. You could see some interesting sights some days. Today, Rosy McNamara was leading it and had the dozen or so seniors doing a warrior pose. I couldn't hear her from here, but I was certain she had some kind of meant-to-inspire monologue about *feeeeeeling* the warrior going on.

The stores were still closed, but there were a few dog walkers and other fitness types out and about. Most of them nodded at us as we jogged past at our warmup speed. The doors of the Fly by Night were propped open, and I could see someone inside, sweeping the floor. The manager at the outdoor gear store on the corner was moving a marquee out front to advertise their kayak sale.

I gave Jake until we looped all the way back to the hardware store before I questioned him again.

"So the blonde? Did you get your birthday wish?"

He shot me the side-eye, which only made me more curious.

Our usual route continued straight down Main for several blocks past the square before we turned left and wound through residential areas, then looped around by the lake. Jake was silent even as we took that first left into a neighborhood, and it wasn't because he was winded. Neither of us was. We did five miles a day, several days a week, and we'd barely gotten started.

"Did she shut you down?" I asked, trying to figure out why he'd gone silent. I didn't want details, but he'd talked so much shit about hooking up that I was sure something had gone wrong, based on his reticence now.

It took a good thirty or forty strides for him to answer. "I had to invoke the three-strike rule."

"Three-strike rule? You struck out and had to try two other women before you got lucky?"

"Dickhead. Last night, getting lucky consisted of escaping the blonde unscathed. The three-strike rule—you know, first strike against her, maybe you can deal with it. Second strike, getting iffy but if you really want some action, it still might be bearable as long as you get out fast afterward."

"Third strike, no way, no how?"

"Precisely."

I chuckled. "What were the strikes?"

"Fuck," he muttered. "You're really gonna make me go there?"

"Reality can't be as crazy as the things going through my head."

It was a quarter mile or so before he gave in. "Well, first, Felisha—that's her name—laughed like a horse."

"Come again?"

"When she laughed, it sounded like a hysterical horse neighing."

"Show me," I said, trying hard to keep a straight face.

"I'm not going to laugh like a fucking horse. Imagine a horse neighing. Now imagine that sound coming out of a woman."

"So just don't make her laugh. You're not that funny of a guy. Should've been fine."

He shot me a look that said if he had more energy, he'd slug me.

"You are kinda funny-looking, I guess," I said. "What about strike two?"

"She's obsessed with selfies."

"She's young. Aren't they all?"

"I was talking to her and her friend for a few minutes, and I kid you not, she must've taken twenty-five selfies."

I let that sink in. "A little excessive, but maybe she was documenting her vacation."

"Six of them she forced me into before I said no more."

My brows shot up. "Okay. That's a red flag."

"All I could think was, who knows where my mug is going to show up. Would she do that when we were naked?"

"Last thing you need is a sex tape going around." I couldn't help laughing some more, because leave it to Jake to pick the crazy ones.

"Jesus."

"What was strike three?"

He shuddered visibly. "Not two minutes after I sat down next to her, she referenced destiny or some shit, saying fate had likely brought me to her side."

I narrowed my eyes, thinking it must've been a joke, because who said stuff like that to someone they'd just met in a crowded bar? "Was she serious?"

"As a heart attack. Within five minutes, she was sure the stars had led us to each other."

"She said that?"

"Direct quote."

"Looney tunes."

"Oh, it got better. Before I could use the john excuse and disappear, she'd used the words *soul mate* and *kismet*."

I let out a howl of laughter. "Sounds like you were two breaths from living happily ever after with your fated mate."

"Happy birthday to me, right?"

"So you left after that? Or did you keep looking for Ms. Birthday Wish?"

"Neither. I gave up the hunt. I may be traumatized for life." He swiped the sweat on his forehead with the hem of his tee. "I stayed and played darts with Dylan, Levi, and Betsy Ballantine. Which means I was there after you left with Ava."

Had I known that before, I might've gone easier on the questions from the start. There was no way he'd be cutting me any slack about this now.

"I walked her home," I said.

"That must've been after you had your tongue down her throat in the back hall."

"My tongue wasn't down her throat." As far as I knew. Although I'd been intense. I could admit, if only to myself, Breckenridge had gotten to me. I hadn't planned to kiss Ava. Hadn't known what I was going to do until she walked out of the ladies' room looking so fresh and pretty and kissable. Hell, I hadn't planned to nearly attack her until my lips were on hers.

"I heard differently," Jake said.

"You know better than to believe what you hear in this town."

"So you didn't kiss her?"

Fuck, it was hot out here already.

"That's what I thought," Jake said. "Then you walked her home. Did you spend the night?"

"I didn't spend the night," I snarled.

"What are you doing getting involved with your ex?"

"We're not getting involved." I sounded defensive and I knew it, but it was nobody's damn business about Ava and me. We *weren't* involved.

"Keep telling yourself that," he said, as if he could hear my thoughts.

"She's only in town for a couple of weeks. Her dream job is knocking at her door, and it's in Los Angeles." I told him about her TV series and how she had to fly back for a meeting next week.

"That's pretty fucking cool," he said.

"It's what she was meant to do. She was talking about writing screenplays even back when we were together."

He blew out something between a breath and a whistle. "I don't know much about the TV world, but head writer sounds like a big deal."

"It is." I'd googled it, the streaming company, and how to

get a job as a head writer. It sounded like a snowball's chance in hell for most people, and Ava was more than halfway to attaining it. "Like I said, her life is fully anchored to California. I'd never want to hold her back."

"Which brings us back to the question of what the hell are you doing?"

"Spending time with her while she's here. She doesn't have a lot of friends in town."

"She was with Magnolia last night, and that's after only being here a week. Seems like she'd be okay without you."

"What difference does it make to you if I spend time with Ava?" I asked, more than a little annoyed. We turned the corner onto the shoulder of Honeysuckle Road to do the last leg, as usual, with a lake view to our right. We had about a mile until we reached Henry's and the intersection with Main.

"I just don't think it's smart to get friendly with someone you have history with," Jake said. "There's too much kindling there and not just the physical kind."

I scowled at him, trying to make sense of his metaphors. "You don't know what you're talking about."

"You used to love each other, the way I remember it," he said. "It's not going to take much for one or both of you to slip back into that. If she's not staying, somebody's going to get their heart crushed like a bug."

"It's not like that," I said automatically. Ava and I were just spending time together, reconnecting on a harmless level for another couple of weeks. Maybe less. I didn't even know how long she planned to stay when she returned. "I like her. That's all. Completely harmless."

I could feel him staring me down from the side, looking for something on my face that went against what I was saying. I blanked my expression, focused on my feet hitting the coarse pavement, even as a hint of unease buzzed in my head.

As we neared the intersection of Honeysuckle and Main, a

siren sounded and seemed to be getting closer. Sure enough, the big fire truck came down Main Street toward us. My first reaction was to glance at my restaurant and Holden's brewery, remembering the fire in the brewery building a few months ago, before Holden opened it. There was no sign of smoke or any other problems in the two lakeshore buildings on the other side of the street, though, thank God.

The truck backed that up when it signaled a left turn onto Honeysuckle, heading out of town. There were houses a couple miles up that way...and Ava's inn. Ava, who'd planned to bake this morning. Ava, who'd been able to scorch a toaster pastry like nobody's business.

"Shit," I said as I took off at a sprint before the truck even turned onto the road that went to the inn.

CHAPTER 12

I'd never felt so defeated in my life.

Or embarrassed.

The siren on the fire truck got closer as my cheeks grew hotter—and not from fire. There was no fire, only smoke, plus an alarm system that was connected to the fire department. *Of course* it was connected to the fire department.

God, please let the earth open up and suck me in right now.

The siren stopped, and I could hear the large truck rumbling down the lane toward me and Gretchen Morris and one of her housekeeping staff, as well as every last Honeysuckle Inn guest. Because naturally the alarms had sounded throughout the inn, and naturally it was necessary to evacuate everybody from the building. Not for the first time, I was relieved there weren't more guests staying with us at the moment, even if it would help the cash flow issue a little.

Gretchen, who was in her mid-fifties and the head of Housekeeping, had come to work bright and early to prepare for most of the guests checking out today. She squeezed my upper arm supportively as the noisy truck pulled up. "Things like this happen all the time. It's okay, hon."

I knew she meant well, and I was thankful she was there and had filled me in on the fire department connection and the evacuation policy. But it didn't feel like things were okay right now.

Four firefighters jumped out of the truck, and one of them asked if the owner was present. With my cheeks still burning, I went toward him.

"There's no fire," I blurted out. "I burned muffins." I pointed to the muffin pan I'd tossed on the ground in front of the porch, thinking maybe that would get the stupid alarm to shut up.

Another one of the firefighters headed over to look at them, and the first one asked, "So there were no flames?"

I shook my head.

"Where did this happen?"

"In the inn's kitchen."

He called out to the other two to go in and check it out.

I explained, "Once you're inside, you go past the desk and—"

"It's okay. I'm familiar with the inn," he said. "You're Phyllis's niece, right?"

I nodded, not for the first time today thinking I was *not* doing Phyllis proud. At that thought, tears gushed into my eyes, and why not? I already felt like a total moron in front of the guests. I might as well cry my eyes out while I was at it.

But if nothing else, I was stubborn, so I squeezed my eyes shut, dragged a finger under each one, trying to dry them, then said, "I turned the oven off, so everything's okay. Not even that smoky."

"We still have to check it out," the guy said. "Shouldn't take long."

"Thanks," I said on an exhale, then glanced at the guests, who were hanging out in front of the east wing. I headed toward them, summoning an apologetic inn-owner smile. "I'm so sorry for the inconvenience," I said for probably the fifth time since we'd herded them outside. "They said it won't take long."

The Bianchi family, a young couple with twin three-year-olds, stood closer to the fire truck than all the others, one girl in her daddy's arms, staring at the truck with wide eyes, and her sister holding her mom's hand while hopping on one foot and talking nonstop about the rig.

"Have you ever seen a fire truck so close?" I asked the mellow girl, and she hid her face in Mr. Bianchi's neck kind of like I wished I could do. Except without Mr. Bianchi, of course.

Mr. and Mrs. Ackhurst, a retired couple from Des Moines, were already dressed for the day, and he'd brought the mug of coffee he'd brewed earlier in their room. Someone had moved two chairs from the porch out to them so they could sit. Mrs. Ackhurst smiled at me. "Looks like you're having that kind of day. At least we got some lookers as first responders."

"That we did," I said with a laugh. One of the firefighters who'd remained outside had taken off his helmet, showing that he was, indeed, a looker.

"You holding up okay?" Knox asked, walking up next to me. He'd been sitting on the curb, his laptop open, typing away as if there was no emergency going on around him. Which there wasn't. Just the smoke and a big truck that made it look so much worse than it was.

"I'm okay," I said. "Embarrassed. You're working early today."

"Couldn't sleep, and my characters were talking. I'm on kind of a roll, so I'm going to go sit in my car and see if I can get to the end of my chapter."

"Good luck."

As he walked off, I turned toward the last three groups,

the Patels, a honeymooning couple from North Dakota, Felisha and Veronica, two besties in their thirties here for a girls' week away, and the Kiplings, a keep-to-themselves couple in their early fifties. They all seemed involved in their own conversations, so I let them be, knowing yet another apology wouldn't make anything better.

I was lucky everyone was so understanding. And that there wasn't actually a fire. This could've been a lot worse.

Two of the firefighters were by the truck now, doing whatever firefighters who got called out on a fluke call did, so I guessed they didn't have any other questions for me. Perfect. I just wanted to be left alone.

I took a few steps away from everyone to try to breathe and calm my emotions. As I turned, I caught movement down the driveway out of the corner of my eye, and when I looked in that direction, I saw the last person I wanted to see right now, coming at me in a sprint.

Except, in spite of telling myself all damn night I needed to avoid Cash Henry as much as possible until I left town, there was an annoying flip in my chest at the sight of him. Because what a sight he made in athletic shorts and a half-drenched-with-sweat T-shirt, his thigh muscles flexing with every long stride, his biceps glistening with perspiration...

"Ava," he said, barely winded. "What's going on?" He stopped beside me, and okay, his chest was heaving a little, but it was nothing like the death I would be experiencing had I sprinted from the main road.

"Everything's fine." I turned my gaze back to the firefighters and the truck and the "action."

"I was on my run and saw the truck turn this way. What happened?"

My eyes fluttered closed. It was embarrassing enough to screw up and have everyone at the inn's morning interrupted, but admitting my amateur mistake to Cash? The professional chef? Especially after he'd teased me that I couldn't bake?

"You were right. I should've gone to Sugar," I said, resigned. "I burned the muffins." I gestured to the pan still on the ground. "The smoke set off the alarm. The alarm's connected to the fire department, and here we all are, just hanging out before seven on a Saturday morning. At least it's not raining."

"Damn. Sorry you're having a bad start." He put an arm around me, squeezed me to his side, then released me. "I'd give you a better hug but I stink," he said.

"I'm fine," I lied. I didn't want him to hug me, and it had nothing to do with sweat. I didn't want *anyone* to hug me. Wasn't sure if I could handle people being nice to me at the moment. "The firefighters should be about done, and then they'll let everyone back in."

He walked several long steps toward the inn, his eyes on the pan, going close enough that he'd definitely notice that not only were the muffins black but they hadn't risen.

When he was back at my side, he asked, "What happened? Was the cooking time wrong?"

"I got distracted and forgot to set a timer."

"It's happened to me. Maybe not to fire department level." His smile was sympathetic instead of teasing. I tried to join him in that smile but I probably wasn't convincing.

"I made the mistake of checking my email while they baked," I said. "There should be a limit on bad news emails before eight a.m. on a weekend."

"What kind of bad news?"

"Let's see… The woman I offered a front desk position took another job. The appraisal on the inn came in lower than expected, so I'll have less to borrow against. And the roof estimate was nearly double what Halstead had guessed and I'd hoped for. For starters."

"That's a hell of a Saturday morning," Cash said.

"Next thing I knew, smoke was coming out of the oven. I switched it off, then made the mistake of opening it."

"Smoke came rolling out?"

I nodded.

He was quiet, pensive, while I watched the two firefighters come back outside and consult with the others.

"This is all recoverable," Cash said, and I raised my brows, because I was ready to walk off the end of the dock and soak my head in the lake. "First I need to wash off the sweat. Mind if I use the shower in the cottage while you finish up with these guys?" He nodded to the firefighter who was approaching, the same guy I'd spoken to before.

"Go ahead," I said, barely thinking about the request. Cash had been in the cottage plenty of times in the past, and he knew where the bathroom was. I stepped toward the firefighter as Cash walked off. "What's the verdict?"

"Everything's fine. You can let people back in," he said. Fire Chief Thomas, I read from his badge.

"I'm so sorry." I'd said that so many times today that I should just get a T-shirt that said it and save my breath.

"You'd be surprised how often this kind of thing happens. Part of the job."

"I'll be more careful the next time I bake muffins," I said, trying to be lighthearted, but the truth was, I didn't know if I would try to bake the damn muffins ever again. Maybe that should be a job requirement of whoever I hired for morning desk shifts.

"Sounds like a plan, Ava. I hope your day gets better."

"I hope the same for you," I said, then walked toward the guests. "Hey, everyone. Thank you for being so understanding. I'm happy to say we've been given the all clear, and you can go back inside. If you're checking out this morning, we'll give you an extra hour if you need it."

Gretchen and Della would have to work a little harder to turn over the five rooms that would need cleaning, in addition to the usual daily cleaning duties in the common areas, but I had no doubt they could do it. If not, I'd pitch in and help. We had ten reservations coming in this afternoon, so it was going to be a busier week all the way around.

As everyone filed into the east wing and Gretchen and Della headed to the housekeeping headquarters, I went into the inn kitchen to see if there were any visible signs remaining of my screwup. It was slightly smoky, with a lingering odor. As I eyed the baking mess I'd left on the counters, my phone buzzed. I pulled it out and saw a message from Cash.

> Bring the muffin ingredients to the cottage. I'll whip some up for your guests while I'm here.

Damn. This was the "nice" I wasn't sure I could handle, and the tears that came to my eyes again were proof.

Another buzz.

> Or you can run to Sugar.

My stubbornness kicked in.

> I'm not going to Sugar. I can mix some more up.

> We need to make sure they rise.

Of course that detail hadn't escaped him.

> Fine. You can bake away.

> With pleasure. Once you bring me the ingredients.

As I gathered the flour, eggs, sugar, cinnamon, and other items, I heard voices in the lobby. I finished stuffing the ingredients in a grocery sack then went out to find the Bianchis there with their luggage, ready to check out. I set the bag on the back counter and checked them out, chatting about their vacation to Dragonfly Lake.

"What was your favorite thing?" I asked Lucy, the bolder of the two little girls.

"Cookies!"

I laughed. "You must've visited Sugar."

She nodded, and even Lilac, her quiet sister, perked up at that, her eyes sparkling.

"We loved Sugar," Mrs. Bianchi said. "And going on a boat and shopping in the toy store and—"

"And pizza!" Lucy hollered, jumping up and down.

"And pizza." Mr. Bianchi smiled and shook his head. "We could've stayed in Cincinnati for cookies and pizza," he muttered to me good-naturedly.

"But maybe not boating?" I asked.

"This lake is breathtaking," Mrs. Bianchi said, "and the town is adorable. We'll definitely be back next year."

"I hope you'll stay with us again. We enjoyed having you." I slid their receipt—handwritten, because that's how Aunt Phyl did it, and we weren't yet set up for anything more advanced—across the counter.

"We wouldn't stay anywhere else. We're so sorry about Mrs. Sharp," Mrs. Bianchi said, more subdued. "You're doing an admirable job stepping in."

I forced a smile, because I could argue that statement but I wouldn't. "Thank you. You have a safe trip home and we'll see you next year. Call anytime to reserve your room."

The family of four said goodbye, and even shy little Lilac blew me a kiss as they walked out the door. With an exhale, I thought, *my first check-out, and the party seemed more than satisfied with their stay at the inn.*

Maybe the morning wasn't a complete disaster after all.

I took out the sign that directed guests to text me if they needed me before I returned, placed it front and center on the counter, grabbed the bag of baking ingredients, and set off for the cottage with mixed emotions.

My plans had been to stay busy and keep my head down, focused on the inn, until I left for my LA meeting on Wednesday. If I concentrated on work, I couldn't think about Cash or last night or kissing him. But here he was, being nice to me again. Seeming to care. Helping me out of a muffin jam and telling me that everything would be okay.

He was turning out to be the friend I needed, just when I needed him, and maybe I needed to just embrace that while I was here. Maybe I deserved a bright spot in an otherwise crap-tastic morning.

I went up the walkway to the front door and entered—and froze.

There, in the open kitchen, was a wet-haired Cash with his back to me, opening cabinets and shutting them, wearing nothing but a towel wrapped around his waist.

CHAPTER 13

Maybe it'd been too long since I'd had sex.

Just looking at Cash across the cozy living room that was open to the kitchen awoke a kernel of desire deep inside me. Okay, more than a kernel. The man might be almost forty and create and sample food for a living, but it was undebatable that he took excellent care of his body.

His back was still to me as he pulled a mixing bowl out of the cabinet, his shoulder muscles firm and flexing with every movement. I admired his biceps and triceps as he reached to the side for something, then I stood there for a few seconds appreciating his total confidence and competency in my aunt's modest, outdated kitchen.

When I closed the door, I should've braced myself, because he spun toward me, giving me a smile and a full view of his chest. It was perfect. Sculpted, with ridges and well-formed pecs, and good lord, those abs… He'd had a baseball player's physique when we were together all those years ago, long and muscular, firm, with an ass that made a girl long to squeeze it, and I'm here to tell you, he'd filled out and firmed up beautifully since then.

I swallowed, shook myself mentally, and attempted to act like I wasn't having a religious moment seeing him nearly naked. "Your clothes disappeared," I managed.

"I rinsed them out and threw them in the dryer. Hope that's okay."

"Of course." Because my body temperature was *not* rising just from looking at him. No, not at all. "It's hot in here," I said before I could stop the words.

"I've got the oven preheating."

"That explains it. I brought what you asked for." I set the bag on the counter and stepped up next to him to unload it. "What's that?" I pointed to a bowl of something he'd already stirred up.

"Glaze. You had what I needed for this on hand. We're making cinnamon roll muffins with glaze."

"I can get behind that. As long as you're doing the making."

"What are you going to do tomorrow morning for muffin time?"

"Serve leftovers?" I said. "Let's bake double."

"We can do that." He was going through the ingredients I'd brought and setting them out according to some kind of order in his head. "Baking isn't hard, Ava. You can master it."

"Obviously," I said dryly. "Just ask Fire Chief Thomas."

"Don't be so hard on yourself," he said in a gentle, encouraging voice as he poured flour into a measuring cup. "If you do two things, you'll have it."

"One, sit on the counter, and two, watch you?"

"I was thinking more of following the directions and setting a timer, but you can sit and watch if you'd rather."

I kicked my flip-flops to the side and hoisted myself up on the counter not far from his workspace. "Muffins might be one of Aunt Phyl's traditions that has to end."

"And that would be okay. You're the owner now and you can do things your way."

I let out a quiet but caustic laugh. "I don't have a way. I don't have the slightest idea what I'm doing here, Cash."

He set aside a third bowl where he'd just dumped the flour and walked over to me. Bracing his hands on the edge of the counter on either side of me, he looked intently into my eyes and said, "I think you're doing an amazing job. You've run this inn for a week now and kept your customers happy, all while grieving."

"More like the inn has run me, most days." Yes, I was trying to be funny when he was stone-cold serious. His praise made me twitchy. I didn't deserve it.

"Ava, your aunt was a sweet, caring lady, and you loved her dearly, but she didn't leave you in a great situation here."

"I don't think she was planning on keeling over at the grocery store."

"What I'm trying to say is that you walked into a mess and you've managed it. Managed it well. You've been busting your ass to make sure the guests are taken care of, the building is taken care of, the employees are okay, all while taking action toward the future to ensure this place will carry on in the spirit of Phyllis Sharp."

He made my eyes water when he said it like that. "I'm trying. I can't find anyone to manage it—"

Cash pressed his finger to my lips to quiet me. "You've been here for five days. Searching for a manager for half of that."

I sucked in a shaky breath and met his gaze. I couldn't deny what he said, though it felt like I'd been here for a month.

"Give yourself a break, Ava."

With him staring into my eyes with so much compassion, I wanted to give whatever he asked of me.

I couldn't help but notice that what he *wasn't* doing, in

spite of how close we were, in spite of those kisses last night, was making a move on me. Not the way I suddenly wanted him to. He was inches away, surrounding me on three sides but not quite touching me. I could feel the heat of him, breathe in the freshly showered scent of him, and I was drowning in those dreamy eyes once again.

"Will you do that?" he persisted. "For me?"

I tried to clear my lust fog enough to remember what he wanted me to do. "Give myself a break," I repeated.

"Be gentle on you."

My gaze dipped down to his lips and I didn't give myself time to think about it. I leaned forward and kissed him, catching his unshaven jaw in my palm, loving the roughness of it.

He kissed me back for several long seconds, then growled and ended the kiss. "Supposed to be baking for your guests."

I wanted to tell him to forget my guests, but after what I'd put them through this morning, I should be giving them each a full dozen sweet treats, plus maybe a complimentary dinner at Cash's restaurant. "I'll give you five minutes to finish up," I said, grinning and pointing at the bowls.

He let out a sort of laugh that told me he didn't think I was serious, and that made me all the more serious. That and the show he put on for those five or so minutes, stirring, whisking, adding ingredients… Someone was missing out on the next reality show here—hot guys in towels making sugary baked goods.

As he mixed the wet ingredients in with the dry, his muscled forearm took a backseat to his abs and that trail of dark hair that bisected his abdomen and disappeared beneath the edge of the worn white towel. I imagined what he would do if I reached out and undid the towel so that it fell to the floor.

"Hungry?" he asked me as he tapped the mixing spoon on the edge of the bowl.

"Starving," I said, not thinking about muffins.

"Let me guess…you forgot breakfast?"

"I scorched breakfast," I reminded him.

"You should eat something." He was pouring batter into the bottom of each muffin cup. Once all of them were partially filled, he sprinkled a layer of the cinnamon-sugar mixture on.

The silverware drawer was directly below me, so I widened my legs, opened it, took a small spoon out, and closed it again. I dipped it into the glaze, then tasted it. Creamy, sugary goodness slid over my tongue, and I let out a sound of appreciation. Cash's gaze leaped to me and he dropped his spoonful of sugar mixture on the counter. I took that as encouragement as he refilled his spoon.

"Five minutes are almost up," I said, then licked the back of my spoon to get every drop of frosting off it.

"Just about done." He picked up the batter again and poured another layer, the cinnamon–sugar smell wafting to my nose.

I watched his easy, practiced movements as he alternated batter with cinnamon-sugar crunch, thinking how talented his hands were to create food that was good enough to bring a girl to tears. As soon as he sprinkled the final layer of cinnamon-sugar on top and stuck the pan in the oven, I grabbed his hand and pulled him in front of me, then laced our fingers together. His brows shot up and I yanked him closer, between my legs, and locked them behind him.

"I'm trying to be good here," he said in a gravelly voice, gazing into my eyes, our faces inches apart.

"There are multiple ways of being good." I brushed my lips lightly over his.

"I don't want to push you into something you don't want."

I let out a soft laugh. "Does this feel like you're pushing me into anything?"

His reply was a slow, sexy growl from deep in his throat as he peered down at me from under heavy lids.

In case he needed further convincing, I dipped a finger of my free hand into the glaze and smeared it down the center of his chest. "Oops." I let go of his hand, slid down from the counter, and licked the frosting off his skin, savoring the mix of sugar from the frosting and saltiness of his skin.

The sound that came out of his chest was half low chuckle, half growl, one-hundred-percent sexy, so I took my time, making sure I got every last drop of glaze, worshipping the firm ridges and valleys with my tongue. I whisked it over one of his nipples, then kissed my way up, over his collarbone, along his neck, to his jaw, waiting for him to either pull me closer or shut me down, praying with every overheated fiber of my being it was the former.

Pausing long enough to look into his eyes, gauging whether he was with me, I barely breathed. My heart pounded as he peered down at me, his lips parted, showing me I was affecting him at least a little.

"Ava…"

I ran my hands up his chest, to his shoulders. "Yes?"

His Adam's apple bobbed as he swallowed. "Is this what you want?"

Letting out a little laugh, I said, breathily, "You really can't tell?"

"You were hesitant last night. Just want you to be sure… No regrets?"

"Only if you turn me away right now."

Our gazes were locked for another five seconds, the longest five seconds of my life, and then his lips lowered to mine, his hands wrapped around my waist and pulled my body into his, and he devoured my mouth without warning in the most thorough, passionate kiss ever, as if holding himself back while I'd eaten the frosting off his skin had taken a toll on him.

He pressed his erection into me, trapping me between him and the counter, leaving no doubt he was as into this as I was. As our tongues swirled and mated, I lowered one hand to the side of his waist, found the lump of towel where it was being held up, and released it. It sprung away from his backside and got caught up where our bodies were touching in front, so I yanked the terry cloth to the side and dropped it on the floor.

The contact between our mouths broke long enough for him to say, "You still turn aggressive when you want something."

"Oops," I said again, grinning into his mouth as I went back to kissing him.

His hands trailed lower, over my butt, and before I knew what was happening, he lifted me. I let out a surprised yelp and my legs went around his waist. I held on tighter to his neck as he turned us away from the kitchen counter.

"Which room are you staying in?" he asked.

"My old one. Upstairs."

He reached the stairs in three long strides, then he darted us up them as if he wasn't carrying another human. That show of fitness and strength did nothing to cool my jets. He went into the room on the right, familiar with where I'd grown up even though we'd rarely spent time there when my aunt and mom lived in the cottage.

At the side of my bed, he set me down, my feet sliding to the floor. There was a huge three-paneled window on the wall facing the lake, but I hadn't bothered to open the blinds yet. The light was filtered, but I could see his naked form when I landed on the mattress. His dick jutted upward, and my body responded to the sight, aching for his intrusion.

"Get naked," he said.

"Mm, you've gotten bossy." I lifted my flowy shirt over my head and playfully tossed it at him.

"You like bossy?" he asked, coming nearer, crowding his legs against mine.

"I like *you*." I unhooked my bra but kept it over my breasts. "I can't get naked if you don't give me space."

"You're taking too long." He backed up half a step, his eyes locked on my chest.

"I'm worth the wait."

I tugged the bra off and flung it so it draped over his shoulder, then stood to unbutton my shorts. Before I could drop them to the floor, Cash was palming my breasts, kneading them, rubbing his thumbs over my nipples, making my breath catch. He lowered his head and took one in his mouth, and my shorts were forgotten as I arched into him, dropped my head back, and held on to his head, my fingers burrowing through his coarse hair.

"Your nipples were always so sensitive," he said between teasing tongue swirls. "Can you still come this way?"

Ten minutes ago, I would've said I didn't know, because I hadn't. Not since him. With his mouth on me though, there was no doubt. "Uh-huh, but I don't want to."

He caught the tip of my nipple between his tongue and teeth, and a shock of sensation zinged straight to my core, making me gasp. "No?" he teased.

"I want—"

His fingers toyed with my other nipple, intensifying the ache between my legs until I squirmed.

Jesus.

"Want you…inside of me. Deep," I finally got out.

"I love your tits, Ava," he said, then laved my nipple slowly, thoroughly. "They're even more perfect than before."

"I need to be naked."

"I agree."

He laid me back on the mattress, my legs hanging over the side, and pulled my shorts and underwear down my legs. I braced my feet on the edge of the bed, bringing my knees up, opening myself to him. Cash feasted his eyes on my most private parts, and the heat in his eyes made the ache inside of me incessant, begging for him to assuage it.

I took his hand and pulled him with me as I scooted farther back on the bed. He followed me partway, then dropped over my legs and kissed the inside of my knee. He trailed his tongue upward, along my inner thigh, laving, nibbling, kissing, driving my need for him higher. When he got to the juncture of my leg and my body, he licked it, one side, then the other, teasing me, not quite hitting the point that throbbed for him.

Trying to divert myself from my impatience, I propped up on my elbows and watched him, the way his head dipped with each movement, and I marveled that we were together again, if only for today. He'd felt like such a vital part of me at one time. He wasn't the same and yet he was in some ways, and beyond the crazy he was making me, there was a deep satisfaction in that.

He spent ages kissing and teasing me with his tongue and lips and fingers. With every pass of his tongue over my center, my need heightened. Though I wanted his mouth all over me, making me come apart, what I wanted even more was for him to fill me. It was the only way to make this deep ache go away.

I pulled at his arm, urging him higher. "Cash."

His gaze lifted and met mine, his eyes so full of lust and heat that I couldn't speak for a few seconds.

I tugged him closer. "Please…"

"You don't like that?"

"I love it but I want…"

He moved up my body with a predatory look in his eyes, his erection nudging my center. "This?"

I answered by dropping my knee, opening more to him.

As he braced himself over me on his forearms, he closed

his eyes for a moment, looking pained. "I don't have a condom. Do you?"

I shook my head, slightly dismayed that I hadn't considered that before this second. "I'm on the pill and clean."

He exhaled. "I'm clean too."

I ran my hands down his back to that delectable former-baseball-player's ass and clasped him to me, running one of my feet up the back of his leg. His dick was cradled in my folds, the hardness and friction lighting up all my nerve endings. I rubbed myself against him, silently begging him.

"I want to take this slow, but if I don't get inside of you in the next two seconds…"

"Get inside of me," I said, then sucked in a breath of anticipation as I felt him at my entrance.

Cash pushed inside, filled me up, drew a moan from me. He stilled and moaned himself, biting his lip as if he had to fight to get control of himself. The ecstasy of the moment meshed with memories, and a sense of rightness settled over me. This was Cash, the first man I'd ever been with. The best.

We'd always been compatible in bed, and it seemed that hadn't changed in nearly two decades, even though we'd both lived so much of life separately. None of that mattered, only this moment when we were as close as two people could be.

With a low rumble in his throat, he withdrew slowly, making sure I felt every millimeter of him, every millisecond of pleasure. It was a familiar play between us, him trying to draw it out, me urging him to give me more, and he smiled down at me.

"It's like no time has passed," he said.

"Mm-hmm."

"Being with you again is incredible."

"Mmm." I moved my hips slowly. "Cash?"

"Yeah, baby?"

"You don't have to sweet-talk me into anything. You got me."

He thrust into me emphatically. "I got you." The corners of his lips curved up in the sexiest hint of a cat-who-ate-the-canary smirk, and then he thrust again, and my eyes fluttered closed and my thoughts dissipated and I just…felt.

Even after all these years, he still knew where to touch me, when to move faster, how to hold me on the precipice, when to push me over the edge until I cried out his name and clung to him and forgot how to breathe, no longer cared how to breathe.

I was just starting to come back into myself when he ground into me harder, tensed, then let go. I watched the ecstasy wash over his face, burned it to my memory, loved that I could still do that to him.

A few seconds later, he opened his eyes slowly, looking dazed but satiated and in as much awe as I was. We'd always been good together. Our sex life had been stupendous and toe-curling. After he'd broken up, though, there'd been so many times if I'd wondered if I'd only imagined how good it had been.

I had my answer. I hadn't imagined it.

We were so damn good together. Physically, of course. Maybe that's where I'd gotten confused in the past.

Locking down on that uncomfortable thought, I brought myself back to the present and ran my fingers through his hair as we both tried to catch our breath.

Cash kissed me slowly, tenderly, as if I were the most precious thing to him— No. As if I were a damn good lay. That's what I was, all I wanted to be. All I could be.

Again, I shut out the wayward thoughts that could only cause trouble. "Almost twice as old as we were before, and look at us."

"We're fucking incredible."

"And incredible at fucking," I said, keeping it light.

He buried his face in my hair, let out a low growl, and said, "Just like I thought it would be."

After another kiss, he lowered his weight to the side of me, propped himself up on his elbow, and ran a finger over my lower lip as he gazed down at me.

"So...you thought about us?" I asked. "About this?" I flicked a hand toward our naked, half-entwined bodies.

"From the second I heard you were coming back to town. Whether I wanted to or not."

I grinned, possibly a little cat-ate-the-canary-ish myself. "And you said you were only concerned about me remembering to eat."

"You didn't ask if I wanted to get you naked."

I thought back to that first night he'd visited me. "I couldn't have handled it then."

"Timing is everything." His cocky grin shouldn't have turned me inside out, but it did.

As we lay there quietly, an aroma besides that of Cash and sex eventually broke through to my consciousness. I sniffed a couple of times, trying to place it. I leaned up on an elbow. "Did you set the—"

"Son of a bitch. The muffins!" He jumped out of bed and hauled his very sexy ass out of the room and down the stairs, naked as the day he was born.

I'll be honest; I watched him until he was out of my sight, and I reveled in every last second of it.

Then I launched out of bed and grabbed my clothes from the floor, wondering if I was about to come face-to-face with Fire Chief Thomas for the second time in an hour.

CHAPTER 14

Still naked, I hovered in the doorway of my bedroom, peeking down to the first floor. I didn't see any smoke. "Cash?"

"Everything's okay," he yelled up at the same time the smoke alarm started screeching. "Got it under control." There was a pause and I heard commotion. "Just gotta get that thing turned off. It's not connected to the fire department."

"Do you need help?"

"I've got it," he said after some swearing at himself or the muffins or the alarm, I wasn't sure which, but it made me grin.

Now that I knew the house wasn't burning down, I couldn't get the smile off my face. My smile was probably audible as I hollered down to him, "I'm taking a quick shower." Or it would've been if the stupid alarm would shut up.

As I hurried into the bathroom and turned the shower on, the alarm went silent at last. I looked at myself in the mirror as the water heated. The grin of a girl who'd been well loved reflected at me, and I let out a giggle. The sound was so foreign that I laughed again. That man made me stupid giddy.

My lips were red and slightly swollen. My nipples showed signs of being ravished, the sensitive tips still protruding and the skin of my breasts pink in areas where Cash's scruff had rubbed.

Goofy grin still in place, I stepped into the shower and let the hot water cascade over my sensitive body. I poured shampoo into my palm and lathered my hair on autopilot, my thoughts consumed by the irresistible guy in my kitchen.

He knew me still. Knew my weaknesses and preferences and most secret desires, just like he always had. He'd remembered, whether intentionally or instinctively, how to turn me inside out like no one else ever had. Seemingly without even trying, he made me feel as if he was made for me, made specifically to take me to the stars and back.

I didn't have the luxury of standing under the hot spray and daydreaming, but that didn't stop me from remembering Cash's touch on my skin as I rubbed body wash over myself. I couldn't wait to get naked with him again, to take our time with each other, spend hours coming apart in each other's arms—

A text message alert sounded from outside the shower, jolting me back to the here and now and sending my heart rate up. I'd forgotten all about the front desk and the fact I could be summoned at any moment.

"Shit."

I rinsed my head and stuck it out from the shower curtain, wondering where my phone had ended up. I saw the corner of it sticking out from my shorts.

As soon as the soap was rinsed off, I flipped the water off, grabbed my towel, and frantically dried myself. I grabbed a brush and went for my hair, letting my body air-dry a little more before pulling my clothes back on. Throwing my hair up would be fast and make it less obvious I was straight from a post-sex shower as I tried to get my inn-owner face back on.

When I was dry enough, I dug out my phone and unlocked it, expecting the message to be from an unknown number, which was how the inn guests would show up. It wasn't though. It was from Willa, my incredible agent.

> Good morning, Ava. I ran into Sheldon Milano at a party in Malibu last night. He brought your name up before I could!

My poor heart couldn't catch a break this morning because now it took off galloping for altogether different reasons. Sheldon Milano was her friend from Stream, the one I was meeting with next week.

> He told me he'd talked to Pete Swain, who raved about your work ethic and your ability to think on your feet back when you were an intern under him. Sheldon said he and his partners are looking forward to meeting you Thursday. I'm taking it as a positive sign that he knew what day our meeting is without me reminding him. I have a really good feeling about this!

"Oh, my god," I whispered, setting my phone on the counter as I pulled my underwear on. I squealed to myself, then pressed my lips together, reining it in long enough to respond to her.

> I can't wait to meet him and his team. Thanks for the update. You're amazing!

I finished dressing, then twisted my hair up on top of my head. I didn't have time to put my mascara or eye liner on, but no one here in Dragonfly Lake seemed to care about that, not like they did in LA.

My whole body buzzing with excitement from Willa's message and lingering bliss from Cash, I hurried toward the stairs, thinking, *Can this day get any better?*

I was halfway down the flight of steps when it hit me that the two things that had me flying high at the moment were not compatible. I paused at the sobering realization.

I was going to have to give up at least one of them. Soon. And for once in my life, I was not going to sacrifice my career.

My breath was shaky as I inhaled slowly. I was terrified that succumbing to the temptation that was Cash this morning might be the dumbest thing I'd ever done.

―――

CASH

When I got to the first floor of the cottage, it was a little smoky, so I rushed to the oven, turned it off, and opened the window above the kitchen sink. I would've swung one or both of the outside doors open, but I was buck-ass naked and didn't figure Ava needed her guests witnessing that.

Now that I knew the house wasn't burning down, I laughed to myself as I fanned the smoky oven with the towel I'd dropped earlier—or rather, Ava had dropped.

Damn, but that woman could still turn me inside out.

"Cash?" she called down.

"Everything's okay." As if to make a liar of me, the smoke alarm went off, shrilling through the house. "Got it under control. Just gotta get that thing turned off. It's not connected to the fire department." I raised my voice to be heard over the damn alarm.

"Do you need help?"

I had half a mind to say yes just so I could watch her march down here naked. "Fucking hell," I muttered to my ridiculous self. "I've got it," I called out to Ava.

"I'm taking a quick shower," she called, and I thought briefly about leaving this mess and joining her.

Instead, I pulled a chair from the kitchen table and climbed up on it to see if there was a button to shut the alarm up. It looked ancient, definitely not hooked up to the house electrical, and I ended up pulling the cover off and taking the battery out.

A few minutes later, I was back up on the chair, trying to replace the battery now that the smoke was gone, standing there like a naked statue on a pedestal, when Ava reached the bottom of the stairs and met my gaze, her eyes wide and alarmed.

"Everything's fine," I reassured her. "No fire department en route. No flames."

Her gaze lowered to my dick and that was enough to make me semi-hard again. That and seeing her all quickly thrown together, her hair pulled up and still wet, her lips still a little swollen. It made me want to get her all undone again.

As I climbed down from the chair, she averted her gaze, still not smiling, and smoothed a hand down the side of her shorts, drawing my attention to her slender, gorgeous legs. They weren't long legs, but they didn't need to be. I could spend hours nibbling on them, running my tongue over them, showing my appreciation of her body. There were subtle changes from the past, like just a few more womanly curves at her waist, and I loved every one of them. Wanted to spend more time learning them in fine detail.

Without saying anything, she went toward her shoes and slid her feet into them. I couldn't help noticing she hadn't looked at me again. I pulled the towel back around my waist, sensing she was uncomfortable, though I wasn't sure why. What we'd shared upstairs had been fucking incredible, and I'd swear, just fifteen minutes ago, she'd agreed.

"Are you okay?" I asked, stepping closer to her, stopping myself from dragging her up against me.

Her phone sounded an alert, and she lifted it and read a message.

"Fine," she said as she read the message on her phone. "That's from the Patels. They're ready to check out, so I have to go." She turned toward the door, then spun back to me, stood on tiptoes, and pressed a quick kiss to my lips, almost like an afterthought.

My hand went to her waist as she did it, but she hurried off, leaving me grasping at air.

"I'll see you later," she said, then hurried out the door, leaving me standing there, staring after her, wondering what the fuck had just happened.

It was nothing good, no question about it. I understood we'd picked an inopportune time to get horizontal, but I couldn't help but be aware of two glaring facts.

One, she'd been rushed and bothered *before* she'd received the text from the inn guests.

And two, she'd used the word *fine*. I had more than enough experience with women to know to never trust it when a woman says she's fine.

CHAPTER 15

Standing outside of the inn, I shoved my misgivings aside, headed to the door, and blazed inside as if I didn't have a doubt in the world.

"Hello," I sang out to the Patels. "It's been one heck of a morning." *Not. A. Lie.* "Thanks for your patience. Let's get you checked out and on your way as quickly as possible."

"Oh, we're in no hurry at all," Janie Patel said as she wrapped herself around her new husband's arm. "We're taking the scenic route home. Driving. No schedule at all. We're going to enjoy the next three days of *us* before we get back to Bismarck."

"You two are so lucky," I said as I went around the counter and pulled out their paperwork.

Janie giggled, exchanged a look with her husband, Ari. "We think so."

I was a newlywed once. I hated to think of Wes now, but I'd loved him at one time—or at least I'd thought I did. If this was what love looked like, where two people couldn't stop touching each other, couldn't stop exchanging private smiles, then I wasn't so sure I could've called it love even back then. These two seemed to have the type of connection everyone searched for.

Cash's image popped into my mind, taunting me, trying to make me confuse lust with love, so I got down to business.

"Other than skipping the early-morning fire alarm, is there anything we could do better here at the Honeysuckle Inn?" I asked them, bracing a little for their response. This was my first time asking that, something I'd seen recommended in one of the hundreds of articles about running an inn I'd read over the past week.

Ari Patel folded the papers I'd handed him and slid them into his pocket. "There were a couple of times we thought it would be nice to have room service."

Janie giggled again, and it was quite clear why they hadn't wanted to leave their room.

"I'm in the food service industry," Ari continued. "I couldn't help noticing that the kitchen here would be more than adequate for some light food service, beyond breakfast pastries. It seems a waste of space as it is."

I tilted my head, considering what he said, unable to argue with any of it. Also unable to wrap my head around how I could manage adding food service to my list, but it was worth thinking about. "That's a great suggestion. Something for me to consider. Thank you."

"I love the loungers out by the lake," Janie said. "They're good for getting some sun—or moonlight. It'd be even better if they had some thick cushions." Again with the giggle and the weighted look at her husband, and I was pretty sure I didn't want to know exactly what they'd done out on the loungers under the moon.

"Cushions for the loungers. Fabulous idea." I jotted both it and the room service idea on a pad of Post-its.

"Our honeymoon has been amazing," Janie continued, "so thank you for your beautiful accommodations. We're thinking of making this an annual tradition."

"We'd love to have you," I said, meaning it. "Let us know when you have dates for next year. We'll save your room for you anytime."

We finished up our business, they went on their way, and I sat down hard on Aunt Phyl's stool. I was exhausted and restless at once. The hot male mistake in my cottage was more on my mind than the encouraging messages from my agent.

That was messed up.

I had three more parties due to check out this morning, but I couldn't stand to sit still and definitely didn't want to be here if Cash came looking for me. I needed time to sort out my brain before I faced him again. I hopped off the stool and left the lobby.

I touched base with Gretchen, who said they were on schedule with their cleaning duties, then took a tape measure from Halstead's maintenance HQ and headed out to the loungers to see what size cushions we'd need. I could handle cushions. They sounded easy and fast, something that could be checked off a list yet today with an online order. Maybe checking something off my list would level out my head.

With the lounger dimensions noted on my phone, I straightened and breathed for a moment. It felt like I hadn't done that yet today. The sun was beaming down, making it a steamy morning. The lake sparkled, and there were several boats out in the center, far from this shore, and lots of activity down toward the marina and the private beach to the west. I'd never needed to soak in my surroundings more than I did right now. I walked toward the inn's docks a short distance from the lounge area.

I went to a section of dock shaded by a towering tree along the shore, knowing the surface in other places would scorch my butt if I sat down. I lowered myself to the shaded worn wood, noting the rough edges, yet I couldn't resist hanging my legs over the side and dipping my feet into the water.

The docks had long needed to be replaced, and it would be a costly but necessary project too. Years ago, we allowed guests to bring their boat and dock it here, but my aunt had been forced to stop that a few years back because of the deteriorating docks.

That would have to be a project for phase two. I didn't know what phase two meant, other than *not right now*, because the roof and the painting and the countless other maintenance projects had to come first. Maybe we could replace the docks in time for the spring season next year. It was something to discuss with the manager I needed to find, once I found them, trained them, and gave them a chance to get acclimated.

I closed my eyes, attempting to close out worries about the inn and about Cash, willing myself to relax. Just for five minutes.

Opening my eyes, I breathed in the humid air, appreciating the lake smell of it like I'd barely had a chance to since I'd arrived on Monday.

Our area of the lake was peaceful. It always had been. To my left was a stretch of undeveloped shoreline, some of which the inn owned—*I* owned, come to think of it. It had been a part of my aunt's original purchase, and she'd kept it wild and untouched. Beyond that, to the east, the shore was lined by modest homes built in the 1960s. To my right, or west, was town, including Henry's Restaurant and McNamara Marina, then a residential area. At night, beyond that, you could see the lights of the new Marks Resort, but I hadn't even had a chance to drive by it yet.

I was working hard to avoid thinking about Cash and this

morning and the implications of all of it. Unfortunately, it wasn't two minutes later that heavy footsteps sounded on the dock behind me, then veered in my direction at the T intersection. The steps were confident and intentional, and I knew without looking they belonged to Cash.

CHAPTER 16

AVA

"Is this spot taken?" Cash asked when his steps halted a foot away from me.

Damn that man. The horrible line said in his sexy voice made me smile in spite of myself.

"Hi." When I looked up at him, I saw he was dressed in his running clothes again, but they were clean and he looked put together, giving no hint of what had happened earlier.

He sat next to me and held out a small bakery bag from Sugar. I took it, opened it, and saw two donuts, one with chocolate chips and white frosting on top, my favorite, and a plain glazed, which had been his usual order when we were together. I'd always teased him for having dull donut taste.

"Even now, with all your chef credentials, you choose glazed?" I asked.

"The beauty is in the simplicity and the textures. The glaze is just thick enough, the center of the donut just soft enough…"

I took out my sugary sphere of perfection. "Frosting and

chocolate chips add even more textural dimension," I said, handing him the bag with his glazed.

"On this, we'll never agree."

"Agree." I took my first bite, and lord, could they still do donuts right at Sugar. I moaned my appreciation, and when I finished savoring the bite, I said, "Thank you. I didn't realize how much I needed this."

"You're welcome. You've burned a few hundred calories already this morning." He rubbed his hand over my thigh and squeezed ever so lightly, just a quick touch, but it took me back to my bedroom, when my body had been bared to him and his hands had been all over it.

"True that." I stuffed another heavenly bite in my mouth.

"I put a dozen in the lobby on the counter with a sign that says, *Help yourself.* In case you still have a few people here."

"I still have a few people here." I glanced at my phone to make sure I hadn't missed a message, fighting the way his thoughtfulness tugged at me. "Thank you, Cash."

"It killed me a little to admit defeat, but by the time I would've cleaned up the mess, remixed a new batch, and baked them, it would've been more of a check-in treat for this afternoon. Which isn't a bad idea, come to think of it."

My heart turned over at his admission. I didn't know this specific chef version of Cash very well, but I knew the man had pride, always had, just like any man, and he obviously was seeing those little muffins as a personal affront. And still, he'd humbled himself and gone out of his way for me.

Damn the man again, getting under my skin.

"I'll add check-in treats to the list of suggestions. As long as there's someone else to bake them," I said. I set the last couple bites of donut on my leg and typed *check-in treats* on the list on my phone. "Ari Patel mentioned room service and making better use of the kitchen space, and his wife suggested thick lounger cushions. Which is why I'm out here." I gestured over my shoulder to the chairs on shore as I stuck the last of my donut in my mouth.

"I agree about the kitchen. A lot of places would kill to have a dedicated commercial kitchen space. Did Phyllis ever do anything besides bake pastries?"

I shook my head. "Most of the equipment is old but barely used."

"We could come up with some ideas. Maybe start small, with breakfast and lunch. Something that could generate extra revenue and add value for your guests."

That was hard to argue with, but the thought of becoming further entwined with Cash made me uneasy. I simply said, "Thanks. I appreciate the offer."

He caught my hand, twined our fingers together. I met his gaze and knew instantly I shouldn't have. His look was intense, searching. "I meant it, Ava."

I looked away, managed to not pull my hand from his, and nodded.

"Hey," he said. "I'm sensing a hesitancy in you. Like you're shutting me out." Still holding my hand, he used his other to brush my cheek with his knuckle.

I wanted to lean into it, and *that* was exactly the problem.

"You better not be having regrets," he said. I could hear that he was smiling, lightening his words.

"Not regrets." I'd be pulling out the memory of this morning later, when I was alone and missed him. When it was safe to spend time with it. "Cash, what are we doing?"

"Same thing we talked about last night."

"Today in the cottage didn't feel like the same thing."

He laughed. "I hope it was even better." In a flash, he went serious, self-conscious. "Was it not okay for you?"

That made me laugh. "It was okay."

He turned more fully toward me. "Just okay?"

"Are you fishing for compliments? It was a hundred times better than okay, and you know it. That's part of the problem." I unlaced my fingers from his, bent over, dipped my hand in the refreshing water because I needed to cool down. "I know I started that. I'm just feeling…doubts. Like, what's the point of getting closer if we have no future?"

I'd thought I could handle "just sex." I'd literally dreamed of Cash all night long after those kisses last night. But then this morning had been intense. Physically, yes. Of course. That was the good part. But the stuff in my mind…

"My brain is confusing the past with the present," I said. "Taking me back to when I thought we weren't temporary."

He didn't reply, and when I dared a glance at him, he was staring straight ahead, toward a boat with a pretty blue and green sail in the distance.

"You don't get that?" I pressed.

"I get it. Being with you is nothing like being with someone I barely know. You're not a one-night stand, Ava. There's a middle ground between a one-night fling and forever though."

"Have you had a lot of one-night stands?" I couldn't stop the question from coming out, even though I had a good guess at the answer and really didn't want to hear it.

"Had enough of them," he said. "Plus the supposed forever."

"How about middle ground? Between a night and forever?"

Cash shook his head. "I've proven neither extreme works for me, though, so maybe the middle ground is worth a try."

"What happened with your ex-wife?" I asked. I was dying to know, but I hated to admit it.

Cash shrugged. "She wanted more than I could give her. Never wanted to be stuck in a small town. Never wanted to be the wife of a chef who works late shifts."

I let that sink in. Waited to see if he'd say more, but he didn't. I could feel it coming off him that he considered his marriage a personal failure, and of course, I didn't really know what had gone on inside of it, but from what he'd just said? His ex sounded like a self-centered, narrow-minded woman who'd never really been in it for forever in the first place.

Dragonfly Lake wouldn't be such a bad place to live. Sure, I'd had all kinds of hesitancy coming back to the place that held so many hard memories and such sadness for me, but the longer I stayed here, the more I was reminded of the good parts—the happy memories with my mom and aunt, the blissful times when Cash and I had been in love. The scenery was unbeatable; looking out over the lake never got old.

And being Cash's wife? If her biggest complaint was that he was scheduled to work late...what, really, had she expected when she'd said I do?

If I were Cash Henry's wife, I'd be happy to welcome him home whenever he got done with the work he was so passionate about. Probably naked.

I sucked in a deep breath and sat up straighter. I was *not* Cash's wife. I wasn't going to *be* Cash's wife. I didn't even *want* to be Cash's wife. I wanted to live my own life, be my own boss, pursue my own dreams for once, just like I'd been planning to do after leaving Wes. Just thinking about the possibility of writing for Stream got my blood pumping.

And so did the idea of sleeping with Cash again. And watching him bake—even if he did it fully clothed. And mapping out a plan for the inn's kitchen with him. I liked spending time with him, but that didn't mean I needed to give up on my goals. I could have both—some scorching-hot times with Cash while I was here and a successful career in television writing if I landed the head writer job. And if I didn't, I'd keep trying, keep knocking on that door until I unlocked it. In California.

I didn't have to choose. I could have him for now and everything else I dreamed of when I got back to LA.

"What about you?" he asked. "What happened with your ex?"

I blew out my breath, knowing I could trust Cash to be sensitive but still hating to talk about this. "He couldn't handle the forsaking all others bit."

"What a shithead."

"That's one of many things I've called him. I take some blame for being stupid too, though."

A caustic laugh came out of Cash. "You're not stupid."

"Let's see…I married him. I put my career on hold for years to support his—"

"No."

I nodded. "We did so much entertaining, to build his career, butter up clients, make connections…" I tried not to let regret seep into my tone, but I had some serious regret. "It sounds like a reality show, but I put so much time and effort into hosting and planning and doing whatever he needed for his career, promising myself I'd get better at sneaking in writing time when he was more established…"

"Is the fucker established yet?" Cash asked.

"He's made partner, but it turns out it's never enough. There are always more clients to woo, more connections to nurture, more nauseating bullshit to spread." I laughed. "I may have some lingering resentment."

"Justified. And your dad is buddies with this guy?"

"Sort of. They're a lot alike," I admitted. "That was hard for me to take when I figured it out. I'd always pinned so much hope on my dad."

"I remember."

"When my mom died and I moved to LA for school, he helped me financially, so there's that. And I know I wouldn't have gotten the settlement I did without my dad being a senior partner in Wes's firm. Wes has always cared more about my dad than about me. It just took me a long time to see that."

Cash put his arm around me, resting his palm on my hip opposite him. "I'm sorry you had to deal with such a selfish prick."

"Me too but I'm out of that situation now. I'm finally giving my career one hundred percent. Or I was until this." I gestured to the inn and swallowed down the sadness of losing my aunt.

"You'll get back to it soon," he said. "In the meantime, I'd like to spend a lot more time with you, a good chunk of it naked if I'm honest, but only if that's what you want, Ava."

"It's what I want," I said, my hesitation gone. "I'm sorry I freaked out. I do want that. No strings. No future, but we know that and agree on that."

"Of course. You'll be writing TV episodes in LA. I'll be here cooking to my heart's content. Maybe you'll even be able to catch me and Henry's on a cable TV show."

Grinning, I said, "I wouldn't miss it. And here's a hint: if you audition for it in a towel, you'll be a shoo-in."

He laughed, the low, gravelly sound sending a flash of desire through me like only Cash could. He leaned toward me and kissed me, and I let him, not worrying about who might see, what people might think, because finally I was straight in my head about what I wanted.

Cash ended the kiss, glanced at the time on his phone, and said, "I need to get to work and you probably need to get back. Any chance you can get away tonight?"

"Deshon's coming in at ten. What do you have in mind?"

"Come to my apartment when you can. I'll feed you. Dinner and dessert."

I heard the double entendre in his words, and I played dumb. "Hummingbird cake?"

Another laugh rumbled from his chest as he leaned to me and pressed a too-short kiss to my lips. "Hummingbird cake and me. Come when you can."

Again with the double meaning. I laughed too and said, "Best offer I've had yet today."

He hopped up and took my hand to help me. We walked back to the inn together, then he went on his way, starting down the lane in a jog toward his apartment.

Not gonna lie, I watched him go until I couldn't see him anymore, appreciating his strong body, looking forward to seeing it naked again. When I headed back inside, I spotted the box of delectable donuts and his handwritten sign on the front desk, and it made me smile wider. His heart was as irresistible as his body.

There was that damn warning bell in my head regarding my heart being in danger no matter what we agreed to, but while I could admit it might be valid, I ignored it. Because trepidation or not, it turned out I couldn't resist spending more time with Cash. With or without clothes. Come what may.

CHAPTER 17

AVA

By Tuesday evening, I'd accomplished a lot, and yet there was still so much to figure out, put in place, make decisions about before I could go back to my life in LA.

I'd seen Knox head out the deck doors a few minutes ago, so as soon as Magnolia arrived for her desk shift, I went out after him. He was sitting on one of the loungers down by the shore.

"I haven't seen you for a couple days," I said as I went down the slight hill.

"Hey, Ava, my pool-shark partner."

"Ha. Five turns, Breckenridge. That's all it took to defeat us. If that's a shark…"

He laughed. "Someone had to lose it all, right?"

"We did it with bells on. So where've you been? If I didn't know better, I'd think you checked out in the middle of the night."

"I just bought a house," he said, his excitement written all over his handsome face. "I heard my offer was accepted less than an hour ago."

"Oh! Congratulations!" I sat on the lounger next to his, stretched my legs out, and leaned back. "I want to know all about it."

"It's an older lakefront four-bedroom. Just down the way from Henry's if you know where that is."

"Of course." Everyone knew where Henry's was, even people who hadn't had the pleasure of sleeping with the head chef for the past few nights.

"The owners were an elderly couple. The man passed away last year and the woman, a Dorothy Sanderson, is moving into assisted living. They never had kids, so she had to sell. I've had a real estate agent keeping his eyes open for me for the past month. He called me Sunday night. I saw it yesterday morning, before it was officially on the market, and put a preemptive offer on it immediately."

"That's so awesome! So you're really not going back to Texas, huh?"

"There's nothing there for me anymore. My biggest tech client is in Dallas, but we communicate online mostly now, and I can fly down if I need to. I mean, look at this." He waved a hand at the lake in front of us. "Why wouldn't you want to wake up to this every day? Well, unless you could have a TV writing job in LA, of course," he added with a laugh. "You ready for your big meeting Thursday?"

I exhaled as I gazed out at the water, sparkling in the early-evening sunshine. A turtle popped its head up beyond the dock, making me smile. I'd always considered it a sign of good luck to catch sight of a turtle right when they popped their head up. "Honestly, I've been so consumed by everything here that I've hardly had time to think about it. Which is messed up, for sure."

"That's part of why you're working so hard while you're

here, right? So you can *not* worry about the inn when you're back in California?"

"It is." It bothered me anyway. The most important meeting of my life was in two days, and I kept forgetting about it because I was so caught up in inn details and resumes and…Cash. "Sort of related, I can't decide if I should thank you or be mad at you."

"Thank me, I'm sure. But what'd I do?"

"I was supposed to fill out a loan application for the bank and price out some of the major expenses and replacements and pick out paint colors and about a thousand other things last night. Instead, I got carried away reading your manuscript. Knox, it's really good."

"Oh." He leaned forward and looked pleased but shy. "Thank you. I'd like to tell you I'm sorry but I'd be lying."

I laughed because I knew exactly what he meant.

"I haven't read a lot of science fiction, but I was pulled in from the first chapter. I fell in love with Aron. He's fabulously flawed and epically lovable."

"Wow. Thank you. That means a lot coming from a seasoned writer."

"I mean it, Knox." I sat up, because his story had legit sucked me in, and I was excited about his writing.

"I'm still waiting for the editor's feedback, so you're the first person who's read it. That's scary as hell."

"I get that. I remember the first time, in my very first writing class, when we were paired with another student and had to critique each other. It's terrifying. But your writing style is so easy to read and your description is vivid yet not overdone and Aron…" I let out an exaggerated dreamy sigh.

"My head's getting bigger as we sit here," he said, laughing. "I appreciate the praise, but there had to be things I could do better. I want constructive criticism too."

I leaned back and cradled my knees into my chest, thinking about his story. I was the one who'd asked him if I could read it, so not knowing whether he wanted feedback, I hadn't taken notes. Even if I'd intended to, I'd been so swept away as a reader, I wasn't sure I'd have noted many things to improve. However… "Have you considered giving Aron a romantic interest?"

He tilted his head thoughtfully. "Honest answer? No. I was all about the action scenes and the saving-his-people bit."

Grinning, I said, "You mean the science fiction?"

"Yeah, that."

"Do you plan to write more in the same world? A series? Sequel?"

"I've played with some ideas. I guess I've been waiting for feedback before I got too carried away. I was thinking I could do more books with different adversaries, link them together with one big, bad power behind it all. I have some ideas in mind, but the book I'm writing now is unrelated."

I nodded. "That's smart. What are you planning to do with the first one after you hear back from the editor?"

"That depends on what she says," he said, sounding self-conscious again. "It's my first book. I'm leaning toward publishing it myself, but I've heard it's wise not to publish your first book."

"That's not bad advice. There are a lot of books out there that shouldn't be published, in my opinion, but this isn't one of them."

"You're good for my ego." He crossed one of his long legs over the other and leaned his head back in thought. "Talk to me about romance."

"In stories, I hope you mean."

"Well, yeah, although I suspect you've got some going on in real life."

He didn't look directly at me, nor did he phrase it as a question, so I didn't comment on Cash. "You know I'm a romance reader and writer, so I come from that bias. But think about it. Everyone loves love. The biggest movies might be action films or sci-fi sagas, but there's almost always a love story at some level. Women eat them up, and men can get into them too as long as they aren't overly done or too flowery. Look at *Star Wars* and *Top Gun*."

"You have a good point. I'm listening."

"Science fiction skews to male readers more than women, right?"

He nodded. "Though more women read it than in the past."

"True. And science fiction romance is actually trending right now. I think by throwing in a love interest at some point—and I'm not advocating for going back and changing this story necessarily, it just depends on what you decide to do with it—you'll open up your readership to include more women. We love romance, and we'll cross genres to get it."

He nodded slowly, as if he was seriously considering what I said.

"I kind of did the opposite with my series. It's romance. Women will be the biggest audience. But it's also sports. Baseball. And there's a *lot* of baseball in it. I put a bunch of research into it when I wrote it, so the hope is that men might get into the series too."

What I didn't mention was that I knew baseball from when Cash and I had been together in the past. He'd gotten me started as a fan, but he'd also given me insight into the politics and the pressure and the behind-the-scenes stuff you don't get as much of from just watching a game on TV. That had sparked my interest in the sport all those years ago, and even after we broke up, I followed it closely. Of course, I switched to being a Dodgers fan instead of Cash's favorite, the Cubs, but I hadn't wanted to quit the sport altogether.

"Pretty smart," he said.

"I know some things," I said, grinning.

"You going to let me read some of your writing?"

"Sure, if you're up for romance."

"As long as it's fiction." He didn't laugh when he said it, and I wondered if there was a story there or if he was just that focused on the writing discussion.

"I'll send you some sports romance. You can focus on the baseball."

"Send me your best romance, sports or not," he said. "I don't read it or watch it and I'm not confident in my ability to write it, but I get what you're saying."

"And Aron is hot. He needs a woman," I joked. "Think how meeting his ideal woman could screw him up good the next time he's fighting to save his people."

"You got that right," he muttered, and I was getting the sense that there was indeed a story in his past that had to do with a relationship gone bad. "Are you in any writing groups you'd recommend?"

"I used to be in several, but now I'm just dialed into one that's for screenwriters. What about you?"

"I'm in some on Facebook, but I mainly lurk and get info. I'm more of a figure-it-out-myselfer in general and learn from books and articles, you know?"

"I get that. I guess I was more of a go-through-an-entire-degree-programmer, spending thousands upon thousands in the process." I laughed at myself. "I loved it though. What about you? Did you go to college?"

"It's been a good long while," Knox said. "I studied the ever-general communications. There was writing involved, but it was the dry kind."

"The majority of successful fiction writers don't have degrees in fiction writing, so you're set."

"What I wouldn't mind is some kind of accountability thing with another writer. Some back-and-forth and some goal setting. Maybe some brainstorming for when I get stuck, which I am right now."

"God, could I use that too. I haven't written a thing since I've been here."

"That's not surprising though, is it?" he asked, and I had to concede.

"No, but it's making me antsy. Like there's something missing from my life."

"You probably won't be able to dive back in for a while, will you?"

I hated that he was right, but he was. "I know people write fiction while having unrelated full-time jobs, but I'm overwhelmed pretty much all the time right now. There's no brain left for creativity."

Knox nodded. "Maybe you should go easy on yourself. When you get back to it, you'll be more than ready."

"I know you're right. It's not easy." An idea occurred to me, and I sat forward and spun my legs to the side he was on. "We could make our own accountability group. I can't write right now, but I can help you brainstorm and feel like I'm keeping a hand in writing at the same time. Kind of a win-win?"

"Hell yes. Let's do it. Send me some of your writing to start with."

"And we can brainstorm where you're stuck."

"I'm only two chapters in, entirely different story and world, like I said, but you have me thinking about the romance angle. Maybe you could read the chapters and give me some insight on this love thing."

I laughed at the way he drew out *love thing*, like it was a foreign language.

"You can so do romance. I'm sure of it," I said.

"Speaking of romance… It looked like there was something going on between you and Cash at the bar the other night. Are you two together?"

I tried to play it cool, but I had a hard time not smiling when I thought about Cash. "Sort of? It's complicated."

"Biggest cliché ever, and I know, as a writer, you don't want to fall back on a cliché," he teased.

Still sitting sideways on the lounger, I entwined my fingers and tried to figure out what to say. Magnolia was the only other person I'd confided in, but I hadn't told her much. "Cash and I have a history. We were together back when I lived here. We hadn't seen each other for seventeen years, when he went off to the Navy."

"Were you serious back then?"

"Pretty serious. He bought a ring." That was something I hadn't told Magnolia, for whatever reason.

Knox let out a whistle.

"He never gave it to me," I said. "He chickened out and broke up instead."

"Ouch."

With a nod, I said, "Years of ouch. I mean, I got over him. I married another guy."

Knox's gaze leapt to my bare ring finger.

"Divorced him, thank you."

"But now you're picking up where you left off."

"No. Just spending time together while I'm here."

"He doesn't like me much," Knox said.

"I don't think he knows you much, does he?"

He shook his head. "He's not the friendliest guy. Holden's the friendly one of the Henrys. Seth was standoffish at first but he's gotten better. It's true what they say about being an outsider in a small town. It's a little rough."

"Cash thinks you're interested in me."

Knox's brows shot up. "You and I hit it off about writing."

"That's what I told him."

"My last relationship ended up going off the rails. I'm not interested in anyone romantically. You can tell him that if it helps."

"I already told him there were no vibes from you. I think he's gotten better about it." Mostly because he'd spent the past couple of nights in my bed.

"I hope so." He said it with a lot more conviction than I'd

expect, and I tilted my head at him. "I don't like having enemies," he said. "You might be leaving, but he and I will be stuck together in this not-so-big town."

I grinned. "I think you'll be fine. He's more bark than bite these days. Anyway, I should get to the list of things I was supposed to do last night, before Aron stole my attention. And you need to send me your chapters of the new book so we can brainstorm."

"I'll do that."

"I might be a little slow, what with my interview that I really need to get my head around."

"I'm in no rush at all, Ava. I appreciate that you offered."

I stood. "Enjoy your view, and congrats again on the house."

After we said our goodbyes, I headed toward the cottage, Cash battling with the inn for space in my mind, and I couldn't help noticing that, once again, California seemed a long way away. If all else failed, I'd spend tomorrow night at my little LA apartment getting my head back in the game. I had to or I'd be kissing my dream goodbye.

CHAPTER 18

My mood was flying high when I got done with work Friday night. I was on my way to see Ava, who'd gotten back in town earlier this evening and was supposed to be waiting for me. But that was only half of it.

I'd driven to work today, something I rarely did when the weather was nice, all so I could get to her faster once we got Henry's shut down for the night. If my time with her was limited—and it was severely—I wasn't going to waste it walking or running all the way out to her place.

I pulled up next to her aunt's beast of a truck, and my body heated at the knowledge that she'd driven that truck to the airport, so its presence verified she was back. When I knocked on the door, though, there was no answer. I grabbed my phone from my jeans pocket.

Where are you, gorgeous?

Her reply came almost immediately, giving me hope that

she'd been waiting for me. We'd made a deal that we wouldn't communicate while she was in LA. She'd be busy and I'd be busy, and I didn't know if she felt the same, but I was a little concerned that we'd been getting *too* close.

> Docks, handsome.

I headed toward the shore, sticking to the shadows between the inn and the cottage as I took inventory of the activity level. I knew there were more people checked in this week and it was a lot livelier. From the treed area, I could see a handful of people on one of the ground-level patios, sitting, drinking, laughing. Over on the main deck was another large group, and they appeared to be roasting marshmallows over a fire pit, even though the day had been hot and it hadn't cooled down much when the sun set. As I walked down the grassy slope, I noted a couple on the loungers on the side opposite the docks.

Thinking there wasn't much privacy at all, I turned my attention to the docks, scanning the darkness for Ava. I spotted her in nearly the same place she'd been a few days ago when I'd brought donuts, and I coached my pulse to calm the hell down as I went toward her.

She turned toward me once I stepped onto the dock. I roved my eyes over her in a glance as she stood. She wore short shorts, a light-colored tank that hugged her torso, and slip-on sneakers without socks. Her hair blew in the breeze, and her smile nearly knocked me on my knees.

"Hey, handsome," she said.

"Hi, Ava." Since there were folks behind us who could see us, I waited for a cue from her as to how cozy she wanted our greeting to be. She closed the last step between us and wrapped her arms around my neck in a hug, so I pulled her body against mine and lifted her. When I let her body slide back down mine, the contact set all my nerves at attention and made my dick go hard. "Fuck, you feel good," I said into her ear, knowing voices could carry over the water a hell of a lot louder than you ever expected.

"Mmm," she said, stretching up to meet my mouth in a too-brief kiss.

I took her hand. "Come on."

"Where?"

"Trust me."

She glanced up at the people on the deck.

"Are you working right now?" I asked.

Ava shook her head. "Magnolia's here until Deshon comes in."

"Then come with me."

"Well, let's go then," she said in a flirty voice. "What are you waiting for?"

Grinning, I yanked our entwined hands and led her off the docks. When we hit land, I took a right and headed away from the inn. The shore here was a narrow stretch of sand for maybe one or two hundred yards, then it got rockier and covered with grasses and bushes and trees. At least it had back in the days when we'd been together. I hadn't had reason to explore this wild section of land since we'd broken up.

"Are you going where I think you're going?" Ava asked as she walked slightly behind me so neither of us had to get our shoes wet.

"Want you to myself." Naked. Panting. Biting my shoulder to keep from yelling out my name.

"I'm down for that."

We hit the end of the sand, and the going got slower through the vegetation, but we both kept moving like our lives depended on it. Hiking through that crap with a hard-on to end all hard-ons was not a comfortable undertaking. The only thing that kept me stepping forward was the hope that relief would come soon.

The shore curved around into a cove of sorts, and once we were there, I searched for the sandy spot I'd once been able to get to practically with my eyes closed. Ava knew exactly where I was heading, and I soon felt her pulling at my hand.

"It's over here," she said.

We were on top of it by the time I saw the small patch of sand, the surrounding brush a lot thicker than it had been before.

"You come here often?" I asked in a cheesy, pickup-line voice.

Ava let out a musical laugh as she turned to face me and pulled me flush with her body. "I did a couple blue moons ago. Always with you." She stood on her toes and pressed a quick kiss to my lips. "Only you."

I wrapped my arms around her and bent down to kiss her good and full, showing her how much I wanted her, not that she needed any encouragement. She ran her hands up under my shirt, shoving the tee I'd changed into before leaving work up to my neck. Putting a few inches between us, I reached back between my shoulder blades, grabbed the fabric, yanked it off, and tossed it to the ground, then tugged the waistband of her shorts toward me and gave her tank the same treatment.

Within thirty seconds, we stood there naked in the moonless night, our mouths going after each other, hands all over. I palmed the globes of her ass and lifted her off the ground, then waded into the lake. The water was refreshing but not what I'd call cool. It could've been icy and it wouldn't have slowed me down tonight.

Ava's legs flew around my waist, her ankles locking at the small of my back, pressing her damp heat to my groin and making my eyes roll back in my head. She ground her pelvis into me, moaning low and so fucking hot that I no longer cared whether our bodies were submerged before I entered her sweet, slick heat.

I managed to get us thigh-deep in the water before she slid just right and impaled herself on my cock.

"Cash," she breathed out as if relieved.

I was too, for about six seconds, then I needed more, needed to feel that friction, needed relief from that incredible pressure.

Clinging to her ass, pulling her as close to me as humanly possible, I bent my legs enough to lower us beneath the surface. Our bodies thrust and ground in a primal rhythm, our intensity climbing, as I lost my ever-loving mind to the ecstasy of sex with Ava. The sight of her white tits in the darkness, bouncing then pressing into my chest, only made me wilder with need. She was perfectly in tune with that as she clenched her muscles around me, moaned that sexy-as-hell groan a few more times, then came apart in my arms. I watched her orgasm raptly, even as it pushed me closer to my own edge, made everything inside of me tense up, reaching, needing.

I came so hard I could barely stand as I clutched her to me and pulsed inside of her, grunting out, "Fuck, Ava."

I felt her teeth on my neck, and that turned me inside out, stopped my fucking breathing, and then had me finally gasping for life-affirming breath.

"Jesus," I managed, panting, my arms still around her as if my life depended on our intimate connection.

"Yeah," she said, and I was gratified to note she could barely get the single syllable out as she tried to catch her breath.

I carried her with me to shallow water, sat my ass down on the sandy bottom where it was just a couple of feet deep, enough to keep our lower bodies submerged and our heads and chests in the open air.

Her lips were on mine as her body settled into me again, her legs straddling me, but the kiss was gentle, sated, lacking the urgency of a few minutes ago.

"It's been a while since we did that here, huh?" she asked between kisses, her lips curling upward. "We could've gone to the cottage."

"That's next," I said, grinning but meaning it. I had no intention of going to my place tonight unless she kicked me out.

The truth was, I hadn't planned to jump her before we could even have a conversation, but here we were.

"I couldn't help myself," I said, running my hands over her lithe back and her slender thighs. "I had every intention of asking you how your interview went first."

"I'm not complaining." She pushed up to a stand, robbing me of the feel of her wet, naked body on top of mine. She held out her hand and I stood, my eyes feasting on every inch of her petite, knockout body now that I wasn't so desperate to get inside of her.

We walked back to our clothes. I spread my T-shirt out for her to sit on and settled my own ass right next to her, on top of my jeans, hoping for no sand in my ass but knowing there was a shower in our near future.

"So tell me about it," I said as she propped her hands behind her and angled her head back, her breasts pointing to the sky. There wasn't any moonlight, but I could see her just fine, and in no time, I was sporting a semi.

"The meeting was really good," Ava said. "I liked all three of the people from Stream a lot, got a good feeling from them, you know?"

"That's important."

"Afterward, Willa told me she got good vibes from all of them. Then early today, Sheldon Milano from Stream reached out to her and was 'very upbeat.'"

"That sounds promising, Ava." I put my arm around her and squeezed her to my side. "I'm so damn happy for you."

"It felt good. Feels good. But I also don't want to jinx anything. So many things could derail it."

I nodded. "They'd be idiots not to hire you."

"My lack of experience is kind of glaring."

"But your talent makes up for it."

With a laugh, she said, "How would you know?"

"I know you. I have every bit of faith that you'll kill it in TV land."

She leaned her head on my upper arm. "Thank you. We'll see what happens."

"When do you think you'll hear something?"

"Probably not as fast as I want. But I'm going to put my head down, dig in here, and try to get the inn settled while I'm waiting."

"Any more leads for a manager?"

"I received a couple more resumes, one guy I might interview, but no one who's exciting me."

"The right person will show up soon." And that would be one more step toward our time together ending, but I locked that thought out of my head the second it popped up.

I didn't know whether she believed it, but she nodded. "How was your week? Any word from the show?"

I couldn't help grinning as I sat up straighter. "Apparently they sent someone out undercover earlier this week. We just got news this evening. They loved our food. We made the cut to the next round."

"Cash! You buried the lead! Congratulations." She grabbed my head and kissed me enthusiastically.

"Thanks, gorgeous. It feels good. The only downside is that the Cove made it too."

"In the Marks Resort?"

"Right."

"You don't think you could both get on the show?"

"They never do two restaurants from the same town."

There were a million small towns in America, and *Small Town Smorgasbord* always liked to mix it up. They'd been to every state, and had only gone back to a handful so far. I'd seen every episode.

"So what's the next step?" Ava asked.

"They're still traveling around, adding to the list of restaurants who made the cut. Sometime next month, they'll start contacting the winners to set up filming."

"So there's nothing to do but wait."

"Right."

"This is going to turn out right, Cash. I can feel it." She squeezed my forearm as she leaned into me from the side.

"For both of us." I kissed her temple, feeling more optimistic than I had in ages. "We both seem to be on the exact track we're meant to be on."

"We are," she agreed. "I believe that."

Her fingers trailed along my bare thigh, distracting me. I wound my arm around her again and pulled her close, trying not to act like a complete insatiable horndog even though that's what she made me. I entwined those fingers with my other hand as we both looked out over the quiet, dark lake. As always, it was peaceful on this side, and this was my favorite time to appreciate it, when there weren't screaming, laughing people ruining the beauty of it.

"Cash?" Ava said a couple minutes later.

"Yeah?"

"I wish it didn't mean we'd end up thousands of miles apart."

"I know." Fuck did I know. I kissed the side of her head again, noting her hair was starting to dry and that our bodies were mostly dry too. We could either get our clothes on and go back and shower or I could take her into the lake and mess her up again. I was open to either. And yet I sat there without moving, appreciating the hell out of this time with her.

"Can I be honest with you?" she asked.

"Always."

She hesitated. "When I go back to California for good, it's going to take a bit to get over you again."

"Same," I said, closing my eyes and breathing in the faint scent of her hair mixed with the smell of the lake.

Ava let out a sigh. "I don't know how to handle that."

"You'll be so busy being a head writer you'll barely remember me," I said lightly at the same time I hoped like hell that wasn't true. I didn't want her to hurt, but I didn't want her to forget about me.

Because it was becoming more and more obvious that I was going to have to fight like hell to be able to forget about her.

I shut down those thoughts again because they didn't do any good. I wanted Ava to have what she dreamed of. Period.

"Want to put our clothes on so we can go back to the cottage and get naked again?" I asked, grinning, my dick full-on hard as I brushed my fingers over her breast.

She leaned into my hand and gasped quietly. "Let's go."

CHAPTER 19

Sunday morning, I crawled out of my bed early, reluctant to leave a slumbering Cash but hoping he'd sleep for another hour or two. To say we hadn't gotten a lot of z's since I got back in town Friday evening was an understatement. I couldn't regret it, though, despite the way my eyes burned with fatigue.

I headed to the maintenance room to get the paint supplies Halstead had picked up. He'd wanted to help me today, but he'd worked lots of overtime the past two weeks, knocking out his items on the Operation Inn Overhaul list, and I'd finally convinced him he could help me paint the interior as he had time over the next week but to take today off. Painting was one thing I'd decided I could handle myself, and I hoped to get a couple of the guest rooms on the west wing done before dinner.

The A/C had been repaired. The roof replacement was scheduled to start on Tuesday with a guarantee it'd be done before Labor Day weekend, when we had seventy percent of the rooms reserved. I'd ordered a new, expensive inn management system and the computers to go with it. Levi Dawson's construction crew was showing up tomorrow morning to screen in part of the deck. I was waiting for bids on the exterior painting, but that was less vital to have completed before our busy end-of-the-summer-season weekend for Labor Day. There were several other smaller projects either in process or waiting for bids, and there was the manager problem yet to be solved, but the to-do list was shrinking.

I unlocked the maintenance room and picked up a paint can, tray, brushes, plastic tarps, a roller, and tape, then headed to the west wing. I set everything down in the guest room closest to the lobby, then went to check in with Deshon and Sadie Brent, who was on her second day of training. After checking in with them and ensuring Deshon's wife hadn't yet gone into labor, I headed to the kitchen to get the donuts I'd stocked up on yesterday. Cash and I had discussed some possibilities for uses of the kitchen, but I hadn't decided on anything yet. Until I did, I'd be using Sugar. No more early-morning baking disasters for me.

By seven, I'd eaten two donuts—I told myself I needed the carbs for the work I was determined to get done today—and was heading back through the lobby when the main door opened and Cash walked in, looking awake and energetic and…not alone. He carried an open-topped box that looked like it held more painting supplies.

Not seeing me, he turned back to whoever was behind him, laughing, and as they entered, I recognized his brother Seth.

"Hey," I called out to them.

They weren't alone. Seth was holding the hand of a pretty brunette. It took about three seconds for me to recognize her —she was one of my favorite country singers, Everly Ash. I tilted my head to the side, unsure what I wanted to find out first, what she was doing here at my inn or why she was holding Seth's hand.

But before I could get answers to either question, Cash's sister, Hayden, came in with a pretty woman about her age. Behind them were Cash's youngest brother, Holden, and two other guys.

"What's going on?" I asked Cash as he came toward the spot where I'd frozen in place near the door to the west wing.

"I told you I'd help you paint today," he said, grinning.

"You did. Hi, Seth. It's good to see you." There might've been a little question in my tone.

Seth let go of Everly Ash's hand long enough to hug me. "Hi, Ava." He pulled Everly closer. "Meet my fiancée, Everly."

"Um, yeah," I said, smiling, "I know of you. I'm a big fan. It's a pleasure to meet you, but"—I addressed Seth—"how the heck did she end up with you?"

"Plain dumb luck," he said humbly. "Best luck of my life."

"It's a story, for sure," Everly said warmly. "It's nice to meet you."

"You can read multiple versions of that story online," Seth said with a scowl.

"But I could probably be convinced to tell you all about how I fell for this guy while we paint," Everly said.

"You're going to paint?" I asked, looking between the three of them.

"We're all going to paint," Hayden, who yanked me into a warm hug, said. "Ava, Ava, it's so good to see you." When she ended the hug, she said, "This is my friend Sierra, her husband, Cole, and this hottie is my husband, Zane. We let Holden tag along as well."

"Tag along. We'll see how many more walls I can paint than you," Holden said to Hayden. He came over and side-hugged me.

I shook Sierra's hand. She had her hair up in a ponytail and wore paint-splattered cargo pants and a cropped tee. "You and Hayden have been friends for a long time, right?" I asked. "I remember hearing her talk about you when I used to live here."

"We met in second grade," Sierra said. "Then we ended up marrying brothers."

"Zane North," Hayden's husband said as he stepped forward and shook my hand. "I'm the good brother. Cole's our black sheep."

"Reformed," Sierra said. "Most days." She nudged her shoulder into his arm as he came forward to shake my hand.

After meeting everyone, I must have looked at Cash stupidly.

"I rounded up painting help," he said. "We'll knock out the whole wing today."

"I… All of you?"

"Dylan's showing up in a couple hours too, and Jake will be here after lunch as long as he can get away from the store," Cash said.

"I… I don't know what to say. You…" I zeroed my gaze in on Cash. Handsome, considerate Cash. "You did this?"

"I asked my people to help. They're the ones who showed up. My dad and Faye said to wish you well. They wanted to pitch in but they're watching Calvin and Jasper, Zane and Cole's nephews."

"So we threw Harrison into the mix," Hayden said. "Don't kid yourself. Faye and our dad wanted to be here, but they wanted to play with their grandbabies more."

"Well, thank you all for coming to help a stranger. It means the world to me," I said.

"Cole and I got married here at the inn," Sierra said, looping her arm through her husband's. "I love this place so much. It has a good soul."

"Sierra owns a remodeling company," Hayden explained. "Restoring historic buildings is her passion. And she's good."

"The best," Cole said.

"You're biased," Sierra said.

"But also right," her husband insisted.

Zane merely nodded at me, as if to back up his brother without having to admit it out loud.

My brows shot up. "We should definitely talk then," I said to Sierra. "This place needs a lot, but I don't want to modern it up too much."

"I'm up for it anytime. Today or another day," Sierra said.

"Yes," I said enthusiastically, "thank you. That would be awesome."

The door opened again and Magnolia came in, followed by more people.

"Hey," I said. "Aren't you supposed to be at the Lily Pad?"

"Dotty gave me the day off," Magnolia said. "Cash told me he was gathering people to help paint, so I brought some friends too."

Three women followed her in, full of warmth and smiles. I recognized one as Olivia, from Sugar.

"I don't know what to say," I said, "other than thank you all, and you're amazing." The last I said to Magnolia as I hugged her. "Lunch is on me for sure. Hey, Olivia. It's good to see you."

"I brought snacks," Olivia said, holding up a large bakery box I guessed was either cookies or donuts.

"Bless you. I'm blown away."

"This is Shawna Jenkins," Magnolia said, indicating the one closest to her, "and Anna Delfico."

"I recognize your names," I said, shaking hands with Shawna and Anna. "Thank you, all. I can't believe this. You're so thoughtful," I said to Magnolia.

"This was all Cash's idea," she said, nodding to him.

I knew it must be true because Cash dodged the credit and said, "I'm taking the supplies in. Join me whenever you're all ready."

The guys went with him, past the ballroom, to the west

wing hall, leaving me with a group of women I barely knew, all who'd shown up to help with a task I'd been dreading.

"I'm so overwhelmed. You don't even know me and you're going to spend your Sunday painting?"

"Hey, we'll have fun," Anna said.

"Painting party," Shawna called out. "But first…give me one of those cookies, Olivia."

"Shawna's just here for the cookies," Magnolia teased.

"I'll take her for whatever reason she showed up," I said, laughing. "Let's take the cookies with us. I've got donuts out here for the guests."

"I'll take those right off your hands," Shawna said as she relieved Olivia of the box, making us all laugh. "Anyone wants one, you can follow me."

"Ava," Magnolia said with a hand on my arm as everyone else except Anna headed toward the west wing. "I assume you haven't had the perfect manager pop up in the past twelve hours?"

"Ah, no," I said, laughing again, because if I didn't laugh, I might cry.

"I was telling Anna you were looking for someone to run this place when you move back to California. Anna's a property manager for Shoreline Rentals."

I turned to the pretty, friendly brunette. "Really? They have rental homes around here somewhere, right?"

"They have a development on the southeast side of the lake, close to Runner. We're currently at thirty-six vacation homes and building another dozen in the next two years."

"I remember now. My aunt mentioned them when they started building. It seems like it was a few years ago?"

"That's right. It'll be five years. I've worked there since the first construction was in progress."

"So you manage all thirty-six homes?"

"Some of them are owned and rented by us, and some have private owners, most of whom have us manage for them. As a matter of fact, Zane and Cole's brother Gabe owns a couple of them."

"Small world."

"Let's just say it's a smart investment," Anna said. "Anyway, I currently manage thirty-two of them. I handle all the rental schedules, the maintenance, the cleaning between renters—"

"She runs the whole place, basically," Magnolia cut in. "Her boss is all about the construction, so he's occupied with that."

"He is. And he can have it. Construction is chock full of delays and problems with supplies these days." Anna laughed, and I found it impossible not to like her. A lot.

"Are you looking for a new job?" I asked.

"I wasn't," Anna said. "I like what I do. I like my boss and the people I work with. I just got back in town from a conference on the East Coast for property managers and learned a lot. I heard about your aunt right before I went—I'm so sorry for your loss." She grasped my wrist with a small hand with gorgeous, modest-length aquamarine-painted nails. "Phyllis was such a sweet lady."

I swallowed, wondering when this would ever get easier. "Thanks. She was." I managed to smile. "She loved this place so much. I want to find someone who will love it too and run it for me."

"I've always liked this place," Anna said, her eyes lighting up, making me believe her. "From the name to the front porch to the view. This place is special to Dragonfly Lake."

"That's how my aunt felt," I said.

"I'm going to help them get the painting going," Magnolia said. "You two can talk."

"Thanks, Magnolia," I said. "Get yourself a cookie. We're going to need our energy."

"You don't have to tell me twice. I haven't had breakfast."

Anna and I laughed. "Let's go in here," I said to Anna,

gesturing toward the gathering room—for one, to give us a little privacy from Deshon and Sadie at the desk, and two, because that lake view was one of the best parts of the inn, and part of me already wanted Anna to fall in love.

She followed me through the doorway, and we ended up by the windows, facing the bright, sunshine-dappled lake. "When Magnolia told me she was working here, she mentioned you were looking for a manager," Anna said. "Like I said, I wasn't looking, but I'd love to know more about what you want, what the position would entail, what role you'll be playing, things like that. Not necessarily now."

"I suddenly have more time than I thought, thanks to a bunch of awesome people."

"Cash is pretty great," Anna said, giving me a knowing look.

"He is." I couldn't help smiling at the thought of him.

Fifteen minutes later, I'd laid out everything for Anna, from the ongoing projects to the marketing rebuild I hoped to do for the inn to the hires I'd made in the past week and the additional ones I'd budgeted for. It wasn't an official interview, but I asked her multiple questions and got a lot of info and, more importantly, got a feel for the kind of person she was. She'd been three years behind me in school. Her grandfather had made the Welcome to Dragonfly Lake sign on the highway coming into town, so her roots ran deep here, and she seemed to love living in this thriving little tourist town. Working as a property manager had provided her with experience that would be a great fit for the inn. She was personable, friendly, and intelligent, and when we agreed to meet for an official interview tomorrow evening, I had a fluttery, optimistic feeling in my gut.

"I see something I need to check out on the deck real quick," I told her as we were about to head toward the west wing and help paint. "Tell Cash and the others I'll be there in five."

"You got it. Can't wait to talk more tomorrow, Ava." She went back through the lobby, and I went outside to straighten the outdoor chairs that'd been left in a cluster by a family reunion group last night.

Outside, the early-morning sunshine felt good after the air-conditioned inn. As I moved the chairs to their usual casual but organized groupings, I tried to get my brain to catch up with the past half hour.

A dozen people had showed up to help me. People who didn't even know me well, some who I'd never met before. It was more than a little incredible and so exactly what I'd needed mentally—not to mention physically.

It was mostly quiet out here, with a trio of twentysome-things on the docks, getting some early-morning rays, and a young family sitting out on one of the upper-level private decks, the parents chatting quietly and their infant son cooing every now and then as they fed him. As I picked up the last chair to carry to its spot, a door must've opened on the west wing because I could suddenly hear a bunch of voices, laugh-ing, talking—probably my insta-paint crew.

When I glanced in that direction, Cash appeared around the corner of the building, walking in my direction.

I set the chair in place, adjusting it just so, and when I straightened, he was at my side, shining his panty-melting smile down on me. I felt it in my chest as well as my nethers.

"Hey." I went up on my toes and kissed him. "Your friends and family are awesome."

"They are. This town is like that," he said, his big palms landing at the sides of my waist. "They jump in to help when someone needs it."

I wrapped my arms around his neck and kissed him again. "Thank you, Cash. The painting will be done about ten times faster because of the help."

He kissed me back, pulling my body into his solid one, and I almost wished there wasn't a crowd of people here to help us so we could blow off the job and disappear back into the cottage.

"Oh," I said, ending the kiss abruptly in my enthusiasm. "And Anna Delfico…what do you know about her?"

"She's good people. One of those types that everyone likes."

I nodded, thrilled that he was backing up my initial impression of her. "We're meeting tomorrow night to discuss the management position."

"For the inn?" His approval was audible.

I nodded again, feeling light enough that I could bounce on my toes.

"I like it. From what I know of her, she'd be good."

I took hold of his hands and peered up at him, my heart overflowing with gratitude. Not only was he thoughtful and generous and really damn good at keeping me fed with out-of-this-world food, but he was my biggest supporter here. Though the inn was mine, there were so many decisions to be made, and he'd heard me out on multitudes of them and weighed in when I'd asked.

"You're incredible, Cash. I appreciate you."

When I went up on my toes again to press one more kiss to his lips before we got back to the painting crew, he caught my head and held me there, lingering over my lips. I felt his attention in every inch of my body. When the kiss ended, he gazed down at me, looking so one-hundred-percent into me. I couldn't deny it—I felt the same about him.

As I lowered back to my heels, the realization hit me with the force of a blunt but deadly object.

I'd gone and done the worst thing ever. I'd fallen in love—again—with Cash Henry.

CHAPTER 20

CASH

"You"—Ava lowered herself to my lap, sitting sideways on the lounger out by the lake—"are wonderful and thoughtful and one of my favorite people in the whole entire world."

"*One* of your favorites?" I teased. I leaned forward and lowered my voice so the group around us couldn't hear. "Guess I'll have to campaign for a higher ranking later tonight."

She laughed and kissed me briefly, touching our foreheads together. "Promise?"

"Count on it." She had me smiling like a dumb ass, which was a feat considering I'd never been known as a smiley guy and certainly not after spending a full day painting.

She went serious, sitting up straighter. "Thank you, Cash. I can't believe how much we got done."

"That was these folks." I waved toward the group surrounding us on the inn's private beach, some of them on loungers like us, some standing in a group closer to the water, all of them in some stage of devouring the pizza Chloe had brought us. Holden's pregnant wife hadn't wanted to inhale paint fumes all day, so she'd taken on the task of keeping us in meals and drinks.

"But you're the one who asked them. Without you doing that, you and I might've managed two guest rooms. Instead we painted the entire west wing."

"That we did. They're wonderful and thoughtful people." I leaned closer again. "I'm just counting the minutes until I can get you naked."

It wasn't a lie, but this moment itself was pretty damn incredible, having this beautiful woman looking down at me with her eyes sparkling and her appreciative, joy-filled smile aimed at me.

She kissed me again, this one lingering a little, sparking my hunger for her instead of sating it. It was over too quickly. "The sun's sinking fast," she said. "I need to close all the doors up there to keep the bugs out."

"Let me do it. You stay here and rest and be social."

She looked about to protest, so I cut her off by touching my finger to her lips. "I insist."

After studying me for a moment, she smiled and rose to her feet so I could get up. "Don't forget to lock them—"

"I'll lock the doors, close the windows, make sure the box fans are on high. I'll lock each interior door too."

"Please." She extended her hand to help me up.

Taking hold of it just to touch her, not because I needed help, I resisted the urge to pull her back down on top of me, stood, and kissed her before heading up to the building.

I went in through one of the open guest room doors and systematically made my way through all of the rooms, closing them up for the night and turning the lights off. The sand color we'd painted all twelve rooms was drying evenly. A second coat wouldn't be necessary thanks to the premium one-coat paint Jake had recommended.

After the first-floor rooms were locked up, I went up to the second and did the same, then went back down, this time through the lobby. Magnolia had left the paint crew early to shower and cover the desk this evening as scheduled. I knew she wasn't particularly liked around town, but I didn't have any bones to pick with her. Now that her rich daddy wasn't controlling her, she seemed to be legitimately trying to make her own way and be a decent person. She'd been good to Ava, between helping at the desk—granted, as a paid employee—and becoming a friend, and that's what mattered to me.

"Hey, Magnolia. Did Chloe drop off some pizza for you?"

"A whole pie," Magnolia said. "I ate two pieces and I'm stuffed. Why don't you take the rest down to the group. Someone will clean it up."

"We've got plenty. How about I put it in the fridge in the kitchen and you can take it home with you. We've got pizza coming out of our ears."

There was a wary look in her eyes for a split second, but then she smiled and nodded. "Sure. If you guys have enough."

"More than. Come down and join us if you want. I'm sure Ava won't mind if you put the sign up."

"I might do that after I make note of the reservation I just took." She pointed to a notepad.

I nodded, started on my way, then paused. "Thanks for rounding up your friends. It means a lot to Ava—and if Anna works out as a manager…"

She smiled genuinely. "I hope it does. I don't know if Anna wants it or if Ava will like her, but to me, it seems like it'd be perfect."

"Can I bring you a drink?" I asked, thinking she wasn't unlikable after all.

"I've got a big ice water, but thanks."

"Okay. See you." I took the pizza box with the leftover pizza to the kitchen and stuck it in the fridge.

When I went out onto the main deck, Knox Breckenridge

was leaning on the railing, peering at the painting crew below. Like a reflex, I gritted my teeth at the sight of his pretty-boy head, but then I caught myself. Loosened my jaw. Let out my breath.

"Knox," I said as I walked up to his side.

"Hey, Cash." He straightened and smiled, as friendly as he always was to me, which only highlighted what a jealous prick I'd been. "Looks like I wasn't invited to the party."

My gaze followed his to the gathering, my eyes zeroing in on Ava. She'd moved from the chair where I'd left her and was ensconced in the middle of the women. It looked like my sister was telling a story, with everyone's attention on her. She made a gesture with her hands, and we could hear the feminine laughter peal from here. My eyes were glued to Ava, who threw her head back as she laughed. I loved seeing her laugh, especially after how down she'd been when she'd first come to town after her aunt's death.

"Don't feel too bad," I told Knox. "It was a painting party. We painted the rooms in the west wing." I hadn't thought about asking him, but even if I had, I wasn't sure I would've. Which was ridiculous. I was the one in Ava's bed every night. I understood, at least now, that the ties between Ava and Knox were only platonic and professional.

"All of them?" he asked.

"Every last one. Ava treated everyone to pizza, beer, and soda."

"Well earned, I'd say. That's a lot of rooms."

"It wasn't bad with so many people."

"Looks like most of your family showed up," Knox said, nodding to the guys who were at the shore now, horsing around.

"I'm related to all four of them," I said. "The two who aren't Henrys are Norths and they're my new stepbrothers, one of them a brother-in-law too." I chuckled at the convoluted family tree we Henrys and Norths made.

"I've met Hayden's husband, Zane."

"The other one is Cole. His wife is Sierra." I pointed her out. "Our dad married Cole and Zane's mom, Faye."

Knox stood up straighter and glanced around, as if looking for the older couple. "They didn't get roped into painting, huh?"

I grinned at the phrase *roped into*. "Actually, I suspect they would've been here helping, but they ended up babysitting Hayden's son and some other grandkids."

He leaned forward on the railing again. "I guess you had a big enough crew to get the job done."

"I'm surprised you didn't hear us. We weren't a quiet bunch. We wouldn't have turned down more help."

He looked at me as if to gauge whether I meant it. Maybe, if he'd shown up, I would've grumbled to myself, but today was about Ava, and I liked to think I would've lived and let live—or painted and let paint.

Turning back to the scene below us, where Zane had swept Hayden up in his arms and was holding her over the water, threatening to drop her, Knox said, "I was downtown for most of the day with my laptop. Spent the morning at the bakery, grabbed lunch at the diner, then found a bench on the square and tried to get unstuck on my book but mostly people watched. A frustrating day overall. Painting would've been more fun and more productive."

I was surprised he'd shared that much with me. God knew we'd never been buddies. My doing, of course. "Ava said your story's good," I offered.

"She read my first one. I appreciate her taking time to read a newbie like me."

"She loves writing, talking writing, reading writing. I'm sure she enjoyed it," I said. "Maybe see if she has suggestions for getting unstuck."

"She volunteered to read what I have, which isn't much. I keep telling myself I did it once. I can write another one. I suspect the first one went so fast because I didn't know any better."

"I don't know how you guys do it," I said, letting the thoughts I'd had toward Ava's writing surface.

"Just like I don't know how you create the dishes at Henry's. Creativity's weird, I guess."

Not everyone understood the creativity involved in being a good chef, and I couldn't help appreciating his comment. Maybe even almost starting to like him. It wasn't that hard if I didn't look at him as someone who was interested in Ava beyond friendship.

Yeah, I might be slow and stupid. Just look at how I'd handled things seventeen years ago. It'd be nice to be able to say I was less stupid now.

My gaze wandered to Ava again, sitting sideways on a lounger, sharing the chair with Everly. Chloe was on the one next to them, with Shawna at the foot of it, and all four of them were leaning in, likely talking about whatever it was women found to talk about anytime they were together.

"Why don't you come down and join us?" I said, knowing Ava would be happy to see him. If I had to remind myself a time or two that she'd be on *my* lap and going home with *me*, chalk it up to old habits dying hard. I could bury the one-sided hatchet, especially for her.

Knox eyed me like he was waiting for the punch line. "You sure about that?"

I let out a self-deprecating laugh. "Fair question. I've been an insecure asshole where you're considered. I'm sorry for that."

He looked at me again, not convinced.

"I know Ava would like it if we made peace." I extended my hand to seal a peace accord.

"This isn't just because you breathed in paint fumes all day?"

It took about a second and a half for me to realize that was his way of being funny. I relaxed my shoulders a degree, grinned, and shook my head, continuing to hold my hand out.

He studied me for a few more seconds, then shook. With a laugh, he said, "Wouldn't mind getting to know the parts of you that aren't an asshole."

"Might be a couple parts," I said, chuckling. "Might not."

We started down the gradual steps side by side. "So if it's not too personal of a question, what'll happen between you two when Ava goes back to LA?"

I shrugged nonchalantly. "We'll go our separate ways."

A few steps later, Knox paused, looked at me, and asked, "You gonna be okay with that?"

I looked from him down to Ava, who happened to glance my way at that moment. The smile she sent my way when she saw I was with her writing buddy was megawatt and made me feel like a million bucks. I smiled back at her, then said to Knox, with raw honesty, "I don't know."

He eyed me for two seconds longer, then said, "Let's go grab a beer."

I pushed down the discomfort from his previous question and followed him, telling myself I'd be just fine.

CHAPTER 21

t was Friday afternoon, two weeks after Cash had organized the painting party, and what a busy, productive, wonderful two weeks it'd been.

I took the sparkling apple juice out of the inn's fridge, popped the cork, and took down two champagne flutes. Though Aunt Phyl had never had a liquor license, I'd seen firsthand that the Diamonds liked cocktails and wine with their poker, so we had a full set of every kind of glass you could want. They would come in handy when we finally opened the bistro Cash and I had dreamed up. The bistro, along with the dock replacement, was part of the official phase two, which would likely begin in the spring.

I carried the bottle and glasses out to the front desk, where Anna Delfico, my hero and inn manager, who'd easily become a friend already, had just finished advising a checked-in couple on dinner options in town.

"We should work out some inn-exclusive discounts with the restaurants," she said off-handedly, and this was exactly why I loved her. She was no stranger to hospitality, knew every crack and crevice of the town, was liked by literally everyone, and was brilliant on top of it all.

"Yes," I said with emphasis as I set the glasses on the counter. "I hope you don't mind this is nonalcoholic."

"Not at all. What are we toasting? The end of computer training?" She brushed her caramel-colored hair out of her face and took hold of the base of one of the flutes while I poured.

I filled the second glass, picked it up. "I mean, that's cheers-worthy too but we're toasting to you."

"Okay then." She stood up straighter and grinned. "What did I do?"

"Only showed up exactly when I needed you with the exact skill set and personality I needed you to have. That's all."

She lightheartedly rolled her eyes. "Don't forget you're paying me well."

"With pleasure." I raised my glass. "Cheers to you, Anna. Because of you, I can go home tomorrow with full confidence that this place is in good hands, which means I can finally get back to writing."

We clinked our glasses and sipped the cold, bubbly apple juice.

"We both have the opportunity to do what we burn to do," Anna said. "This job is a dream for me. I liked my old job, at least until my ex-boss turned into an angry jerk at the end there, but this inn…our vision for it, the history, the fact that it's in the town I love instead of across the lake… is perfect for me, so you shouldn't give me too much praise."

"You're getting the praise, so deal with it."

"Yes, boss."

"And you're banned from calling me boss," I said, laughing. "You're the boss, anyway. I have every bit of faith in you, so once you get comfortable, I trust you're going to run it like you own it."

"Mostly," Anna said. "Consulting with you on the big decisions."

When Anna and I had met the day after the painting party, we'd clicked. Her experience was a great match, and more importantly, I trusted her implicitly. I'd hired her on the spot, and she hadn't even had to think it over. She'd accepted, with the condition she would give her employer two weeks' notice. Except her boss had been pissed that she was quitting less than a week after going to a conference on his dime, to work at what he deemed a competitor, no less, so he'd asked her to leave immediately. You know, so she didn't take all his trade secrets to the Honeysuckle Inn. As if.

His stupidity was my gain. Anna had started on Wednesday last week, just in time for the installation of the property management computer system. The inn had sprung into the twenty-first century, with key cards, a reservation system, and more. She and I, along with Sadie, Magnolia, and Deshon, had spent this week being trained on the system. We'd finished late this morning, as planned, and tomorrow I was heading back to LA for good.

In addition to the computer system, the roof had been replaced, the whole inn had been painted inside and out, and a lot of the smaller projects had been knocked out as well. Anna was meeting with Sierra North—and me via online conference call—in a couple weeks regarding sprucing up the interior while honoring the inn's hundred-year-old roots.

The Honeysuckle Inn was poised to grow and flourish, and I couldn't feel better about everything I'd gotten done in the past month, with lots of help, of course.

I hadn't heard from Stream yet, but Willa was still optimistic. Most days, I was too. Even if I didn't get that job, I was itching to get back to writing. I'd come up with multiple ideas for more screenplays. I'd been invited to a party at a big-name producer's house in a couple weeks, and I knew it'd be crawling with writers and producers I wanted to meet and get face time with.

Everything was working out as I'd hoped. The only downside was leaving Cash. I swallowed at that thought and pushed it away. He was due to pick me up in a few minutes for our last evening together, and we'd agreed there'd be no sad, heavy stuff before tomorrow. We were both pursuing our dreams, and my leaving was part of the plan.

"I'll be back...as much as I can get back," I said. Yet another factor in Anna's favor was that she already lived in Dragonfly Lake, already had a home, so I hadn't had to throw in my cottage to sweeten the deal. It was mine, and I'd always have a place to stay when I visited. "It depends—"

"On how long the Hollywood guys take to get off their butts and hire you," she said generously. "And if and when you get swept away by your soon-to-be new, amazing job, you know I've got this."

"I know." Glasses still in both our hands, I hugged her. "God, I know, and I love you for it."

The door opened before we could separate, and Cash's voice rang out, "Am I interrupting something?"

We laughed and ended our hug.

"You wish, Cash Henry," Anna said.

I looked up to see his smile that made my insides melt every time. "Hey, handsome."

"Hi, gorgeous."

I finished the juice in my glass. "We were toasting Anna."

"Seems justified," he said warmly. He knew exactly what a godsend she was.

For the past two weeks, he'd practically moved into the cottage. It was as if there was an unspoken agreement that neither one of us wanted to play games by acting like we didn't want to spend as much time together as possible before I left. He'd helped me with the inn when he wasn't working, and he'd even taken a day off here and there from the restaurant, which I'd gathered was nearly unheard of.

Truth bomb: I didn't hate it. At all.

"Are you ready to go? If we don't get there soon, all the good berries will be gone."

"Kinsey's making cobbler?" I asked.

"Kinsey's making cobbler."

Kinsey's cobbler was almost as good as Cash's hummingbird cake.

"I don't want to be the reason Kinsey can't make cobbler," I said.

"Highly recommend against that," Anna said. "Get out of here, you two. I've got everything under control."

As Cash wrapped his big hand around mine, I said, "Text if you need anything."

"Just some cobbler," Anna said.

We went out the door with a wave.

"She knows cobbler won't be ready till tomorrow, right?" Cash asked, and the T word made something sink in my gut.

"She knows."

"I'll bring some by for her," he said, leaving it unspoken that I'd be gone by then. My flight out of Nashville was an early one. As if to brush over that fact, he rushed on to say, "You ready to rock the farmers market?"

"I'm always good for a farmers market." I grinned, because before Cash had taken me to the weekly Friday market in Dragonfly Lake, I'd never been to one. Here, everyone went, it seemed. It was an Event with a capital E, small-town style. The stalls were open on the square for several hours, from late afternoon to early evening, and fresh produce was only a fraction of the offerings. There were handcrafted items, soaps, candles, specialty breads, food stands, and more. The market ended with live entertainment, usually locals or regional bands, on a makeshift stage on the green.

Nearly an hour and a half later, we'd grabbed the last flat of "good" blackberries, plus some plump raspberries as well, and a whole basketful of other produce for Henry's. Cash had dropped it off at his place to take to work tomorrow morning so it would be out of the sun and heat, and now we were walking back toward the square to hit the taco truck. It was owned by an acquaintance of Cash, and Cash swore they were the best street tacos he'd ever had.

Rosy McNamara, Nancy Solon, and Kona Powers waved from their picnic blanket on the grass, where Kona's two big dogs rested, their eyes on the action. In the other direction, a couple of the McNamara brothers—I couldn't keep them straight—were flirting with some girls I didn't recognize. Jewel, the bartender from Humble's, wore her Humble's T-shirt and denim shorts, looking like she was heading in for a Friday-night shift, but she stopped at the Thai food truck on the corner.

As we were walking by one of the many benches, a couple stood and walked away, freeing up a coveted place to sit.

"Want me to grab this and you can order for both of us?" I asked Cash.

"Hell yes. What do you want?"

"Surprise me," I told him, not knowing the menu, trusting him with my food as I'd been for the past month anyway.

He kissed me, then headed off to get in line.

As I leaned against the back, I spotted Chloe, Holden, Olivia, and a couple of guys I didn't recognize from here, sitting in a group on the grass near the stage, eating and drinking. Olivia saw me and waved, then gestured to me to join them.

I waved back and shook my head, then pointed toward Cash. She gave me a thumbs-up with an exaggerated smile, making me laugh.

This was people-watching at its best. All ages. Friend groups and families. Locals and tourists, although the number of out-of-towners had dropped to a fraction now that Labor Day had passed and we were officially in the off-season.

My phone rang and I pulled it out of my pocket, expecting it to be Cash with a question about my dinner preference. Instead, it was Willa, and my heart skipped a beat.

"Hi, Willa."

Willa, my seasoned, normally sedate fifty-something agent, let out a squeal like I'd never heard from her. "Avaaaaa!" She cleared her throat and said in a more level voice, "You did it, hon. I just talked to Sheldon. They want you for the job."

"Oh, my god." I popped up off the bench, put my finger over my ear to hear better because I didn't want to miss a single word of this. My heart was galloping and it was all I could do not to squee in joy myself. "Is this for real?"

"It's a thousand-percent real, honey, and it is a sweet offer."

I listened as she rattled off all the details, only retaining half of it in my state of utter disbelief. Somewhere along the line, Cash came up beside me, a look of confusion on his face and a bag of tacos and two bottled waters in his hands. He set the bag and bottles on the bench and sat on the edge of it, as if to respect my phone call.

I held up a finger to tell him I was almost done as Willa promised to email me a summary of the details and the contract so I could sort through it all. I already knew I'd missed about half of what she'd told me as I tried to keep my cool and not come across as someone having a conniption fit in the middle of the town square.

When Willa and I disconnected, I squeezed my eyes shut and pressed my lips together, which was the only thing I could do other than scream with joy.

"Is it the job?" Cash asked, grinning widely as if my happiness was contagious. "Was that Stream?"

"My agent," I said breathlessly. "Yes. Yes! I'm trying to not lose my mind, but they offered me the head writer job!" I clasped both of his hands and squeezed excitedly.

"Holy shit, Ava. Fuck yeah. I'm so damn proud of you. Hell yes!"

I laughed sort of hysterically, in a good way, and bounced on my feet, then I threw my arms around him.

Cash pulled me close. "Congratulations, my little writing powerhouse. You deserve this and more."

With his arms around me, I closed my eyes again, over-come. So overcome. With elation and disbelief and a measure of hell yes thrown in.

I breathed in Cash's scent, savored every inch of his firm, big body pressing into me, cherished the low growl of emotion that came from his chest. I felt his support and genuine happiness for me in every cell. He was my biggest supporter, and in his arms celebrating was exactly where I wanted to be.

Even if it was only for a short while longer.

When we finally pulled apart, I ignored the sinking feeling in my chest and plastered the goofy grin back on. There'd be time later to miss Cash, but right now, I didn't want to miss a single second.

"What do you say we take our tacos back to my place and celebrate privately?" I suggested.

With another sexy growl, he banded an arm around me, pulled me to him as he grabbed the food with his other hand, and laid another toe-curling kiss on my lips. "I say yes. One-hundred-percent yes."

CHAPTER 22

CASH

t felt like I'd been asleep for an hour tops when the mattress dipped beside me and I felt a light touch on my arm.

"Cash, my car will be here in ten minutes."

I cracked one eye open enough to see it was still dark outside. The bathroom light was on, the door pulled nearly closed, letting only a small beam through.

Ava.

Saturday. Predawn.

She was flying out this morning.

Fuck.

I let out a grunt to show I'd heard her, all the while fighting the urge to pull her in with me, strip her down, bury myself in her, and make her forget the time so she'd miss her flight.

Second choice would be to yank the blankets over my head and shut out reality.

"I hated to wake you," she said, her voice barely above a

whisper, so soothing when this day was anything but soothing.

We'd agreed not to make it a big, sad ordeal though.

I could shut things out with the best of them, so I ran my hand up her arm, over her shoulder, to the back of her neck and pulled her down to me. Her fresh, hint-of-flowers scent and the slight moisture beneath her hair told me she'd showered and was ready to go. Starting something would be pointless right now as the old-school clock on the nightstand told me she hadn't left a lot of wiggle room for getting to the airport. I pressed a gentle, almost chaste kiss to her lips.

"Morning, gorgeous." My voice was gravelly as hell.

"Hey, handsome." She stood so I could crawl out of her bed for one final time.

Quit thinking like that, dumb ass. Only makes it harder. Denial, denial, denial.

I sat up to face the day I'd been dreading from the second she'd reserved her flight.

"I need to finish tidying up downstairs," she said. "See you down there when you're dressed."

I mumbled some kind of halfhearted affirmative as she hurried out of the room.

Three minutes later, I'd rinsed with mouthwash, splashed cold water on my face, and pulled my clothes from yesterday on, then went heavily down the stairs, telling myself fatigue was my main problem this morning. It was a factor for sure—we'd stayed up till all hours, talking, making love, snacking on dry cereal sometime after two, then doing it all over again. It was as if neither of us could bear to let the night end, because we both knew after it did, *we* ended too.

Yes, I actually thought the words *making love*. There was no denying it. I'd fallen in love with Ava again, or maybe it was still. But I hadn't spoken of it. Telling her how I felt would only complicate everything, make it harder when she left today, and we'd agreed to make her departure no big deal. Not an emotional, wrung-out goodbye.

This—her leaving—was what we'd agreed on all along. This was the right decision, the way it had to be. But fuck, did it suck ass-balls.

Ava's luggage was sitting sentinel by the door, her clutch at the ready on top. The lamp closest to the door was on a dim setting, allowing me to see the place was tidied to within an inch of its life. Ready to be empty for a prolonged period.

I swallowed down the need to say something, anything to stop her from leaving.

A glance out the door told me the car she'd hired hadn't arrived yet, but the clock on the stove said the witching hour was two minutes away.

"I'll take these out," I said, grabbing the two suitcases.

Without a sound, Ava picked up the clutch and her carry-on, and we stacked them out by her aunt's truck.

"Okay," she said nervously, not like my Ava at all, and I got it.

And then reminded myself she wasn't *my* Ava.

We'd agreed this was it. We would let each other know how the important stuff went—her first week on the job, whether or not Henry's got onto *Small Town Smorgasbord*—but we were making this break as clean as possible. I'd offered to drive her to the airport, but that would be *too boyfriendly*, she'd determined.

I wasn't her boyfriend.

She wasn't my anything except ex.

What would happen if you told her you loved her?

That was an easy one, the answer at the top of my mind because I'd turned it over in my head so many damn times.

Not a fucking thing. It wouldn't change that her dream job is in California and your livelihood is here in Tennessee.

All it would do was complicate a no-win situation.

Ava would be fine without me. She had so much to

accomplish, and I wanted her to accomplish the hell out of all of it. I knew she would kick some Hollywood ass and take names. I wasn't about to do anything that would distract her from her goals.

Right decision. The way it had to be.

Enough internal whining. *Jesus.*

I needed to get the hell out of there before her ride arrived, before she climbed into some generic car with some generic driver and drove away from me. I couldn't watch it. Didn't want that to be the last image in my head of Ava, at least until the next time she was back in town and I happened to run into her on the sidewalk or at the bar or…

Fuck.

"Come here," I said.

She walked into my arms and pressed her face into my chest and I just fucking held on. No words would make this better. I didn't know if she was feeling the same dread I was. Asking wouldn't make anything better, even if we hadn't agreed to not address it.

I blew out a breath, determined to make this suck less. Ava was making her dreams come true. Not only was I *not* going to stand in her way but I was going to send her off with the hope and optimism she deserved. I wanted her walking out of here feeling on top of the world as she went to take on the job she was meant for. It was more than a job for her; it was a passion.

I pulled back and grasped her shoulders, looking her in the eye. "You're going to kill it, Ava." Managing to smile, I continued, "I can't wait to watch every episode and pause it when *Head Writer—Ava Dean* pops up on the screen so I can think, *I knew her when.*"

Ava's beautiful dark-chocolate eyes lit up and a grin crawled across her pretty face, growing bigger and truer. *That* was the Ava I wanted to remember. *That* was the picture I needed burned in my mind. Well, that and the one where she was naked and hovering over me, her hair cascading down between us, her milky skin glimmering in the moonlight…

"Sexiest fucking head writer ever," I said.

She laughed, which was what I'd hoped for. "You're biased." She ran her fingers over my unshaven jaw.

"You like me that way." I kissed her, trying to keep it brief.

"I do," she said, grinning. "Thank you for everything you've done, Cash. The painting, the work around here, the food…the really incredible food…" She laughed again. "You've spoiled me and it's going to suck going back to carryout and frozen pizza."

I cringed. "I'd send you a good, simple cookbook, but I know better."

She nodded. "You do." Her smile faded and she took in a slow breath and blew it out as she glanced around her. The inn was quiet, the only lights coming from the fixture on the porch and the security light in the parking lot. The sky was just beginning to lighten in the east, and a single determined cricket serenaded us from close by. "I'll miss this place. I'll miss you."

"No you won't," I said, forcing a smile. "You'll be too busy to miss me."

The sound of tires driving down the inn's road toward us registered. I didn't bother to turn and look for headlights. Palming the side of her face, I ran my thumb over her lip, then lowered my mouth to hers and kissed her. Not brief. Not chaste. I poured everything I felt for her into that kiss, willing her to feel it, to know she was loved, that she'd always have a place in my heart.

I ended it abruptly so I could escape before the car pulled up.

"Later, Ava," I said, mindful that we'd agreed we wouldn't say goodbye. "Safe travels."

She gazed up at me, her lips pressed together, and merely

nodded. Then I turned away, walked to my car, and drove off without a glance back.

———

AVA

I kept up my strong, happy, going-off-to-fulfill-my-dreams front until I was safely tucked in the backseat by myself.

The timing of Cash's departure had been ideal, with my ride showing up at just the right moment so I couldn't watch Cash drive off. But now that I was alone, my throat felt swollen with sadness and my eyes burned and brimmed with tears, the same but different as when I'd arrived at the inn nearly a month ago.

This is totally different, I told myself. *That was grief for my aunt. This is just leaving Cash and the inn and everything I'd grown to love. Not grief.*

Cash would be here, living his best life, blowing people away with his fantastic cooking. That was exactly what he was meant to be doing, just as writing was my destiny.

Everything was going to plan, both of our plans.

Still, I sort of wished he'd asked me to stay. Both of us knew I couldn't, but it somehow would've made me feel a tiny bit better if he'd asked. Would've told me he felt something. More than a little something.

My inhale was deep but shaky as I told myself it didn't matter. It was better for Cash if he didn't have deep feelings for me, because this sucked.

If I put my magnanimous hat on for a second, I didn't want Cash to hurt, didn't want him to feel this wrenching pain I felt in my chest. I wanted him to live happy. He deserved so much to live happy. He could do that here in Dragonfly Lake, as the owner and head chef of his family's restaurant. This was where he belonged.

And I was going where I belonged.

I would embrace that and be happy and grateful as soon as I got there. In the meantime, I'd try to get through the traveling without losing my composure and bawling my eyes out in public.

CHAPTER 23

CASH

By the time Seth and I were sitting in the empty dining room at not-yet-open Henry's for our weekly Monday morning meeting, Ava had been gone for more than fifty-four hours. I didn't know why the fuck I was counting but I couldn't help it. Maybe I was hoping it'd get easier the more time that passed.

I mainly grunted while my brother rambled on about social media crap and the events on the Rusty Anchor beer patio the rest of the month, but then grunting through a meeting wasn't unusual for me. Seth ran our business the way it needed to be run and basically updated me during our meetings. I had more of an opinion if the food itself was involved, or the kitchen.

Today, I didn't give a flying fuck about any of it.

"Have you heard from Ava?" Seth asked out of nowhere.

I glared at him. "Why the hell would I?"

His brows rose. "You two were pretty close the past couple weeks," he said. "I just thought—"

"Save yourself the thinking. We agreed to end whatever it

was we had." I crumpled the agenda my anal brother always printed out and clenched it in my fist. "You got anything else about the restaurant or are we done here?"

"That's all I've got. Just…sorry you're hurting."

"I'm fine." I shoved my chair back, stood, and pushed it back in, knowing I was being an unbearable asshole but not caring. With a glare out the window, where it was rainy and gray and perfect for my state of mind, I trudged off to my office tucked in the corner of the kitchen, slamming the door behind me when I got there.

I knew I needed to get over this crap and stop being a jackass. It was no surprise that I missed the shit out of Ava, but I'd known this was coming. Hell, I'd known it would end this way from the first time we'd talked at the inn last month. In my messed-up mind, I'd taken the fact she was going back to California as a sort of security. We could spend time together *because* there was a definite end to it. There was no possibility of a future. I hadn't *wanted* a future with her.

My gut knotted up.

Did I want a future with her now?

It didn't matter anyway. I wasn't going to have one.

I just needed to get back to doing what I did—the food business.

Out of habit, I sat down and opened one of my social media apps to check the latest on *Small Town Smorgasbord's* hashtag. I knew Kennedy Clayborne's people had likely posted for us over the weekend, but I hadn't bothered to check in once. I also needed to like or comment to any customers who gave us a plug.

The show's account itself appeared at the top of my feed. Before I even finished skimming it, the knot in my gut hardened to a rock and sank.

"Son of a bitch." I bit out each word clearly and separately, as if enunciating could make them count more.

I fisted my hand and held it up to my mouth, my elbow

lodged on the desk, reining in everything so as not to do what I felt like doing—pounding a hole through the wall.

Join us in congratulating Chef Nola Simms and the Cove in Dragonfly Lake, Tennessee, for being selected for an upcoming episode of Small Town Smorgasbord! Filming will begin this fall. Watch for episodes in the spring.

I sat there in stunned silence, my jaw clenched so hard I might pop a molar or three.

I'd been so sure Henry's would get the nod for Tennessee.

We were better than the Cove. Our food was outstanding and creative and top quality. Our service was commendable. And our history was decades longer and stronger than the Cove's.

Did none of that count for jack shit?

The door whipped opened and Seth's ugly face appeared. I glared at him silently, my fist still clenched in front of my mouth, and he studied me with a question in his expression.

"Did you see?" he asked.

"I fucking saw."

He came in, shut the door calmly, and sat in the chair opposite mine. After blowing out a sigh, he said, "It's not necessarily a no for us."

"Bullshit. They don't do two places from the same side of a state, let alone the same small town."

"Yeah. I think you're probably right," Seth acknowledged. He shut up for a few seconds, then said, "It's all subjective. You know that."

"Mm-hmm."

"Their opinions don't mean a fucking thing. We've been here for years running our family's restaurant. That show doesn't get a say in what we're doing or how we're doing it."

I didn't respond. Just waited for him to get it all out and then get out of my office.

"You're a damn good chef, Cash, and you know it."

My brother sat there and stared at me, even though I wasn't looking directly at him. I waited him out.

"This on top of Ava leaving sucks, huh?"

Rain smacked against the window, as if it was coming at me too.

"How 'bout you leave me alone?" I lashed out, meeting his gaze finally, my eyes hopefully flashing with my toxic anger so he'd get the message.

His eyes flashed right back at me with a satisfying dose of pissed-off. Good. Bring it on. A fight would feel fan-fucking-tastic.

"Get over yourself," he said, his voice low, controlled, but undeniably angry.

"You don't know anything about it," I growled.

"I know more than you think."

The fuck he did.

"You run this place from the safety of your precious office," I rumbled. "You have no idea how it is when it's *your* creations being judged, *your* work being deemed not good enough. I put my heart into every dish on that menu, so don't tell me you know what it's like to have some upstart fuckers across town come in and get chosen over me."

His jaw ticked as he stared me down for several seconds, no doubt calming his unflusterable self the way I obviously didn't care to do. "I might not create the food, but I put my heart into everything else. I oversee the marketing and the atmosphere and every other thing about this restaurant. We're a partnership, in this together. So hell yes I take that shit personally. Whether it's exactly the same or not isn't the issue."

"What's the fucking issue?"

"The issue," he bit out at me, "is that you have some screwed-up idea that you're not good enough. You have for years. Not just about the food, but let's talk about the food.

You know you're an excellent chef. I know you know that. And yet you've been targeting this show as if you can't exist without their seal of approval."

"Their seal of approval would have a tangible result in sales," I explained to him as if he wasn't more intelligent than the rest of us Henrys put together.

"Fuck the tangible result. This isn't about that."

"Then what's it about?" I snarled.

Seth leaned back, crossed his arms, and looked me straight in the eyes. "It's about you, Cash. That show might bring in business but it wouldn't change *you*. You'd still walk around discontented all the time, with something to prove."

"What the fuck are you talking about?" I growled, acting like he was insane even as his words hit a raw spot inside of me that I refused to acknowledge.

"I don't know what your dysfunction is," he said, leaning forward, "but for some reason, nothing's ever good enough for you."

"Because I want Henry's to be featured on the show instead of some shiny new start-up?"

"You're unhappy, and a show isn't going to fix it, Cash. You're searching for some kind of career gold medal, but you've already gotten accolades out the ass for your food, for Henry's. Everyone buys into it, everyone knows how good you are—except you."

"I know I'm good."

Seth nodded, his jaw rigid. "We don't need the show. Henry's is all good. But you aren't. You're searching, always searching. Once you get over this show, there'll be something else you'll go after, thinking it'll make you happy, but it won't. Whatever it is, it won't."

I leaned back and crossed my arms, hoping that would curtail the urge to punch his know-it-all face. "I suppose you're gonna tell me what will?" I said with the utmost sarcasm.

Seth stared me down. His brows shot up, as if he really thought I had an idea of what he was thinking. His voice was quieter when he said, "You've been a different person for the past two or three weeks. Like, pleasant. I heard you whistling while you were working on the kitchen schedule, for fuck's sake. You hate doing the schedule."

He kept staring. Leaning forward, I planted my elbows on my desk, wove my fingers together, and brought both my hands in front of my chin, not meeting his gaze, waiting him out, refusing to acknowledge where I knew he was going.

"Three little letters," he said, smug as fuck, and I snapped.

"Ava lives in California. Two thousand miles away. Living out her dream, and that doesn't include me."

"Did she say that?"

I scowled at the dense fucker. "She didn't have to. She's there, isn't she?"

"Did you ever once ask her to stay?"

An acidic chuckle came out of me. "How would that go in your head? 'Hey, Ava, I know you just got a once-in-a-lifetime offer for the job of your dreams, but how 'bout you skip that to be a small-town chef's girlfriend.'" I scoffed and shook my head.

"Maybe it doesn't have to be either/or."

"Why are you in here playing counselor?" I snarled, pushing down the faintest spark of hope that ignited at what he'd just said.

"Just returning the favor from when you set me straight a few weeks ago."

Obviously he meant when I'd told him to pull his head out about Everly. "Our situations have nothing in common."

"Let's see. I fell in love with a girl who lived somewhere else, had a career somewhere else, and I was too chickenshit to go after her and ask her to stay," Seth rattled off, as if I hadn't been there.

"Key differences: Everly was an hour away in Nashville;

Ava's on the opposite side of the country. Everly was already doing her dream job and could do it anywhere. Ava's just about to get started and she has to report to the studio five days a week."

"There are options. What if you tried long-distance for a while? Her show won't last forever, right? No show ever has."

"It could last for years."

"They still have breaks between seasons," Seth said. "And you've got Zinnia here. She's not you but she does a decent impression, all but the perpetual grumpy snarl. She can hold the fort down if you spend half your time in LA."

I stared him down. I wanted to fight. I wanted to bite his head off and tell him how stupid his idea was. But there was a part of me that wanted to believe it was possible.

"Look, this isn't your first time around with Ava," he carried on. "It seems to me that, regardless of whatever you did to fuck it up in the past, there's something there. Something that might be worth fighting for instead of just throwing up your hands, walking away, and being a dick every day for the rest of your life."

I bided my time, my jaw clenched, hands still fisted together in front of me, not making eye contact, not giving my brother any indication that anything he was saying might resonate. But there were parts of it that fucking resonated.

"If you're good with letting it end the same way it did before, then I guess that's safe, familiar territory for you and you should go with it. But if you want a different outcome"— Seth stood and shrugged—"then you'd have to do something different than before. Now I need to get some work done. We open in less than half an hour."

Which meant I had shit to do.

But I also had a staff in the kitchen, prepping away, including Zin. I was screwed up enough at the moment that they'd do better without me.

After another three seconds of watching me to see what I'd do, he turned, walked out of my office, and shut the door calmly behind him.

A storm raged inside of my head, making me want to come out of my skin. It'd been stirring for two days, building, but then my brother had known the buttons to push to blow it up.

I was torn between needing to explode and wanting to curl up under my desk and cry like a fucking baby. Neither would be okay, so I stood and shoved my chair back so hard it crashed into the wall, then went to my office door, whipped it open, and marched the six feet or so to the side exit and thrust it open, not so much as glancing toward my staff.

The rain was coming down in sheets, but I didn't fucking care. The beer patio was in front of me, so I took a right and stormed to the shore, not giving a shit where I wound up, just needing to clear the noise in my head.

I ended up at the water's edge, the rain pounding down on me, water washing down my face, my whites already soaked clear through.

There wasn't another soul in sight, neither on the lake nor onshore, not even one of the McNamara pussies at their marina next door.

As much as I wanted to blow off everything my brother had said, that bit about the past… It was jabbing at me.

I'd fucked up with Ava before. I could one-hundred-percent admit that. I'd wanted to marry her then, for fuck's sake, but instead, I'd dumped her? What kind of sense did that make?

A fuck lot of sense if you stopped to consider what made me do it.

Fear. Of not being good enough. Of screwing it up. Of losing her later down the road, when it would allegedly hurt more.

If I was honest, the only thing that got me through the

pain of breaking up with Ava the first time had been that the Navy worked my ass so hard I didn't have time to mourn the loss. I'd been too damn tired at night to lie there and let it burrow in too deeply.

Now here I was, seventeen years later, and had I learned a damn thing? Was I still just as stupid and fearful?

Seemed like it, because I'd just let the best part of my life go without a fight. I'd let fear convince me there were no options other than letting Ava go back to LA.

But maybe there were options.

As much as it chafed me to admit Seth might have had some decent suggestions, he had. If it meant having Ava in my life, I could try long-distance. I could try splitting our time, some here, some in LA. I wouldn't care what bed I woke up in as long as I woke up next to Ava.

The question was, could I convince Ava I was worth it? We were worth it? Did she care enough about me to make room in her California head-writer life for me? Or had she already moved on?

As the noise in my head calmed and made room for a glimmer of hope, I lifted my head to the sky and let it rain down on me, turning over my options. It was vital that I spoke to Ava in person. The sooner the better.

I turned back to the restaurant and made my way toward the side door, standing under the overhang as I took out my phone. I scrolled to my pilot brother-in-law's contact info and tapped his number, hoping he answered.

"Hey, Zane," I said when he did. "I have a giant favor to ask."

CHAPTER 24

AVA

Late Monday morning, I parked my car in the garage under my apartment building and killed the engine.

I sat there staring at the ugly concrete wall in the dim light. The underground parking had been my one nod to safety since the place I could afford wasn't in a spectacular neighborhood. Because this was LA. Not Dragonfly Lake, where people didn't break into cars or steal them.

Dragonfly Lake people also didn't spend a significant percentage of their life stuck in traffic. Two days back here and my jaw already hurt from clenching it and yelling at stupid drivers.

I'd gone into the doggy daycare this morning to quit, and it'd been weird. Even though I liked and respected Mrs. Cassidy, the owner, just fine, I'd had a harder time saying goodbye to the dogs than the humans. I got the feeling Mrs. Cassidy wasn't too surprised or upset to see me go either, as she'd kindly told me not to worry about working the rest of this week. She'd already hired an extra person, so they were good without me.

I thought of the teary goodbye Friday evening with Magnolia, noting the two were night and day. I'd worked for Mrs. Cassidy for almost two years and had only known Magnolia for a month, but the ties back in Tennessee were stronger. I suspected that's just how a small town was.

Naturally, thoughts of that small town sent my mind straight to Cash. My lids lowered as the ongoing ache in my chest intensified.

Saturday I'd cried my eyes out, and unfortunately, I hadn't been able to wait till I was home to do that, silently blubbering my way through both legs of my flight and the Dallas airport, as well as the Uber ride to my apartment.

Yesterday I'd picked up my phone a thousand times to text Cash about something, anything. Little things. Big things. Funny things. Hunger. And a killer craving for hummingbird cake. Or maybe it was really just a killer craving for him. But we'd agreed not to be in touch daily. Only for the big things.

God, I missed him.

For the zillionth time this morning, I wiped tears from my eyes, took a deep breath, and reminded myself I had my big-girl panties on today.

I might need to go online and buy a whole case of big-girl panties.

Each time I got sad about Cash, I forced my brain to thoughts of Stream and my new job. Some of the time I was able to summon that rush of excitement and optimism about the opportunity.

After quitting the dog job, I'd decided to drive to the Stream studio, where I had an appointment to fill out paperwork on Wednesday and I'd be reporting for work starting next week. I didn't have a lot of other things pressing me for time, and I'd wanted to look at it, let it soak in that I'd be working there.

It was just over an hour's drive on a good day, at nonpeak hours. Today, even though it'd been well after the morning rush, it hadn't been a good traffic day.

I'd sat in my car, staring at the place where I'd be working, and it was surreal. Looking at the buildings, I couldn't help but wonder if any actors I'd recognize were working away in them. That had finally diminished the traffic frustration and sent a buzz of excitement through my veins.

I'd spent ten minutes staring at my new employer's studio, and then, trying to avoid lunch-hour traffic, I'd headed back home. An hour and forty minutes later, here I was.

Maybe after I got a few paychecks, I could afford to move a little closer and shave a few minutes off my drive. You know, cut it down to a flat hour. Ugh. So traffic and commute time would suck. Surely the excitement of leading a creative team of three would make it all worthwhile.

I knew there'd be downsides to the job. Willa had warned me the head writer position would be demanding, nonstop, require extra hours, and would be under constant scrutiny, so I'd been trying to prepare myself for all of that. It was true with almost any job, right? Well, not the doggy daycare, but then the hourly wage reflected the difference.

I was going to miss those dogs.

But not nearly as much as I missed Cash, Magnolia, Knox, Anna, and…others. So many others. It was odd that all those years ago, I'd never really fit in in Dragonfly Lake, never had time to fit in. Now I'd gone back for less than a month, and I had all these connections, with so many different people. Besides the ones I'd developed deeper friendships with, there were the Diamonds, who'd continued to spend their Thursday evening poker sessions at the inn, allowing me to join them, adopting me as if I was one of their own, making me feel closer to Aunt Phyl and to each of the ladies. There were Cash's family and people in town, like Jake Bergman and Jewel, the bartender at Humble's. Olivia and Shawna and Everly and Kemp.

After living in this apartment for over a year, I didn't know more than about two people who lived in the building. While I had a growing list of contacts and acquaintances in the TV industry, none of them were what I'd consider a close friend. The only other people I knew were my coworkers at the dog place and the doggy dads and moms who brought their pups in regularly.

That was depressing. Remarkably, it had never bothered me until this moment.

With a noisy exhalation, I opened the car door and climbed out into the stale air of the parking garage. I'd gotten in the habit of breathing in the humid lake air, and I stopped mid-breath now when all that registered were a dirty concrete smell and the faint odor of gasoline and motor oil.

I took the elevator up to the third floor. As I exited, my next-door neighbor, Aubrey or Audrey, I could never remember which, was carrying a floor lamp and waiting to get on, alongside a tall, muscled guy who was carrying a moving box.

"Hey," I said, "are you moving out?"

"I am." Aubrey or Audrey looked at the guy and smiled a lot like the newlywed Patels had smiled back at the inn that first week. "I'm moving in with my fiancé, Bart."

"Wow. Congratulations," I said, smiling. I hadn't seen the guy before, hadn't known she was serious with anyone, but then I probably wouldn't. We mostly ran into each other at the mailboxes and elevator.

"Thank you," my neighbor said. "We're excited, aren't we?" She and Bart shared an elated look, then she went up on her toes and pressed a brief kiss to his lips.

"Can't wait for you to be my wife, babe," Bart said.

The elevator doors started to close, so I caught one and let the blissed-up couple get on.

"Good to see you," Audrey or Aubrey called out to me, her tone friendly and happy. So damn happy.

I smiled to myself as I walked toward my unit. With every step, my smile faded, and as I unlocked my door, that heaviness set into my chest again.

I wanted what she had.

I'd almost *had* what she had.

Maybe… Maybe I could still have what my neighbor had?

No. I'd made my choice.

After entering my tiny one-bedroom apartment and getting that same antsy, angsty sensation I'd gotten every other time I'd walked in since Saturday, I shut the door and went to the personality-less sofa that, like the rest of the furniture, had come with the place. With a soul-deep sigh, I flopped down on it, wondering how long I'd feel this way, this raw and sad and uninspired. Discontented.

The unease that had accompanied me the whole way home from Tennessee and been present every second since I'd arrived reared its head and made me gasp for breath.

Had I made a mistake?

Hugging a throw pillow to my chest, I rationalized with myself yet again. A girl didn't get a dream job offer every day. A head writer position for a relative newbie like me? That didn't happen. Even selling a series to a network didn't often happen to thousands of writers who spent their entire lives trying.

I'd told myself for the past year plus, since before my divorce was final, that this was *my* time. My chance to see to *my* needs that had been sacrificed for years and years, first for my mom, then for my ex.

Toppling over to lie on my side, I squeezed my eyes shut and tried to drown out the unsure voice in my head that asked ever so politely whether my needs had changed.

I was in this now. I'd said yes to Stream. I'd be insane to tell them no.

Wouldn't I?

The silence of the apartment echoed in my ears, mocking me. I was alone now. I was the boss of me, just like I'd always wanted to be.

Yay, me.

I took my phone out and checked for messages, wishing there was someone to talk to. All was quiet. Everyone was carrying on with their lives, just as they should be. Even Cash. It was two hours later in Tennessee, so the lunch rush was probably over. The restaurant would close soon for the break between lunch and dinner service, and someone would be preparing to start the staff's daily meal together, something Cash had usually told me all about, from an experimental dish that had blown his mind to someone's specialty dish that he was considering adding to the Henry's menu.

I wondered how Anna was handling the new week and whether her interviews for more desk help had panned out. I could text her, but I didn't want her to think I didn't trust her.

And Magnolia… I knew she wasn't working at the inn tonight because the Lily Pad was having an artist exhibit week, and she'd planned to stay late for the kickoff mixer after the store closed. She'd been happily up to her eyeballs doing most of the planning for the special event.

When I'd checked the Dragonfly Lake weather earlier, the radar had shown rain, and I wondered if it would clear off enough for people to get out on the lake for a few hours later.

I let out a groan. "You're making yourself crazy," I said into the quiet.

It was lunchtime, but my appetite was MIA, so I rolled to my back and opened my email. I skimmed through the junk and the ads, and when I saw an email from Knox, I broke out into a smile. I opened it and read:

You are stinking incredible! I'm blown away by the chapter you wrote. It jostled all sorts of stuff free inside my thick skull. I see what you mean about romance now. And no, I don't take a single bit of offense at your "presumptuousness." Quite the opposite, Ms. Head Writer. There's a reason you are where you are. If you ever want to lower your standards and co-write a book with me, you know where to find me.

I laughed, relieved he'd liked what I'd done.

I'd finally had a chance to read the first chapters of his new book yesterday morning, now that I was no longer in charge of the inn's day-to-day. Once again, I'd loved his writing style, and I'd been drawn into his hero's story conundrum from page one. And then an idea had struck me to take a female character who appeared in chapter one and turn her into a heroine. She and a romance storyline could add another layer to the book.

It'd been weeks since I'd written anything on my own projects, of which I'd had two going before the call about my aunt's passing. I hadn't had time or energy to be creative, but something about Knox's project had sparked me. I'd pulled out my laptop, opened a blank document, then debated. I didn't want to come across like a know-it-all or infringe on Knox's creation in any way. But the entire day had been looming over me, stretching out with all kinds of unhappy thoughts. I could face that, or I could take a stab at writing a couple pages from the potential heroine's point of view.

I'd decided to go for it and email it to Knox, emphasizing that it was strictly for fun and thanking him for helping me back into my writing habit after so long away. I also told him if there was anything he wanted to use in the chapter that had poured out of me, to feel free.

I reread his email and laughed again, and then my eyes went back to that last line.

If you ever want to lower your standards and co-write a book with me, you know where to find me.

My grin faded and I jolted upright, swinging my legs around to sit on the edge of the sofa.

I would love to co-write with Knox.

A torrent of story possibilities flooded my mind, just like that—something that hadn't happened with my solo screen-writing for ages, not even last night when I'd read through one of my works in progress.

I hopped up off the sofa and paced, my mind racing at full tilt, my heart thundering, because all of a sudden, literally in between heartbeats, a different possibility coalesced in my brain.

What if I moved to Dragonfly Lake permanently?

What if I chose to walk away from Stream because my needs had changed without me even noticing?

Tears ran out of my eyes, and I legit didn't know if they were from fear or sadness or elation or all of the above.

I could live in the cozy, homey cottage at the inn and be there when Anna needed me and be involved with the business more directly and yet not full-time.

I could spend time on the inn's deck with friends—and at Henry's and the Rusty Anchor and the Fly by Night and Humble's.

I could switch my focus from screenwriting to novel writing. I knew a decent amount about indie publishing. If Knox was serious about co-writing, I was all about trying it, and if not, well, I could go solo just fine. It would take a few months to get ramped up, but my living expenses would be almost nothing.

Most importantly, there was a chance I could be with Cash. Maybe he was as miserable as I was and... God, it scared the shit out of me to even think it, but maybe we could have a future.

But what if that wasn't what he wanted?

My mouth went bone-dry and I tried to swallow. He might not want something long-term. He might not want the downsides of a relationship. He might not end up wanting any of that with *me*.

But I didn't know that, and I wanted a future with Cash so badly that my chest ached with it nonstop.

If I went back to Dragonfly Lake, I would fight for him with everything I had.

But if he ultimately turned me down, would I still prefer small-town Tennessee life over what I had here in LA?

I had trouble catching my breath. I stopped by the counter that separated the living room from the minuscule kitchen and leaned both my arms on it, trying to breathe.

Because I was honest-to-god considering doing this.

I suspected Cash loved me even though we hadn't said the words, but what did I really know?

Was I willing to throw away my golden opportunity with Stream to move to Dragonfly Lake? With or without Cash?

It would crush me if Cash said no, but I was already crushed to be here by myself.

Without my lake.

Without my inn.

Without my new friends.

Without a single chance with the man I loved.

Moving back to Tennessee would mean a life without hours of traffic, without a depressing, soulless apartment, without a solitary existence where I didn't have close friends or people who cared about me.

Though my heart was in my throat, I knew what my answer was.

I wasn't a gambler, but this was too important. I was going to take the highest-stakes risk of my life.

First things first. I took my phone out and tapped on my agent's number before I lost my courage.

CHAPTER 25

AVA

When I left my ex-husband, I'd walked away from our oversized, pretentious house with very little—by choice. I hadn't needed all the crap that filled the five-thousand-square-foot place, and I hadn't wanted the reminder of him or our life together.

If I'd ever had anyone visit me in my apartment, my lack of worldly possessions would've been glaringly obvious and slightly pathetic for a thirty-seven-year-old woman. My place was void of character and signs that someone lived there permanently. But now that I was packing what little I had to take east, it was as if this was how it was meant to be all along. It'd just taken me a while to see it.

A quick trip to the liquor store down the street had netted me some empty boxes, and I'd picked up a pile of those free shopper-type newspapers you never think about until you need packing paper for a move. I was wrapping my Target set of four dinner place settings and putting the last of it into a Tito's vodka box when someone knocked on the door, startling me.

It was likely Aubrey or Audrey, in need of something she'd already packed or wanting to say goodbye, which would be weird but nice of her. I looked through the peephole and…

My heart screeched to a halt.

I looked again.

A couple seconds passed while my brain caught up with my eyes, and then my heart restarted out of sheer necessity, and then, my mouth likely gaping, I opened the door.

"Cash!" I resisted the urge to throw my arms around him because apparently my brain still hadn't caught up. "What are you doing here?"

"I was worried you'd forget to eat." He held up a takeout bag I hadn't yet noticed because I was too busy taking in his handsome, familiar, beloved face.

He was smiling, and I couldn't *not* touch him for another second, despite my confusion. I threw my arms around his neck right there in the hallway, breathed in his scent, and let myself get lost in the moment. Cash wrapped one arm around me and lifted me with a moan that told me he was just as happy to see me and feel me and breathe me as I was him. He carried me through the doorway, set me down, then placed the food bag on the bar counter, which was right there. Everything was right there when your apartment was so small.

A dozen questions roared through my mind, but the thing that came out of my mouth was, "Lottie's?" as I read it off the side of the bag. "I've never heard of it."

"Southern cuisine. Closest place I could find that mentioned hummingbird cake online, and by close, I mean I would've been here an hour earlier if I hadn't tracked down dinner—"

"And cake," I said, my eyes filling with tears yet again.

"And cake. I hope it doesn't suck." He chuckled, then moved in on me again. "Come here."

I went into his arms with zero hesitation even though the

questions only multiplied. Cash kissed me, but it was a short, controlled kiss, not the twenty-minute meshing of our mouths I longed for.

He glanced around, from the big box on the kitchen counter to the stack of three others in the path to the bathroom to the barren living room. "So this is where you live," he said as he stepped toward the utilitarian sofa.

"This is my apartment," I said, because it'd occurred to me over the past few hours that you couldn't really call what I'd been doing here *living*. "Cash." There was light scolding in my tone, because he was acting like he'd come from next door, not two thousand miles away. "What are you doing here?"

He turned and faced me, looking suddenly nervous. "Come sit down."

His seriousness made *me* nervous, and I wondered if something bad had happened. I went over to him and we both sat on the couch, me with one leg under me, sitting sideways, facing him.

I held still and quiet, watching him, waiting, finally understanding what people meant when they said their heart was in their throat. As he inhaled, his gaze on his hands, which were on his thighs, I said, "Cash!"

I took his hand and held on to it, for me as much as for him if he needed it. He apparently needed it, as he flipped his hand and wove our fingers together.

"I made a mistake," he finally said, meeting my gaze, and between those hazel eyes and his words, I melted. "I don't want us to end, Ava. I don't know what that looks like, but I'm ready to do long-distance when we have to. I can fly here sometimes, and you'll have breaks between seasons, right?"

I shook my head, trying to let everything he said soak in. Unable to stop the wide grin from stretching across my face, I struggled to decide what to say first.

"You won't have breaks?" he asked.

"Oh. Yes, I'll have— I mean no." *Holy crap.* "You'd be okay leaving the restaurant for a few days here and there?" I asked, stunned. He'd taken a couple full days off that last week I'd been in town, but as I understood it, those days were rare, usually not consecutive, and he'd never left it for more than a weekend at a stretch in the entire time he'd been an owner.

"To fly out here and be with you? I would. I've got Zinnia. She can handle anything that comes up. And I could hire an assistant for her or maybe a clone." His expression went from determined to solemn. "Unless that's not what you want. I know we said no strings, but…" He bit down on his words, seemed to gather his courage, then continued, "I want more time with you. I want strings. I fucked it up in the past, and I've regretted that for years. I thought the regret was just for being such a bastard with my blindside breakup, but the problem wasn't *how* I broke up but that I did. Because you're it for me, Ava. No one else. I never gave my ex-wife a chance to work out because I think, on some level deep down, I knew it was supposed to be you. It was always supposed to be you. I love you, Ava. I don't know exactly how we make us work, but the one thing I'm sure of is I want to try."

My mouth hung open and more tears gathered like an army getting into formation, at the ready. "Really?"

"Really," he said earnestly. "If I need to, I'll take a sabbatical from Henry's while we figure out how to make us work."

This man…

"Henry's means everything to you," I said.

"You mean more."

That intense, loving look in his eyes slayed me in the best possible way.

My eyes fluttered closed as I was overcome, and sure as anything, the tears poured over the rims.

"I need to know if you want the same thing," he said, sounding worried, and a laughing sob broke from me.

"Cash…" I quickly said, needing to reassure him but

struggling to take everything in. I lifted our entwined hands and kissed his knuckles as tears dropped onto them. "I do. I want the same thing. Well..." I laughed awkwardly. "Not exactly the same thing."

He squeezed my hand, his face registering distress, and really, could I screw this up any more?

"I want to be with you," I clarified, sniffling and swiping a finger under each eye in a fruitless attempt to stop the tears. "But I don't want to do long-distance. I..." I sucked in a belly-deep breath and expelled it, trying to prepare myself for his reaction. "I turned down the Stream job today."

"Ava, no."

I smiled, nodding. "I'm moving back to Dragonfly Lake." I pointed at the boxes.

"You're..." He studied my face, as though waiting for a punch line.

"Moving home. It turns out I love that little town. And the inn. *My* inn. And you. I love you, Cash. I don't even need the town or the inn if I have you."

"You have me," he said, his voice teeming with love and happiness. He palmed both sides of my face, pulled me closer, and we kissed, with me leaning awkwardly on my knees, hovering over him, not caring about anything but that connection, not even when I lost my balance and toppled to the side.

We both laughed, and then I somehow ended up on my back on the couch with Cash stretched over me.

"Hello, gorgeous," he said, gazing into my eyes.

"Hi, handsome. I wasn't done." I pulled his head to mine and kissed him some more, loving the weight of his lower body pressing into mine.

He pulled his head back before I was remotely close to done kissing him.

"Get back here," I said, hardly recognizing my own lust-filled voice.

"In a minute." He rolled to the side, lodging himself between me and the back of the too-small sofa, his arm around my middle. "I don't want you to give up Stream for me. I could never ask you to do that."

"Um, you didn't," I said in a Captain Obvious voice.

"It's your dream, Ava."

I ran my fingers over his rough jaw. "It was. My dream changed though."

"You're just going to be an innkeeper?" The look on his face was scandalized, and it made me laugh.

"I'm going to be an innkeeper and a writer. But mostly a writer, which I can do because I have Anna." I told him about Knox's email and his off-hand remark about co-writing. "I don't know if he was serious, but we could combine our genres and collaborate on something like sci-fi romance, which happens to be big right now. And if he isn't interested—"

"He'd be an idiot."

I laughed again. "Then I'll write solo, same as I always have, but I'll do novels instead of screenplays. Or I could still do screenplays if my agent ever talks to me again. The only thing I won't be able to do is work in a studio, and I'm okay with that. As long as I'm with you."

"But your baseball series…"

"Is still being done. Just without me in the writing room."

"That's a giant sacrifice."

I met his gaze head on to make sure he would *hear* what I said. Really hear me. "It doesn't feel like a sacrifice to me. Not at all. Not with everything I'm getting."

Those hazel eyes peered down at me, seemed to see inside of me, and slowly, the smile I loved crept across his face.

He was starting to lean in when his phone rang and a puzzled expression overtook his smile. Rolling his weight off me, he pulled his phone out of his back pocket and said, "It's late back home. It's Seth."

With an apologetic look, he swiped to answer, and I sat up, concerned.

"Hey," he said. "What's wrong?"

"Sorry to bother you." I could hear Seth's voice over the connection. "Nothing's wrong and I know you're *busy*"—he drew out that word and even I could hear the teasing in his voice—"but you need to know tonight—"

"Know what?" Cash interrupted, his impatience tangible.

"We made it. We got the show," Seth said and then let out a howl that sounded as if he was in the room with us even though he wasn't on speaker. "They posted a few minutes ago."

Cash jumped off the couch. "What? You better not be fucking with me."

With a joyful gasp, I sat up, got my phone out, opened the social media app, and searched for *Small Town Smorgasbord.* There it was, at the top of their posts.

"Oh, my god, Cash!" I squealed. "He's not kidding!"

Seth was still talking in his ear but I couldn't hear him anymore, didn't need to hear him. Cash took my hand and pulled me off the couch. I read the post to him.

"Join us in congratulating Chef Cash Henry and Henry's Restaurant in Dragonfly Lake, Tennessee! We've added them to our esteemed list for *Small Town Smorgasbord's* spring season."

Cash threw his head back and let out a cackle. "Yes! Fuck yes! We did it!" He pulled the phone back to his ear. "We fucking did it, Seth."

Seth said something back, but I wasn't paying attention anymore, just waiting for Cash to end the call so I could jump on him.

"Hell yes. You too. Thanks for calling." He paused while Seth spoke. "All good. I'll talk to you tomorrow. Later."

He ended the call and held his arms out. I was in them before he could say a word.

"Congratulations, Cash." I kissed him, laughing. "You deserve it. I'm so happy for you!" I bounced on my feet and kissed him again, and then he picked me up and whirled me around.

"This is the best day of my life. A feather in my chef hat and the girl of my dreams by my side." He whirled me around again with a bellow, and I held on for dear life, laughing with him, ecstatic for him.

For us.

"We need to get back home so you can get your butt in the kitchen," I said once he'd set me down.

"Home," he said. "I love the sound of that coming out of your mouth. When can we go home, Ava?"

"I was planning to leave tomorrow morning, but my packing was interrupted." I couldn't get the grin off my face if you paid me to.

"I know a guy who could help you pack and we'll get it done in half the time."

"That's perfect."

"The boxes are going to have to wait a little longer though because that guy has something more important to see to."

"Yeah?" I asked as he inched his mouth closer to mine.

"Yeah. And it's going to take a while. Probably most of the night." He pulled me into him, pressing every inch of his hardness into me, making my body ache for him.

"Mmm. That so works for me."

"Just one thing though," he said. "Is there a bed in this joint? That couch is horrible."

I laughed. "There is. Through the door that isn't the bathroom."

He took a step back and held out his hand. "Come with me, my love."

I placed my hand in his and tugged until he paused and met my gaze so I could make my point. "I'll follow you wherever you want to go, Cash Henry."

Never had I ever thought I'd want to go back to Dragonfly Lake permanently, with Cash, but it turned out that was exactly where I was meant to be.

EPILOGUE

CASH

I t was a Tuesday evening, and the beer patio at the Rusty Anchor was teeming with people. Anticipation buzzed through me more potently than the Kayak Smack Ale in my glass.

Ava and I had been home from LA for two and a half weeks after packing her California life and driving her car across the country. Though we weren't officially cohabitating, we'd stayed together every single night, either at my place or the cottage. We'd talked about me moving into the cottage with her, and I couldn't wait for that day, but I planned to make an even bigger move first.

Today, I'd taken Jake ring shopping with me. The little box with the oval-cut diamond ring was burning a hole in the pocket of my cargo shorts. I didn't have specific plans for a proposal, but I wasn't going to be able to wait long. I'd been thinking I'd do it later tonight, after we left the patio, but as I watched her, Everly, Hayden, and Chloe standing two tables over, saying hello to "the girls," as Ava called her new group of friends that included Magnolia, Anna, Olivia, and a host of others, I didn't know how I'd wait a couple more hours.

My whole family had taken over the biggest high-top table—Seth and Everly, Holden and Chloe, Hayden and Zane, and even our dad and Faye. The weather was about as perfect as an early-October evening could get, but tomorrow, a cold front was coming through. People had flocked to the beer patio for one last outdoor hurrah. When Hayden's in-laws, Mason and Eliza, who—fun fact—were my stepbrother and stepsister-in-law as well, had volunteered to watch Harrison, Hayden had convinced Zane and our dad and his wife to drive in from the city to enjoy it.

The women returned, Ava sitting by my side, just as Chelsea arrived with our food. Zinnia was running the kitchen, and she'd ensured every dish looked exactly the way it should. I was confident it'd all taste right too. I'd come to trust Zinnia that much. I had to, because, as Seth had commented, I'd turned into something closer to a normal human and was learning to take a couple days off each week.

As soon as the food was served and Chelsea made sure we didn't need anything else, Holden held up his beer glass. "We need a toast," he said. "To a spur-of-the-moment end-of-the-season dinner on the beer patio with a pretty kick-ass fam. Glad you city people drove in tonight."

We all raised our glasses, most of them filled with various beers brewed by Kemp, the brewmaster, and Ava and Chloe sticking to nonalcoholic drinks. With a chorus of *hear, hears*, we clinked.

"And here's to a full house at Rusty Anchor," Hayden added, sweeping an arm out at the patio. "I hope this is exactly what you envisioned, Holden."

"We're proud of you, son," our dad added.

Holden closed his eyes, bowed his head for a second, then nodded, gazing around the circle at each of us. He ended with his eyes on Chloe. "Couldn't have done it without you all."

There was a second round of clinks, then we all got to the business of eating some damn good food if I did say so myself.

Conversation flowed as dinner progressed, with my siblings and me flipping each other the usual amount of shit and Zane joining in around the edges, even though he was the quietest of the bunch. There were compliments on the food and drinks, a collective pause to appreciate the sunset over the lake, several local folks stopping by the table to say hi, and more than one joke about who was running the restaurant and brewery since all of us Henrys were sitting here stuffing our faces.

As Finn McNamara and Carter Costello walked away from us, Holden straightened and addressed the family again. "Hey, all, Chloe had a doctor's appointment today and we have some news."

Everyone's attention locked on the couple. Chloe had passed the halfway point on her pregnancy, and we were all itching to know whether they were having a girl or a boy. They'd previously decided not to find out, but the way Holden spoke now…

Chloe eyed her husband, as if wondering what confidence he was about to break, but she tilted her head, waiting like the rest of us.

"We're having a…" Our youngest brother's brows shot up as he glanced around to make sure he had everyone at the table's attention. He did, of course. We'd all stopped breathing, waiting. "Baby!"

There was a half second of silence as it sank in that he'd tricked us, and then, laughing, Seth said, "You're a douche, man."

"You really didn't find out the gender?" Hayden asked, her expression crestfallen.

Chloe shook her head, grinning, and said, "We *genderly* don't care either way, as long as the baby's healthy."

"Boo," Zane said, and there were groans and laughs around the table. Holden, on the other hand, high-fived her for the lousy pun.

I shook my head and shared a look with Ava, who was still getting used to this nutty group I called my family.

"I respect your decision," Everly said to Chloe, "but you two are stronger than I'll ever be. I'd be dying to know. I *am* dying to know!"

"Are you preggers?" Hayden asked her.

Everly's quick answer was a head shake. "Bite your tongue. We'd like to get married first please."

"Old-fashioned," Hayden declared, and everyone laughed because Hayden and Zane had done things all out of order, with an oops, then a relationship, and then the marriage in time for Harrison's birth.

"Not to sound like a nosy stepmother-in-law-to-be, but have you made any plans for your wedding yet?" Faye asked.

Everly ducked her head with an exaggerated cringe. "Not yet but soon. I promise you you'll be one of the first to know, Stepmother-in-law-to-be." Her voice was warm and affectionate.

"Ev's been burning it up in the studio," Seth said.

"Now that I'm indie, there's no deadline," Everly said, "but for the first time ever, the songs are coming to me fast and furiously. Go figure."

"Since she's at the Hale Street Studio, I got to listen in the other day," Hayden said, her tone bubbling with enthusiasm. "It's sounding incredible."

Everly beamed. "Gin Steele is amazing. I can come in in the morning with a rudimentary melody and lyrics, and by the end of the day, she's turned it into a song that's ready for release. It's making my creativity explode in a good way."

"I can't wait to hear it. Do you have any idea when you'll release your album?" Ava asked.

"Not officially, but that will be announced soon, I think. And then...full steam ahead on marrying this patient guy." Everly leaned into Seth's shoulder. My brother put his arm around her.

"You two are so cute," Hayden said.

"Nauseating," I added, grinning.

"You've got no room to talk, bro," Holden said.

I turned to Ava, grasped her chin, and kissed her hard just for Holden's benefit, making everyone laugh and throw some more shade, but I didn't care.

"I'm just happy you guys worked things out," Zane said. "If Ava had rejected you, my conversation with Mason about emergency use of the company plane would've had a whole different tone to it."

Laughing, I held up my glass to him for another toast. "You're my hero, Lieutenant North. Thanks again for the ride."

Ava ran her fingers down my forearm as she nodded and smiled. "Or Captain North. Whichever is better," she said.

As Hayden clarified her husband preferred *captain*, Ava's attention went to the patio entrance, where Knox and Kemp wandered in. She waved them over, and I'm happy to say the animosity between Knox and me was completely gone. Even when she stood and hugged him. In fact, she threw her arms around him as if she hadn't seen him two days ago. The guy couldn't seem to get his bearings. He might as well get used to it.

A couple days after we got back, Ava had met with Knox to see how serious he was about co-writing. Turned out the man was a lot smarter than I'd given him credit for, and he'd jumped at the opportunity. They'd had some brainstorming sessions, and Ava had been devouring science fiction romances as research. Knox had been occupied with moving into his house, so they planned to ramp up in the next week or two. Frequently, out of nowhere, Ava would start spouting off what-ifs to me regarding plot possibilities and characters and conflicts and whatnot, then apologize for "boring" me, but the truth was, what she referred to as her ramblings fascinated me, and I loved listening to her, getting more insight into that brain of hers.

Kemp wandered over to Holden and Chloe and fist-bumped his business partners about how full the patio was, while Ava asked Knox whether his belongings had arrived from Texas.

"This morning. The garage is stacked full of all the boxes," he said with a grimace. "I figure I'll get to them as I get to them."

"Sounds like a plan," Ava said. "Do you know everyone here?" She swept her hand out at the table at large.

"Hey, Cash," Knox said as he stepped back and had the chance to acknowledge everyone else.

I could swear he stiffened as he looked around the table, but I couldn't imagine why.

"Hello, everyone," he said.

"You probably haven't met our dad," Holden said. "Simon Henry and his wife, Faye. This is Knox Breckenridge. He just bought the Sanderson place."

Our dad stood with a smile, leaning across the table to shake Knox's hand. "Hi, Knox. Congratulations on the house."

Knox went serious and seemed nervous as he said, "Thank you. Pleased to meet you, sir," then turned to Faye, who'd also stood.

"You're the one who's writing with Ava," Faye said warmly as she clasped Knox's hand.

"Yes, ma'am," Knox said, smiling a little. "Planning to. Until she fires me."

"As if," Ava said with a laugh and an eye roll.

"So Kemp, you just can't stay away from this place or what?" I asked the brewmaster, fully aware that none of us Henrys had room to talk about hanging out at our own business during off hours.

Kemp came back to our end of the table, grinning. "Promised this guy a tour of the facility," he said, nodding toward Knox, who'd followed him back toward Ava and me. "We just got done and now we're going to enjoy the fruits of my labor."

"What'd you think?" I asked Knox.

"It's fascinating. I worked up a big thirst."

"Do you want to join us?" Ava asked.

Without a glance at the table, Knox said, "You guys do your family thing."

"That table over there has more single ladies," Kemp added, gesturing to the one with Anna, Magnolia, and company.

"Good point." Knox glanced at the other end of the table again, to my dad and Faye, nodded respectfully, then he and Kemp headed off toward the estrogen contingency.

Ava leaned over and kissed me.

"What's that for, gorgeous?" I asked, tasting the hint of salty onion rings on her lips.

"You making friends with Knox," she said with an irresistible smile that made me want to push the rest of my beer-battered walleye aside, throw her over my shoulder, and spirit her away to the cottage for the night.

I shrugged. "Old news." With a wink, I stole one of her onion rings and bit down on it. The crispy golden batter was just right tonight.

Conversation continued around the table, everything from placing bets on which North brother couple would lose the anti-pregnancy campaign and get knocked up first—Drake and McKenzie or Cole and Sierra—to Hayden's latest big-deal design clients, country-star power couple Ellie Grant and Thomas Maywood, and the memorial bench the Diamonds were working on for Ava's aunt. Ava explained how they were going in on a custom-made wood bench that would sit on the slope at the inn, overlooking the lake her aunt had loved, with a plaque on the back in remembrance of Phyllis Sharp.

As dinner plates were removed and desserts ordered—Ava and I were splitting a slice of hummingbird cake—Ava excused herself to go to the restroom. The restaurant had just closed to diners, but the kitchen was still open for the tail end of the patio crowd.

I watched the love of my life walk toward the door, and it hit me that I should've arranged some kind of clever proposal with a ring in her hummingbird cake. I shook my head at myself, thinking that wasn't very original, and I wasn't a planner anyway. I was better flying by the seat of my pants. And then I thought, *So why not do that now?*

I popped up out of my chair, excused myself as if I needed the restroom, and went inside Henry's. Riley, one of our managers, was totaling receipts back in Seth's office, but the dining area was otherwise deserted.

Like I'd done that night at the Fly, when I'd first kissed Ava, I went to the hallway outside of the ladies' room and leaned against the wall to wait.

———

AVA

I finished in the restroom, put some lip gloss on, and ran a comb through my perpetually mussed hair.

Cash's family was wonderful and warm and entertaining, and though I hadn't known what to expect from our impromptu dinner, I'd loved it. But I couldn't help thinking about being alone with him later. We couldn't seem to get enough of each other, and I refused to apologize to myself or anyone else for that. But I would try to mind my manners and not make it obvious I was in need of some one-on-one attention from my sexy chef.

I walked out of the ladies' room, and my attention was drawn to the hallway wall opposite the door. Cash stood there, watching me, with heat and love in his eyes. My heart started beating faster just at the sight of all that maleness focused on me. He took a light grasp of my wrist and gently tugged me closer, reminding me of that night at the Fly when he'd first kissed me. That night he'd had the slightest predatory gleam in his eyes. Tonight he was more intense but less intimidating.

"Hi, handsome," I said, catching my balance with a hand on his chest. "What are you up to?"

"Can't a guy miss his girl?"

I laughed, because that was cheesy even for him.

"Come here." He laced our fingers together and lightly tugged me again, this time toward the emergency exit at the end of the hallway. He punched in a code on a keypad, then opened the door without the alarm going off.

"Where are we going?" I asked. This door opened on the side opposite the patio, away from everyone, facing the marina instead, which seemed to be deserted.

"Little walk. Beautiful night," he said into my ear as we followed the walkway toward the water.

"What about your family?"

"I needed to get you alone for a bit. That okay?"

"Always." We walked some more. "But…what about cake?"

He let out a low growl of a laugh. "You like cake better than me?"

"Never, but I was hoping I could have both tonight."

He laughed again and put his arm around my waist,

pulling me into his side. At the intersection with the sidewalk that ran parallel to the shore, he veered us right, toward the marina, instead of left toward the beer patio, and slowed our pace way down.

We were in the shadows between the lights that illuminated the Henry's docks and the marina, with a half-moon glimmering down on us. The din of people on the beer patio reached us but barely. Cash stopped us next to one of the honeysuckle bushes along the walkway. The bush was still lush and full, but the blooms had been replaced by little round berries. He turned us to face the lake, his arm still around me. I wound mine around his middle too and sank into his side, breathing in his familiar scent.

"You like my family?" he asked out of nowhere. His voice was low but still broke into our silence.

"Of course. I've met them before. Lots of times." I'd met most of them in the past and then spent more time with his brothers and Chloe and Everly lately, so his question confused me.

"Like, well enough to have them be *your* family?" he asked, still gazing out over the water.

I stopped breathing for a second as I processed his question. "What are you saying?" I asked, afraid to jump to conclusions.

Cash was quiet for so long I was about to whack him in the gut with the back of my hand, then I heard him rustling around, fidgeting with his pocket. Then, before I could think another thought, he moved between me and the beautiful moonlit lake, faced me, took my hand, and lowered himself to one knee.

I inhaled sharply, my eyes wide, all my focus on his handsome, earnest face. "Cash?"

"You're so pretty, Ava."

A half-crazy giggle erupted from me. "What are you doing?"

Staring up into my eyes, he inhaled. Exhaled. His gaze dropped down to his hands, and mine followed in time to see him open a ring box, take out a ring, and hold it up between his thumb and forefinger. "Will you marry me?"

My gaze popped back to his eyes, and I saw his heart and his soul and his love there. I saw my future there. *Our* future.

"Yes," I said on a breathy exhale. "God yes, I'll marry you!" I leaned down awkwardly to kiss him, and the next thing I knew, he was lifting from his knee, one arm banded around me tightly enough to lift me too.

Our lips crashed together in a clumsy kiss as he slid me down his solid body. We laughed into each other's mouth, then he leaned down and kissed me again, hitting his target and holding it and loving it and pouring so much joy and hope into me. I gave him all of my heart in return.

When we finally pulled back, he cradled my face with one hand. "I love you, Ava. Feels like I have forever."

"I love you, Cash. For even longer."

We kissed again, and he cut it off abruptly to let out a howl of happiness as he took my hand. "Come on. I want to tell the world. Or at least my family. Soon to be your family too."

When we walked onto the patio, the crowd had thinned out so that it was just Cash's family, Magnolia's table of girls, and Kemp and Knox.

"Ava Dean said she'd marry me," Cash announced to everyone present and probably half the rest of the town.

Cheers erupted from everyone, and in a heartbeat, we were engulfed in hugs and congratulations and *Welcome to the family* and *Are you sure you want to be stuck with this guy forever?*

Chelsea was the last server working, and as I grabbed my cake and dug into it—because it turned out getting engaged worked up a sugar craving—she brought two bottles of champagne, plus some sparkling grape juice for those of us who didn't or couldn't drink.

We'd abandoned our table and were standing around in a happy, noisy group when Mr. Henry said, "Listen up. It seems fitting that I offer up a toast."

Everyone quieted, all laughs and smiles and expectant looks.

"I'm not a man of many words, so I'll keep this short and sweet."

"You're definitely sweet," his wife said, eliciting some *aww*s from the group.

"Your mom would be over the moon to see our four children happily marrying such good, loving folks." He raised his glass to the stars. Then he put his arm around his wife. "And nothing could make Faye and me happier, right, honey?"

Grinning widely, Faye tilted her head, lifted a brow, and said, "Right. Nothing except for more grandbabies."

Mr. Henry lifted his glass. "To Cash and Ava…and maybe, eventually, someday, when they're ready, grandbabies."

We all toasted, with more laughter and teasing and wisecracks. Cash pulled me in for a champagne-flavored kiss. "Happy?" he asked.

"I've never been happier."

———

KNOX

The mood on the Rusty Anchor patio was jovial and hopeful and would've been contagious if I wasn't so lost in my head. I was happy as hell for Ava and Cash, so it was easy to raise a glass for them.

But the longer I stood here in silence, the more I felt like a liar, and I'd never been okay with dishonesty. It'd gone on for too long already—my doing, plus a little bit of fate. I feared there would be damage to undo when the truth came out.

Now that I stood here with the entire Henry family, I couldn't not act. I knew full well that this was not an opportune time. This was probably one of the worst times, but the happenstance of having the entire family in one place... I couldn't ignore that sign.

Magnolia, Olivia, and Anna finally said their goodbyes with another round of hugs and congrats. Kemp stood next to me, peering after the trio, then tipped his glass up to empty it.

"I'm going to take off too. What about you?" he asked me.

With a glance back at the Henry clan to ensure they were all still here, I said, "Going to stay a few more minutes. You go ahead. Thanks for the tour, Kemp."

"Happy to share the beer-love." He looked down the walkway to the parking lot and street again, and I vaguely wondered what his interest was, or rather, which one of those women his interest was in if any, then he called out a collective good night and took his leave.

Leaving me there with ten Henrys or Henrys-to-be.

This was the opportunity I'd been waiting for, and even though my timing sucked, if I didn't do it now, I didn't know when I'd get a better chance.

I stepped up to the group, between Ava and Hayden, across from Simon Henry, my heart about to pound out of my chest.

"Hey, everyone," I said above their conversations. "I'm sorry to intrude on a private family moment, but I have something I need to say."

They quieted relatively quickly for this group, expectant smiles and welcome expressions focused on me.

That would change in a heartbeat.

I cleared my throat. "I know this isn't the best time to say this, but I need to level with you all about the reason I came to this small town in the first place."

I was semi-aware of Ava clasping on to my wrist. "What's going on, Knox?"

Focusing fully on the patriarch of the group, who stood mere feet from me for the first time, I said, "I found out a few months ago that you, sir, are my biological father."

BONUS EPILOGUE

AVA

The closer we got to Dragonfly Lake, the harder it was to not come out of my skin with anticipation.

Our honeymoon had been magical. Maybe that was a cliché, but it was one-hundred-percent fitting.

After our wedding—an intimate affair with less than fifty guests, at the inn, overlooking the shimmering lake, with my aunt's gorgeous memorial bench in the midst of it all as if she were with us too—we flew to Caribou Creek, Colorado, and stayed in Gabe North's family lodge in the mountains. The home was beautiful, private, everything we could ask for and more, with a hot tub, a fully stocked state-of-the-art kitchen for Cash, and breathtaking, life-affirming views of mountains —some still tipped in snow—forests, and sky in every direction. The early-June air had been crisp and fresher than anything I'd ever breathed in.

We'd explored the adorable little mountain town, hiked some of the trails, visited waterfalls and lakes and rushing mountain springs, and spent some full days in bed, soaking up all the alone time we could get. We'd shared our desire to start a family as soon as possible and set aside birth control on our first night in Colorado. I couldn't help but wonder if there was a new life taking hold deep within me at this moment. We'd certainly given the mission our all, taking advantage of our alone time to the hilt, knowing full well when we got back to "real life," we'd both be perpetually busy with our careers and lucky to have extended periods of time together.

Tomorrow. The craziness of our daily life would start tomorrow. Cash was still all mine, newlywed version, for the rest of tonight, and I knew without a doubt, after the surprise I had in store for him at home, it would be a memorable, hopefully toe-curling night.

"You're fidgety this evening," Cash said, glancing at me from the driver's seat as he drove us home from the airport. He reached over and took my hand in his, and I realized I'd been tapping my fingers on my thigh.

"I'm just happy," I said with a smile. "I got this handsome new husband, you see."

"Yeah? Sounds like you're a lucky girl."

I laughed at the cockiness, then conceded, "So freaking lucky. But so is he."

Cash laughed too. "I'm the luckiest bastard alive. Colorado was incredible. Thank you for convincing me we deserved two full weeks."

Two weeks had been a stretch for both of us to make peace with leaving our jobs and responsibilities behind, but I had a good reason for insisting on it. He'd understand that when we got back to the cottage in a few minutes. I pressed my lips together and caught my legs bouncing on the car seat and stilled them.

"Home, sweet home," I said as we drove past the Welcome to Dragonfly Lake sign.

Cash peered at me again, flicking his gaze to the mostly

empty road from time to time. "How does it feel? Is it really home for you now?"

With zero hesitation, I said, "It's felt like home since we drove back from LA. This is where we belong. I belong wherever you are."

"Damn straight you do."

In the months since I'd moved back, Cash and I had started creating our life together. He'd moved into the cottage the day after he'd proposed. We'd switched out my dear aunt's master bedroom furniture for his and moved in there, then turned the upstairs rooms into an office for me and a guest room.

Our social lives were busy and fulfilling. This time around for me, life in a small town meant taking time for people first, getting to know them, making deeper friendships. I hadn't had the time or the confidence for that when I was growing up. I'd missed out, because the group of people I was getting to know—Anna, Magnolia, Shawna, Olivia, my sisters-in-law, and Cash's brothers and friends—made my life, our life, so much fuller.

Anna was rocking the hell out of running the Honeysuckle Inn. We'd hired two assistant managers, delved into phase two of renovations, enlisted Kennedy Clayborne's marketing help, and managed to book about ninety percent of the inn's rooms through the end of the season. I got to keep my hand in my aunt's legacy but could rest knowing Anna was taking on the lion's share of responsibility. The rest of the days, I spent co-writing with Knox and thriving as we built up our fiction-writing empire. We'd published two books and were almost ready to put out the third in the series.

Cash slowed down as we got into town. It was just after seven p.m., so downtown was still crawling with tourists and locals alike, our little town buzzing with its summer-season energy.

As we went by the hardware store with Cash's former

apartment on top of it, I asked, "Is it weird not going back to your old place?"

"Let's see, a lonely bachelor pad with no view other than Jake's ugly mug next door or a cozy, homey cottage overlooking the lake with the woman of my dreams. No contest, gorgeous."

We pulled up to the stop sign at the T-intersection of Main Street and Honeysuckle Road. Across the road and in front of us was Rusty Anchor Brewing, and Henry's was to the right of that. I sat up straighter as I took in the scene.

"Holy shit," Cash said. "It's a Monday night, right? Not a weekend?"

"It's Monday," I verified. "Cash, look at all the people waiting."

The car behind us honked, and I realized we'd been stopped too long. Cash took a right and an immediate left into the restaurant parking lot, which was overflowing with cars, even though lots of people hit downtown and this area on foot.

"The show," I said, grinning.

The Henry's episode of *Small Town Smorgasbord* had aired a week and a half before our wedding. We'd had a watch party at Henry's in the bar, and Anna had broadcast it at the inn as well. In fact, several businesses had tuned all their TVs into it, from Humble's to the Fly and even the Barn Bar, from what I'd heard.

The episode couldn't have gone better. The show's host had raved over everything Cash had presented him with. The footage of the food had managed to convey how incredible it looked in person, so that you could practically smell it through your screen. And Henry's and Rusty Anchor's social media had exploded before the episode was even over.

That week before we went out of town, both the restaurant and the beer patio had been busier than before, but it coincided with beautiful spring weather and an influx of tourists, so it'd been hard to name the cause. Seth had reported a significant increase in overall revenue while we were gone, and from the looks of it—the wait line was out the door, the spillover deck for people waiting for tables was full, and there was even a line of folks waiting to get on the beer patio—that increase had only continued. When Cash pulled up in a non-spot next to the dumpster and lowered his window a crack, we could hear the din of diners and drinkers from both the patio and the lakefront deck; in fact, *din* didn't do the noise justice. It was closer to a distant roar.

"Holy shit," he said again, his face split with a wide grin that filled me with joy—and yet I couldn't help but wonder if I could eclipse that with my own surprise...whenever we finally got there.

We'll get there soon, I coached my impatient self. *Let him bask in this for as long as he wants. It's incredible and wonderful and what he's been dreaming of for years.*

As I watched him—because seeing the emotions flit over his face was even more fulfilling to me than the crowd—it was as if he was fighting to sit still.

"I'm gonna go in," he said. "Just for a minute. I'll see if Seth is there or check in with Riley. I just… This is unreal."

"I'll go with you," I said, hopping out, wanting to be at my husband's side as he took in this moment.

Thirty-five minutes later, my enthusiasm had waned and my fatigue from a day of traveling had set in. I'd said hi to the employees as they hurried here and there, but mostly I just tried to stay out of the way and let them do their thing. When the end seat at the bar opened up, I slid onto it to wait, trying to summon all my patience.

"Can I get you anything to drink?" Dakota, who was working the bar, asked in a rush.

I shook my head and smiled, not wanting to give her

anything else to do. She was earning her paycheck, her tips, and more tonight from what I'd seen. She gave me a thumbs-up and moved down to the next customer in need.

My phone buzzed with a text message. I saw it was from Hayden.

> Are you home yet?

In town but we had to stop at the restaurant.

> So he still doesn't know?

No. I'm trying to be patient.

> What's he doing?

I looked over my shoulder, around the bar and the one dining area I could see from here, but Cash wasn't in sight.

I suspect he's in the kitchen.

> Working? ARE YOU KIDDING ME?

I laughed because I could hear Hayden's exclamation in my head.

You know your brother.

> My brother is an idiot.

I'll give him a few more minutes. He's seriously being so cute.

> Yuck. Let me know his reaction when you can though. And welcome home!

Thanks!

I added some heart emojis and thought, as I hit send, how weird and awesome it was to have sisters. All of them knew about my surprise, as did Cash's brothers. I'd had to let them in on it, otherwise there would've been questions while we were out of town.

After checking the time again and noting it'd now been nearly forty-five minutes since we'd come in, I leaned my elbow on the bar and summoned a little more patience, reminding myself Cash had no idea there was any reason to hurry home. My surprise would be revealed soon enough.

CASH

The kitchen was slammed, and Zinnia reported it'd been like this since five o'clock.

Seth had gone home for the day, as was his usual, and Riley was managing tonight. She'd only had a second to talk, and she'd confirmed that this was how it'd been seven days a week since we'd gone on our honeymoon.

As soon as I'd wandered into the kitchen, I'd jumped on helping Zin with expo, making sure everything that left the kitchen was exactly right. We'd expanded our staff for the season, so we had a couple extra bodies, but it was barely controlled chaos, and Zin looked like she might fall over from exhaustion.

Zin and I had just sent out a ten-cover when she looked at me and said, "Thanks for the help, but what the hell are you doing here, Cash? Aren't you supposed to be on your honeymoon?"

"Shit. I left Ava out there."

I walked out of the kitchen and glanced around for my wife. I didn't see her until I peeked around the corner into the bar area. She sat alone at the end of the bar, looking…sad. Not at all like the woman who'd been so excited to get home that she'd been bouncing in the passenger seat.

Dammit.

It'd been tough to learn to step back from work to a more "normal" level these past few months, but I'd managed to do it and even embrace it. Taking a two-week vacation out of state had also been out of my comfort zone at first, but once we'd arrived in Colorado, I'd savored the time with Ava and had even gone a few days at a stretch without checking in back here. But we'd been back in town for a grand total of two minutes before I'd fallen right back into my workaholic habits. In doing so, I was letting my wife down big-time.

Guess I'd have to make it up to her when we got home, I thought with a faint grin, not hating any part of that idea.

I strode toward her without letting Zin know I was leaving—she'd figure out I'd pulled my head out of my ass—and put my arms around Ava from behind. "I'm sorry, I'm sorry, I'm sorry. I got carried away," I said in her ear, then I whispered exactly what I was going to do when I got her naked, to make up for it.

She laughed as she spun around to face me and slid off the barstool. "What are we waiting for then?"

Feeling like an insatiable caveman and not caring if I caused a scene, I picked her up with an arm under her knees and one supporting her shoulders. She shrieked and laughed, but the sounds just meshed with the crowd noise. A couple of locals called out encouragement from a table by the wall as I spirited her out of the restaurant and jogged toward the car.

"Put me down," she said, laughing more than speaking.

I did exactly that when we got to the passenger door, setting her on the seat and closing her in. I jogged around to the driver's side, let myself in, started the engine, and got us out of there.

"I'm sorry, Ava. I got swept away by the craziness. I should never have poked my head into the kitchen."

"Well," she said, shrugging, "that's pretty much the guy I fell in love with. I forgive you. Or I will once you atone." Her voice turned a little breathy, telling me she'd heard every word I whispered into her ear and was looking forward to it as much as I was.

"Thirty seconds after we get in the door," I promised.

"Mm, we'll see." Her voice was smug, knowing, and I glanced her way as I turned down the Honeysuckle Inn's entrance. She looked like she was up to something, but I couldn't imagine what.

I parked on the gravel by the cottage and we both got out.

"Luggage later," Ava said, meeting me near the trunk and yanking me toward the house.

"Whatever the lady desires," I said, grinning and following eagerly.

She already had the key out, which was not the norm at all. When the door was open, she reached in, flipped on the lights, stepped inside, and turned to look at me. She was so gorgeous I'd never get tired of looking right back at her.

"Cash," she said.

"Mm-hmm."

She gestured to the kitchen and I froze in my tracks, my jaw gaping as I took in what my eyes were seeing.

"What the…"

"Happy wedding present," she said.

I darted my gaze to her for a second but went right back to taking in the… "New kitchen? What? What in the world did you do?"

Ava laughed and bounced on her feet as she took my hand and tugged me forward. "I hired Sierra North. I was going for a chef's dream, though I was a little held back by square footage."

I went into the open kitchen space that had been completely renovated in some kind of fucking two-week miracle that took the cottage's modest but sufficient kitchen and turned it gourmet and state-of-the-art. "How…?"

I slowly pivoted, salivating over the bigger island with a

second sink, the six-burner gas stove and double ovens, the additional counter space that'd been eked out by rearranging the space and extending a couple of feet into our living area. It was cozier but still livable, and the kitchen…

"This is… This is fucking incredible, Ava." I swallowed, as if that could clear up some of the emotions flooding me and help my brain work right. I went over and opened drawers and cupboards, all brand-new cabinetry, and ran my hands over the granite surface.

"You like it?" she asked, coming up to my side and sounding hopeful.

"No, I don't like it. I fucking love it. This is…" I shook my head, unable to find words good enough. "You know I was okay with what we had before, right?"

Looking nonchalant, she shrugged. "I suppose we could have Sierra put it all back."

"Not on your life. Come here." I pulled her into my arms and pressed her into the brand-new cabinets with my hard, happy body as I kissed her irresistible lips and leaned her back over the counter. My body pulsed with need for her because I loved her so damn much, but I finally managed to stop kissing her for long enough to speak again. "I'm stunned, Ava. The happiest man alive. Thank you."

"I figure if you're going to feed me for the rest of my life, I better give you as gourmet of a kitchen as we could fit in here."

My joy burst out of me in a howling, loving laugh. "You're so perfect for me."

"Just like you're perfect for me." She threw her arms around my neck again. "I love you, Cash."

"I love you too, Ava. You want me to cook you something right now?"

She pulled back and met my gaze with an expression of mock horror. "Not even a little bit. I want you to do exactly what you promised me back in the bar. Right here in our new kitchen…if you dare."

I laughed. "Oh, I dare. I like to think I'm a man who keeps his promises. In fact, I plan to spend the rest of my life keeping promises to my gorgeous, sexy wife."

NOTE FROM THE AUTHOR

Thanks for reading *Undone*! I hope you loved Cash and Ava.

Knox, the unexpected Henry half brother, gets his story next! Knox has been hanging on to his secret for months, but find out what happens when he gets the surprise of his life in *Unexpected*.

If you missed the North Brothers series, you can dive into book one, *True North*, in ebook format for free! Find out what happens when Mr. Socially Awkward spontaneously volunteers to be his beautiful boss's fake date.

Find both books and more in my author store at amyknuppbooks.com!

———

If you liked *Undone*, I hope you'll consider leaving a review for it. Reviews help other readers find books and can be as short (or long) as you feel comfortable with. Just a couple sentences is all it takes. I appreciate all honest reviews.

———

Undone is part of the Henry Brothers series, which includes:

- Untold (prequel)
- Unraveled
- Unsung
- Undone
- Unexpected

The Henry Brothers series is a spin-off of the North Brothers series, which includes these stand-alone stories:

- True North
- True Colors
- True Blue
- True Harmony
- True Hero

ALSO BY AMY KNUPP

Henry Brothers Series

Untold (prequel)

Unraveled

Unsung

Undone

Unexpected

North Brothers Series

True North

True Colors

True Blue

True Harmony

True Hero

North Brothers Box Sets:

North Brothers Books 1-3

North Brothers Books 4-5

North Brothers: The Complete Series

Hale Street Series:

Sweet Spot

Sweet Dreams

Soft Spot

One and Only

Last First Kiss

Heartstrings

<u>Hale Street Box Sets:</u>
Meet Me at Clayborne's
Clayborne's After Hours
It Happened on Hale Street

<u>Island Fire Series</u>:
Playing with Fire
Heat of the Night
Fully Involved
Firestorm
Afterburn
Up in Flames
Flash Point
Fire Within
Impulse
Slow Burn

Island Fire Box Sets:
Sparked (books 1-3)
Ignited (books 4-6)
Enflamed (books 7-10)
OR
Island Fire: The Complete Series

Themed Box Sets:
Friends to Forever (Friends to Lovers Romance)
Working It (Workplace Romance)

ABOUT THE AUTHOR

Amy Knupp is a *USA Today* Best-Selling Author of contemporary romance and a freelance copy editor. She loves words and grammar and meaty, engrossing stories with complex characters.

Amy lives in Wisconsin with her husband and has two adult children, three cats, and a box turtle. She graduated from the University of Kansas with degrees in French and journalism. In her spare time, she enjoys traveling, breaking up cat fights, watching college hoops, and annoying her family by correcting their grammar.

For more information:
amyknuppbooks.com